Universe Olympics

Heat 1

By

Amanda S. Dubin

In Loving Memory of

Matilda "Tillie" Timmes

What if winning the gold medal at the Olympics

wasn't the end?

What if… it was only the beginning?

~ Ambassador Liew

List of Athletes:

Amy Ride – United States of America, Swimming

Dmitri Pedrovich – Russia, Wrestling

Zhang Yosi Chen – China, Gymnastics

Marvin "Pappie" Rapperhand – Great Britain, Triathlon

Jaysen William Powell – United States of America, Decathlon

Jenefer Washington Lee – United States of America, Track and Field

Ramon Stead – Jamaica, Bobsled

Margit Housman – Norway, Cross-Country Skiing and Biathlon

Stoke the Jam Townsend – United States of America, Half-Pipe, Slopestyle

Eric Verheinen – Netherlands, Speed Skating

Moses Al-Nair Shabbat – Kenya, Marathon, 5,000-meter, 10,000-meter

Louis Emmanuelle Suarez, Cuba, Springboard, Platform Diving

Yogitako Sito – Japan, Sport Climbing

Jodie McQuenzy, Australia, Artistic (Synchronized) Swimming

Josie McQuenzy, Australia, Artistic (Synchronized) Swimming

Ariel "Ari" Arianna Foxx – Federated States of Micronesia, Surfing

Gretta Von Strither – Germany, Alpine Skiing

Mark Hallperan – Canada, Pairs Figure Skating

Justine Hallperan – Canada, Pairs Figure Skating

Onorina Di Mateo – Italy, Pentathlon

Chapter 1

The Meeting

They were given only a time, location, floor number, and date: 9:30 a.m., United Nations Secretariat Building, 22nd floor, Sunday, October 19, 2036. Any and all digital or wearable devices were to be left outside on the table next to the door. As people slowly started trickling in, signs reading "UNOOSA" directed them to a long, rectangular, wood-paneled conference room. Its design was reminiscent of the 1970s.

Men and women, both young and old, cautiously walked in. There was a silent recognition among the attendees; everyone was an athlete who had competed at an Olympic Games. One by one, the athletes, each with a coach by their side, sat down at an elongated wooden conference table with a name card in front of each chair.

It was an odd choice of location for a meeting of world-class athletes. The UN building in New York normally invited only a few athletes at a time to speak in front of the General Assembly for their separate causes, but the Assembly was quiet today. And this was the first time that so many athletes had come together at the UN without being told why. There had been absolute secrecy. Before opening the invitation to the meeting, the recipient had to sign a nondisclosure agreement of confidentiality. If the media were informed about this meeting, whoever leaked it to the press would be excluded. They would also be prosecuted, based on the agreement's terms. Most of the athletes complied. One person, who shall remain nameless, did leak the meeting plan to a media source, who was fortunately close to the UN Director. That athlete's invitation was immediately revoked—the lawsuit is pending—and exclusive first-reporting rights on what was about to occur, effective at the appropriate time and place, were offered to that powerful news outlet.

There were some familiar faces loitering around the room. Sitting by himself at the far end of the conference table was the most famous athlete of all. He had become the face of the Summer Olympics completed two months ago in Nairobi, Kenya. More than half of the people sitting at the table, had in one way or another, gained notoriety during those Games. It was the first time Kenya had ever held the Olympics, and for the most part it was able to put on a good show. African nations had become players on the world Olympic stage.

As the tardy athletes and coaches settled in, the room gradually grew silent in quiet expectation. The lights changed and a stillness descended as a very smartly dressed Asian woman walked in. She spoke in English, as was the custom in this almost century-old New

York building. "Good morning, ladies and gentlemen. Thank you for coming to the satellite office of the UNOOSA. Usually, we would have met in our headquarters in Vienna, but for various reasons, this meeting needed to be held here in New York. I am UNOOSA Director Xi, and I am here to welcome you and congratulate you."

The crowd of people sitting around the conference table stirred for a moment and mumbled in confusion.

"Most of you were in either the recent 36th Olympiad Summer Games in Nairobi or the 2034 Winter Olympic Games in Harbin, China. It is because of your special achievements in those Games that you all have been asked here today. But let me go no further without introducing the real reason you are here. Please let me introduce… Ambassador Liew."

Every one of the athletes sitting around the table audibly gasped. Ambassador Liew was known around the world, and not a single person in the room, but for Director Xi, had ever met him before. A very tall, gangly person meandered into the room and up to the head of the conference table—at well over seven feet tall, he was almost too big and proportionable for the table. He had two arms, two legs, forward-facing eyes, light hair, and skin, and was wearing an appropriate gender-neutral outfit, but one characteristic set him apart from everyone in the room: He wasn't human.

Almost two years had passed since *it* had happened. The world, as every person at that table knew it, had changed. Nothing had changed individually per se, but something had changed for the whole of Humanity.

It started slowly, as such things often do. One night, an astronomer in Australia discovered a rapid moving object through her telescope. At first, she thought it was a new asteroid, but as days crawled into weeks, the object went from an asteroid approaching our moon—with a bright illumination and odd trajectory that no asteroid could ever have—to a shimmery silver ship. This vessel became a worldwide sensation, thanks to the internet and the smartphones in the hands of almost every human being on the planet. Billions of people watched as the large, silvery, cigar-shaped ship slowly made its way to a position halfway between our moon and the new International Space Station and stopped. At that point, all doubt dissipated. It wasn't a man-made object that originated from Earth—it was alien.

The Americans, Europeans, Russians, and Chinese jointly sent out a small emergency vehicle to the spot in space where the ship had waited motionless for over a week. The combined mission was made up of a top-secret American Orion "spare" command module that had been kept ready by the U.S. Space Force in case of emergency—and this was deemed enough of an emergency for launch. The module was a refurbished SpaceX booster rocket, and it jumped off from another smaller space station which was positioned halfway to the moon. The Europeans happened to be represented, because a British astronaut had just started his five-month rotation on the space station a few weeks prior.

Small zero–G mini-drone cameras floated along with the four astronauts—American, Russian, Chinese, and the British—as they journeyed to the silver ship waiting patiently, in the emptiness of space. It made for the best reality programming in history; the guesstimate was that 6.7 billion people were watching. Almost no work was done by any nation with an internet or television connection for one solid week. Billions and billions of dollars' worth of productivity were lost. The stock exchange was shut down for fear of a catastrophic sell off, or worse. And most of Earth's inhabitants were riveted as they watched the sortie from a space capsule now deemed by the media as, "Humanity One."

When the astronauts docked with the silver ship, sitting inside waiting, alone, was Liew. He explained, in multiple languages, that Humanity was currently in a quarantine zone, as it had been for millennia. The zone reached past Pluto into the Kuiper Belt, and only one ship and one ambassador, Liew, were permitted to make initial public contact. He specifically had been chosen because it would be easier for humans to accept another anthropomorphic biped like themselves. And until Liew felt Humanity was ready, no further alien contact would be permitted. A waiting period of one to fifty years would be implemented until Humanity no longer felt threatened by first contact, accepted they weren't alone, and took comfort in the fact that they were one of many life forms in the universe. In time, humans would join with the others, *if* and *when* humans chose.

After the initial live feed from the astronauts, Liew was hardly ever seen in public. For over a year and a half, there were the rare meetings and photo ops with presidents, premiers, heads of state, and religious leaders from all over the world. But the true whereabouts and comings and goings were kept top secret. The spaceship, once it landed in Antarctica without its main passenger, was never seen again, and Liew had made no other public statements or announcements in the almost eighteen months, which was in a way a very good thing.

The first month after he showed up, about half the world was convinced they were going to be attacked at any point by alien invaders, like in some bad 1950's science-fiction film. Some headed to their bolt-hole secret bunkers, waiting for the doomsday Armageddon that never happened. And the other half went about their daily lives. But life on planet Earth continued as it had for millennia. Almost a year and a half after first contact, most people didn't care anymore. Liew was out of sight, so he was out of mind. Everyone got back to living their normal daily lives; worrying about an alien with a spaceship didn't put food on their tables or a roof over their heads.

There was a recent public sighting of Liew—the first in almost a year. He was a guest at the opening ceremony of the Summer Olympic Games in Nairobi. And this 36th Olympiad was special, unlike any before it. All the countries and athletes acknowledged it as such. It was the first Olympics to truly bring all of Humanity together; there was a spirit of camaraderie like never before. Perhaps it was the knowledge that Humanity was no longer alone, as evidenced by Liew gazing upon them. Whatever the true reason, the media was still discussing the Olympics. Not since 1896 when the first modern games were held in Athens had an event brought in such a global audience. They said it reminded Humanity of all the great things it could do when working together and made people glad to be human on planet Earth.

Back on the 22nd floor, in the UN conference room, Liew stepped forward at the head of the conference table lined with Olympic athletes. "Greetings and salutations to you all," he said in a voice that melded deep and high registers and sounded as though two people were speaking at the same time. It was both a little off-putting and beautifully melodious at the same time.

"I hope each of you knows who I am, but if you don't, I am Liew, Ambassador to Earth. I come from a planet three-quarters of the way across the Milky Way Galaxy. In many respects it is similar to Earth—a green planet on an outer band of this galaxy. But my home planet isn't the specific topic of discussion here today."

All the athletes glanced toward their coaches sitting by their sides, but for one very well-built man who never broke eye contact with Liew.

"Let me start with the reason I am here. This is first and foremost an invitation." Liew opened up his hand and reached upward.

Out of his hand flew four spheres, each revolving in concentric circles around a fifth yellow rotating orb. The small spheres drifted further apart, hovering over the table. Closest to the center was the red sphere, then the green, blue, and white ones revolving around the larger, glowing yellow orb. A hush fell over the large room as the awed athletes realized they were likely the first humans to witness such advanced technology.

"Each athlete here today is formally invited to join me on a trip back to my home quadrant of the galaxy to take part in Games."

"Games?" questioned one of two identical girls on the far side of the table.

Director Xi stepped forward and spoke in a commanding tone, "Please, no questions until after Ambassador Liew is done speaking. Thank you."

"These Games are very similar to what you humans just had with your Summer Olympic Games in Kenya," continued Liew. "Every member planet in the Milky Way Galaxy sends their best athletes to partake in a wide variety of sporting events."

"You mean we will be seeing aliens?" burst out a young man with an American accent.

"Well, that is the point. You will be competing with other life forms from other worlds, yes." Liew pointedly answered the young man's question. "This is a great honor, but there are a few compromises and rules if you wish to come to these Games."

The very spritely young man with light brown hair looked quizzically at his coach and elbowed his side, in a 'see I told you so' gesture.

"First: only the athletes are invited and not the coaches. If you choose to come, you come individually."

Almost every coach in the room looked horrified and quickly glanced over to their protégés. One noticeably older coach shouted, "BUT!"

Liew continued, ignoring objections. "Second:" He paused and put his hand up. The coach immediately grew silent. "No one else can know you are going off to compete in these Games. No friends, family, or heads of state of your individual countries. You all must sign another confidentiality agreement, immediately."

"Then why go?" interrupted one of the older female coaches.

"Please, let me get to rule three. If everything goes well, you all will be allowed, when you all return home, to share with the people of Earth your time and competitions at the Games. But if it doesn't go well, then you will never be allowed to speak of it again."

There was a giant rustle of movement and grumbling in the room. "Doesn't go well?" someone mumbled in broken English with a heavy accent. "What does that mean?" asked another.

Liew paused in front of the table until the room regained its silence.

"I'm not sure if you all understand what a great honor this is for you," he continued. "Humanity has been asked, *well ahead of schedule*, to take part in the greatest Games in the galaxy. You have been asked to introduce yourselves and your planet to the wider universe of other worlds and to be ambassadors for your beautiful planet.

"You will be the first human beings to meet other life forms, besides myself, from other worlds, as well as show the galaxy what human beings are capable of doing. This is a chance for Earth.

"Do well and Earth's mandatory introductory program could jump ahead by a full generation or more."

Ambassador Liew looked around the table at each of the now silent athletes. "Please understand, we have not asked any of Earth's politicians, heads of state, famous personalities, celebrities, astronauts, world renowned scientists, authors, or religious leaders to go out and make first contact for Humanity. It is you, Humanity's finest athletes, who will be the first."

The men and women around the table were left speechless. It was a humbling statement and offer. Liew was correct, except during the Olympics, when were these athletes the *first* and the *chosen*.

Liew turned to Director Xi, who handed him a small paper list. "As has been done for millennia, please let me announce each potential candidate for the Universe Olympics," stated Liew.

Director Xi stepped forward holding a large pile of papers. "If you agree to the terms and conditions, this is the agreement you *and* your coaches will sign. There will be no digital copy of this agreement; this is legally binding not only on our planet, Earth, but all others in the galaxy, as well."

Liew looked down at the paper Xi had handed to him and started at the top. "This is in no particular order, so let us begin. We, the Universe Olympic Committee, and I, as your Ambassador, are proud to invite from Planet Earth," he looked across the long wooden table to a cheerful face, "Amy Ride, from the United States of America for swimming."

A young woman who looked about seventeen-eighteen with long brown hair nodded. She was wearing a T-shirt printed with the words, *"Let's Ride"* in bright red letters on a wave of water, and underneath it in smaller red, white, and blue letters, "Go Team USA." Amy took in a breath and let out a giant squeal, "Thank you," she said to Liew.

Director Xi handed her a large stack of papers. "Please, read this carefully."

Liew continued, "Dmitri Pedrovich, from Russia for wrestling."

A very large man with long light brown hair pulled back in a ponytail, and muscles that could rival Hercules, grunted a sound that was neither a yes nor a no, more like "present."

"Zhang Yosi Chen, from China for gymnastics." The small (both in frame and in height) Asian girl, who appeared to be barely fifteen years old, smiled a little and bowed her head in acknowledgement.

"Marvin Rapperhand, from Great Britain for triathlon."

"Cheers, and call me Pappie, please. Good morning, everyone," he said, nodding to Liew and waving to the other athletes at the table.

"Jaysen William Powell, from the United States of America for decathlon."

A young man smiled. He had light brown skin and bright blue eyes. He was also wearing a T-shirt, but his read *"Pow–Wow"* in front of a silhouette of him throwing a javelin.

"Jenefer Washington Lee, from the United States of America for track and field events."

"Thank you, Lord Jesus," said Jenefer, who bowed her head down for a brief moment, thanking God for this second chance. She had won every short distance running event but one, the 100 meter hurdles. Her foot caught the second to last hurdle and she tripped, disqualifying. It was a regret that reached deep down in her heart. This opportunity was another chance. "And thank you, Ambassador."

"Ramon Stead, from Jamaica for bobsled," continued Liew.

The whole room let out a snicker, then an audible laugh at his home country and sport. Ramon quickly glanced at the other participants, almost defiant, before he smiled a bright white grin against his dark black skin. He joined in with good humor. "That's aight… That's aight…," he said in a thick Jamaican accent, nodding his head. "You, wait and see clear…"

"I thought it was only gold medalists, Ambassador Liew?" asked Jenefer Washington Lee, the African American woman sitting across the table from Ramon.

"I never implied that, Mrs. Washington Lee," answered Liew sternly.

Jenefer Washington Lee quickly closed her mouth and looked around the room. Every athlete in it, including herself, had won a gold medal for his or her individual event in the most recent Summer or Winter Olympic Games. Ramon Stead from Jamaica was the *only* person without a gold medal in any individual or team event, and whose ranking was below tenth in any world standing for their sport. In fact, if her memory served since it was a couple of years ago, the Jamaican bobsled team came in twenty-ninth in Harbin, China.

"Margit Housman, from Norway," continued Liew, "for cross-country skiing and biathlon." A beautiful blond with her hair pulled back in a ponytail smiled and nodded to the other athletes.

"'Stoke the Jam' Townsend, from the United States of America for half-pipe, and slopestyle."

"Stoked!" yelled the very young-looking kid, who appeared all of sixteen, at the mere mention of his name. "So stoked!" he screeched again even louder, pointing both hands up to the sky.

"Eric Verheinen, from the Netherlands for speed skating."

Eric turned and smiled at his fellow athletes at the table, a bright smile that matched his bright House of Orange shirt.

"Moses Al-Nair Shabbat, from Kenya for marathon, 5,000-meter, and 10,000-meter."

A few athletes gasped in the room, then turned to stare at Mo. He was by far the most famous and immediately recognizable athlete there, having become the face for the most recent Nairobi Summer Games. Moses was only the third man to win a marathon gold for Kenya since 1956. But with his home country as the host country, and to almost everyone's surprise, including his own, he also won the gold medals in both the 5,000-meter and 10,000-meter events. No one had ever done that trifecta before. And with the three wins in long distance running, both in track and field, and the marathon, he became the most famous athlete in the world overnight, giving rise to the hashtag "MO-mentum." Keep on going and never give up were his MO-mantras, and now the world's.

But his famous outward persona did not mesh well with his inward persona. He grew up dirt poor, running the countryside in Kenya, dreaming of one day winning the gold medal. The endorsements and prestige weren't the goals for him; they were, unfortunately, a necessary side effect to pay for his equipment, coaches, and training. He made sure at least half of the endorsements paid for the expenses of the rest of the Kenyan Olympic team. He didn't mind sharing. He grew up with eight brothers and sisters. So, in his mind, it went with the territory.

Mo hated all the attention of the room on him and he pretended to put his head down to examine the paperwork Director Xi put in front of him.

"Louis Emmanuelle Suarez, from Cuba for springboard and platform diving."

"*Gracias*, Manny, *por favor*," he said making the sign of the cross, kissing the St. Mary medal hanging around his neck, and putting his hand over his heart nodding slightly to the group.

"Yogitako Sito, from Japan for sport climbing."

A very well groomed, meticulously dressed man bowed his head reverently to Ambassador Liew.

"Josie and Jodie McQuenzy, from Australia for artistic-synchronized swimming."

The identical twins turned and smiled at each other in perfect unison, as if a mirror were next to a single person. Both were impeccably dressed in green sequined tops and makeup that would rival any drag queen in a New York nightclub.

"Ariel Arianna Foxx, from the Federated States of Micronesia for surfing."

A striking young woman with dark hair, dark eyes, and light brown skin, who exuded the essence of laid-back cool that accompanied most surfers, leaned forward and smiled. "Ari, please. Good… good!" She had almost an American accent, waving hello.

"And finally, Gretta Von Strither, from Germany for alpine skiing."

The blond with piercing blue eyes nodded her head. *"Danke schön."*

Liew put down the list and continued, "Every athlete will be allowed to bring any and all equipment required for their sport on this trip. Your coaches are allowed to record training sessions for each of you, but once we leave Earth all communications with your home world will cease."

"What if we say no?" a sheepish Moses asked while looking down at the privacy agreement, not making eye contact with any other athlete or Liew.

"This is your individual decision and I leave it up to you. But seeing worlds other than your own, meeting other life forms, and being a part of a historic first for Humanity are only the beginning of what awaits if you agree. Most importantly, for each of you, it allows you another chance to win.

"You each have twenty-four hours to discuss this with your coaches and make your decision. This is a once-in-a-lifetime experience, ladies and gentlemen. Humanity will only ever be introduced to the galaxy once, and you all have been chosen to be a part of this momentous event. It is an honor for you and for me to be a part of this with planet Earth. Thank you."

As Ambassador Liew turned and reached out, the revolving orbs flew back into his possession. He quietly left the room through a wooden panel that would never be mistaken for a door, as Director Xi stepped up to the head of the conference table. "We look forward to your answers, and please before you leave this room, today's nondisclosure agreement must be signed—that's the single sheet in front of you. Even if you choose not to go, this meeting must be kept above top secret. Thank you."

One of the older coaches immediately barged up to Director Xi, peppering her with questions, "Where are these Games taking place? How are they going to get there? What will they eat? Where will they stay? Are there going to be facilities for training? What specific events are at the Games? How long are they going to be gone? Who will watch over them—some of these athletes are minors?" Mr. Sayers eyed not only his prodigy Amy Ride, but Stoke the Jam, and Zhang Yosi Chen, as well.

"Not to worry, Mr. Sayers. It's all in the agreement," she said, tapping on the thick contract he had grabbed out of Ms. Ride's hands.

"Excuse me, Director Xi," said Amy who stepped beside her coach, "What does UNOOSA stand for? I've never heard of it before."

Director Xi smiled at the young athlete, "United Nations Office of Outer Space Affairs."

"Oh, *Outer Space* Affairs, well, this would qualify," she smiled at the Director, while taking back the contract from her coach.

"Yes, Ms. Ride. It does."

Chapter 2

Decisions

Moses went running that afternoon, like he always did when there was something important to decide. Running up and down the length of Manhattan three times wasn't exactly his idea of a quiet peaceful time, but it was what he needed to make up his mind; there was a big decision to make. He wasn't sure if he wanted to accept Ambassador Liew's offer to participate in the Milky Way Galaxy's version of the Olympic Games on another world. And he found it hard to focus while running amongst the loud honking cars, crowds, and never-ending ambient noise of New York City. He longed for the quiet countryside of Kenya where his mind could focus and make the important decision.

It had all been too much since winning three gold medals in the Summer Games in his home country. He didn't want all of this public attention, and *if* he went on this trip to the games, he knew what it meant—he would go down in the history of Humanity as one of the first people to step foot on another planet. He would be like Neil Armstrong and Buzz Aldrin, who until the day they died, and even after that, were best known for being the first men on the moon. He wondered if he would ever be able to move on from this. If he attended these Olympic Games, the world would *never* leave him alone.

Mo conjectured, as he crossed 51st Street again for the third time, that the other athletes didn't think about what would happen once they came home from these games. They, like all good competitors, only thought of the competition itself. He was once like that, but that all changed after the Kenyan Olympic Games. So much was expected of him, not only by his country, but merchandisers, media, fans, and the general public. He'd been swarmed every day since the games ended, and there was no end in sight. This wasn't what he expected or wanted when he won the gold medals: the constant recognition, notoriety, and fame. He thought it would have died down by now, but as time went by his notoriety has only amplified tenfold. It used to be all about winning for him and showing the world he was the best at his sport. Now, it was about sponsorships, endorsements, magazine covers, interviews, commercials, appearances, etc.—all the things he hated about sports.

And if he thought it was bad now, imagine how dreadful it would be when the world found out he not only traveled to another planet and was introduced to other life forms, but he also competed in *sports* against them as well. It would be a type of infamy he didn't want.

In fact, it was the closest thing to hell he could imagine. There would be no place left on planet Earth where he could be safe and find some peace and quiet. He knew his answer. And with that, Mo stopped running and headed back to his hotel.

*   *   *

Coach Sayers looked over the two-hundred-and-fifty-page single spaced contract and turned to Amy Ride, who was sitting across from him in the swanky hotel living room of their suite, comped by the UNOOSA.

"It's too many pages to go through in twenty-four hours, Amy. There is no way anyone can pinpoint all the particulars within this contract without a lawyer going through it with a fine-toothed comb."

"I guess this is a matter of faith and trusting Liew to do what is best for us," she said.

"See, Amy, I have two issues," said Sayers. "One, I don't trust Liew. He's not a human being and doesn't know the necessities of what goes into caring for a human. And two, he's not a coach. He has no idea—the workouts, regimes, sleep, food, training, cross-training, massage therapy, and everything else that goes into creating and maintaining an Olympic athlete."

"So… you don't want me to go," said Amy with a flat affect in her voice and raised eyebrows.

"No, I don't. We don't know anything about these games, what you'll face, what if there's an injury, or," his voice hesitated, "how long you'll be gone."

"I thought it said here," Amy grabbed the contract and flipped through the pages, "OK, yeah. Notice of affirmation or declination within twenty-four hours; a week to gather materials, equipment, wardrobe, and necessities before the team leaves Earth; and returning before December 25." Amy gleefully smiled, hoping to reassure her worried coach. "See, we'll be back before Christmas! There's nothing to worry about."

Coach Sayers snatched the contract from her hands and read out loud. "Yeah, but it doesn't specify which *year* you come back. Could be Christmas Eve, 2052."

Amy looked over her coach's shoulder and closely analyzed the contract. "Oh, good point."

"The devil is *always* in the details, Amy. It could take you a decade of our time to get there, with what we know about Einstein's Theory of Relativity."

She turned and sat down next to him. "True, but Coach, I *really* want to go."

"Amy, no. It's too big a risk. What if something were to happen to you? I'm not going to be there to help you out in any way. I barely have enough time to create all these 'coaching videos' in the next week. And I'm still not sure where the hell this thing is taking place." Coach

Sayers flipped to the beginning of the contract and put on his reading glasses. "It says you will be 'conveyed,' note that it doesn't say *how* you're conveyed nor how long it takes to get there, to the 3rd galactic quadrant - $180° \leq l \leq 270°$ near the Dranthlin nebulae, in the Outer Arm, wherever the hell that is!"

"The Dranthlin nebulae isn't ringing any bells over here," said Amy thoughtfully. "And I just took Astronomy class in school. Well, it was high school Astronomy; we mainly studied our tiny eight-planet solar system—still arguing Pluto is nine, but whatever."

"What about training facilities, training equipment, weights, a gym, lap pool?" Coach Sayers said pointing to the paper. "It only states, and I quote, 'Everything the athlete needs will be provided to prepare for his or her event' end quote." He boldly snatched the glasses off his face. "Amy, how are you going to swim in space?"

"Um, I don't know, Coach. Hold my breath."

"And you still have two, maybe three, more Olympics in you. Also, what about college next year? *AND* how the hell do I explain where you are to your parents? You know they check in with you every day. You are incommunicado once you board that ship. They will think you were kidnapped."

"I guess we could make up something about sending me to South America for Inca high altitude training, and the internet satellites don't work down there," she said, sounding as though she didn't even believe her own words. "OK, we need to come up with something better. Like pre-recorded video messages to them, or something. I hate lying to them like that…"

"I'm telling you, Amy. NO!"

"But Coach, this is it. There is no greater opportunity than this one, right now on Earth. The human Olympics are over. And to me it's worth the risk. Does this scare me? Yeah, a little bit, OK, a lot. I don't know these people, and worst-case scenario is that I don't swim for the next two months. I can make up for it when I get back with extra training and doubling my workout schedule till I start summer swim at college. I would rather take this gamble and not swim for two months than miss the chance to swim on another planet."

Coach Sayers was just sitting there. "Believe me, that's *NOT* the worst-case scenario, Amy," he said, shaking his head no, over and over.

"I wonder sometimes if I knew this was coming all along."

"What do you mean?"

"It's weird. During Astronomy class last semester, I kept imagining other planets in other galaxies. That's why I took that class, you know. I wanted to see new worlds. Learn about water on other planets. Would it be like the oceans of Europa and Enceladus, frozen all over, or just at the poles like ours and Mars? Were there any complex life forms in that water? If so, what would it be like to evolve on a purely ocean planet? And most importantly," she smiled at her Coach. "Could I swim in it?"

Amy stared for a moment at Coach Sayers. "Please, I think—I feel, I'm supposed to go."

*   *   *

Gretta did something unusual that Sunday afternoon. Well, it was unusual for her. She slowly walked into the American Museum of Natural History on 81st Street. Though she frequented museums all the time in Europe, those were art museums. This was a science museum. It had probably been fifteen years since she walked into any science museum, and this was her first visit to a planetarium.

She proceeded through the museum's first floor, not stopping to view any of the North American mammals, or the giant blue whale model. She headed straight to the pre-show area for the next Hayden Planetarium Space Show. It was called "Liew's Light."

As she walked into the theater at the bottom of the hour, she half expected to see other athletes from this morning's meeting to be seated around the semispherical planetarium. She took a long hard look around. Gretta was mildly surprised that she was the only Olympian in there. But maybe, she rationalized, some might have come to an earlier show. They did run every half hour.

Gretta had to witness with her own eyes where they were going. This new space show was an exploration of the neighborhood of the Milky Way Galaxy where Liew came from, and he did say the games were taking place near his "home quadrant." So, she figured if she saw the vicinity of where they were going, it would help her grasp how far away she was going to be from home.

The lights dimmed and above her head, in the concave sixty-seven-foot-wide dome, she saw Earth being projected and slowly rotating. It took up her entire field of vision.

"Earth, home to us all, but for one," began a narrator's voice with the soothing cadence and baritone resonance of James Earl Jones but was most probably Neil deGrasse Tyson. "The colors of our home world: the greens, blues, and whites, shine bright in our hearts."

The scene slowly pulled back, with Earth becoming smaller and smaller on the screen, passing a small space station. "Let us today leave the comfort and safety of our planet, and travel to the home star of Ambassador Liew." The title, "Liew's Light," appeared floating in space, next to the half-lit sphere of Earth. "If we were to travel at the speed of light, it would take us about eight minutes just to get to the source of our nourishment, the sun."

The view quickly flashed past our bright yellow star and continued on through space, approaching the first planet. "The light from our sun reaches Mercury in 3.2 minutes." A small planet whizzed by, to be taken over by another larger planet, that gleamed all white. "Venus, in 6 minutes, and going further reaching Mars (a red planet swiftly came into view) would take us twelve minutes, still traveling at the speed of light." The picture zoomed by Mars and onward past an asteroid belt nearing Jupiter as swirls of browns, reds, and whites enveloped the screen. "Jupiter in 45 minutes, again traveling at the fastest rate human beings know how to travel." The images began speeding up immensely.

"Past our other gas giants; Saturn, 79 minutes; Uranus, just over 2 hours; and finally, Neptune, 4.1 hours." All three planets quickly whooshed by and the pale-yellow dot that is our sun became smaller and smaller in the distance.

"Even at the speed of light, we won't reach Pluto and the Kuiper Belt for 5.5 hours. And that is just our humble solar system." The images pull past Pluto and the Kuiper belt into interstellar space. A plethora of small lights, suns, scattered in front of Gretta's eye.

"We have to cross a vastness of space and a hundred thousand other suns, too many to name, past our arm of the Milky Way Galaxy where we live, the Orion Arm. We need to proceed through another arm of the Milky Way Galaxy on the road to our destination. It takes us ten thousand light years to make it into the Perseus Arm." A star view of every color in the imagination—nebulae, stardust, gasses, white dwarfs, red dwarfs, yellow dwarfs, blue giants, red giants, and red supergiant suns, and planets—passed her eyes almost too quickly for the brain to take in all the information.

"It will take us another ten thousand light years until we reach our final destination today: the newly discovered Outer Arm of the Milky Way Galaxy, now known as Liew's Arm. As we arrive at Ambassador Liew's home solar system, even at the speed of light, it would take a human being more than thirty thousand years to conventionally arrive at his home planet."

The distances were too far and too great for Gretta to fathom realistically. The time needed and the enormity of space between Earth and Liew's part of the galaxy daunted her. She stared, wide-eyed, up at the star view above her head.

The narrator's voice comes in, "Finally we reach the nineteen-planet solar system of Liew's Arm." There were two binary red dwarf suns on the outskirts, revolving around each other, and a large third yellow dwarf star, much like Earth's sun, residing in the center of that solar system. "It would be hard for us to fathom a planet as far out as Liew's containing complex life forms, but the universe is a miraculous place and life always finds a way."

"We have finally reached the light that is the nourishment of Liew's home world, Beiahisa." A very healthy yellow dwarf sun shines on a large green planet far in the distance. "This sun, which they call Jeen, is the light of Liew."

"Let's hop, skip, and jump across the outer Liew's Arm, past the Perseus Arm, back to our Orion Arm, which is really a spur, only to realize the light emitted from Liew's civilization hasn't even reached our eyes on Earth yet," said the narrator. But it was three jumps too far for Gretta. She quietly got out of her seat. Her head, and now her heart, knew her answer.

*   *   *

It happened naturally; even though it was never specified in the contract, or agreed upon by any athlete, coach, Director Xi, or Liew. The very next morning, Monday, October 20, 2036, at 8:55 a.m., a line started to form outside the door of the conference room, United Nations Secretariat building.

Pappie was at the head of the queue and very proud of it. He waited patiently, vigilantly watching the closed door. The British pride themselves on their ability to form a proper queue, in an orderly fashion, showing the rest how it's done.

The line of other Olympians slowly started to form behind him. Ari arrived second, placing herself directly behind Pappie, then Dmitri, until three turned into five, and five to eight, then twelve, all standing quietly. It seemed instinctual to a group of people who waited their turn in order to compete. It went with sports.

At precisely 9:30 a.m., twenty-four hours to the minute, the door opened, and Director Xi popped her head out. "Oh good. Mr. Rapperhand, please come in, first."

Pappie looked back at the others and gave a slight smile. He followed the Director into the wood paneled room, and sitting in the closest seat to the door, not the head of the conference table, was Liew. He looked up.

"Good morning, Mr. Rapperhand."

"Good morning, Ambassador, call me Pappie, please."

"Do you have your answer, Pappie?"

"Yes, sir. I do. I would be privileged to join this team representing Earth."

"I'm so pleased to hear it," said Liew, holding out his hand waiting for the contract. Such a large packet of paperwork was rare nowadays, considering nearly everything was digital and using physical paper was considered wasteful. But tradition was tradition. These had to be physical contracts with no other electronic trail.

Pappie handed him the papers.

"All signed, then?"

"Yes, Sir."

"Please be ready to go in one week. You will be instructed as to the rendezvous point, presently."

"Thank you, sir." Pappie turned and walked out of the conference room grinning wildly.

Ari waited for Pappie to exit and only when he walked back out of the door did she enter.

As soon as she entered the room, Liew spoke. "My dear girl, will you join us?"

"I would be honored to, Ambassador Liew," said Ari, placing the contract on the table in front of Liew.

"Ms. Foxx, please be ready in one week. That would be Monday, October 27th."

"Yes, Ambassador. I'll be ready." Ari nodded to Liew and immediately turned around, heading out of the room.

As she departed, Dmitri briskly walked in. Without another word, he went straight up to Liew and said, *"Da!"* He handed Liew the paperwork, turned, and marched out of the room just as quickly, not waiting for a response from the Ambassador.

"Mr. Pedrovich is a yes," chuckled Director Xi, who had been hovering just behind Liew the whole time. "I'll inform him the departure date is next week, Ambassador."

"Thank you," answered Liew.

Following Dmitri was Amy and her coach Mr. Sayers. Amy skipped in and bobbed up to Ambassador Liew at the conference table.

Mr. Sayers spoke first. "It's against my better judgment."

Amy interrupted, "I'm going!" She handed Liew the huge, signed stack of paperwork.

"Wonderful, Ms. Ride. And we are very happy to have you."

Mr. Sayers stopped her just before she walked off. "BUT, I have one concession I need from you, Liew."

Amy jolted to a halt, surprised by his announcement.

"Please name it, Mr. Sayers," said Liew.

"We need alternates for her. I don't want her, or any athlete competing, to feel they need to participate because there is no one else there to replace them nor is there a coach to advise them on pushing their bodies too far. To have my consent, not that you need it, but *she* does, I request at least two alternates."

"Understandable, Mr. Sayers." Liew pondered for a minute. "Yes, consider it done. I think it is a very good suggestion. We can do that for the team. We leave in one week."

"OK, then, Amy can go." Mr. Sayers looked at Amy, who jumped up and down repeatedly, silently mouthing the words, "YES!"

Mr. Sayers had a resigned stare as he followed her jubilant steps out the door.

Next in sauntered a very large well-built man with confidence in his stride. "My answer is, yes, Mr. Ambassador. I wouldn't miss this for the world, or yours." said Ramon laughing, as he dropped the papers on the conference table.

"Wonderful to hear it, Mr. Stead. You will be an *invaluable* member of this team. We leave in a week."

Behind him was Yogitako Sito, well dressed and perfectly manicured in a well-tailored suit, no tie, clean-cut lines, and jacket. He bowed when he reached Liew. "*Hai, Ambassadoe Liew. Dōmo arigatōgozaimashita,*" said Sito as he handed Liew the contract then bowed again.

"Please prepare and be ready in one week, *Yogitako-san,*" answered Liew in Japanese.

"*Hai,*" replied Sito, who turned and left the room.

Waiting in the doorway was a tall blonde. She walked over to Liew. "I am pleased to come, *Tusen takk,*" said Margit handing over the papers.

"Perfect, Ms. Housman. Please be ready in one week."

Jaysen was the next through the door. He headed up to Liew. "We're all good, Ambassador Liew."

"Is that a yes, Mr. Powell?"

"Yup. Pow-Wow *in*." Jaysen made a punching motion in the air, pointed up to the sky, and threw the contract on the table.

"Fine. Please be ready in one week."

Zhang Yosi Chen walked through the door; her grumbling coach hardly a step behind her. Her English was broken, but passable. "I want to, Ambassador Liew, but my coach doesn't want me to go without him."

"Ms. Zhang, you were the one invited, not your coach. The decision is yours alone."

Yosi hurriedly handed Liew the papers. "*Shì, Xièxiè.*" She bowed to the Ambassador.

"Good, be ready in one week, Ms. Zhang," he responded in Chinese.

She bowed again, smiling at hearing her native language, and quickly ran out the door with her coach protesting loudly in Chinese behind her.

Next up, looking perfectly coordinated and in matching blue outfits, were the McQuenzy twins. Jodie strolled up and handed Liew her paperwork. "Can't wait, Mate!"

Half a step behind her, her identical twin Josie concurred, "Rock yeah, Liew."

"Girls, we leave in one week. Please have everything ready."

Both nodded and spoke in perfect unison, "Cheers!" They caught each other's eye and screamed, "Jinx!" at the same time.

Jodie leaned into Liew, "It happens so often, it's not even funny anymore."

"Oi! It *IS!*" howled Josie. "Very funny!" They both turned, again in perfect unison with a bit of a hand flare and glided away triumphantly.

Following the twins, Eric rolled in.

"How about you, Mr. Verheinen?"

"*Goedemorgen,* Ambassador Liew. Yes, I would be pleased to attend these games."

"*Goed,* please be ready by next Monday," replied Liew.

"I will, and thank you for this opportunity, Ambassador." Eric placed his contract on the conference table next to the other papers, and promptly left the conference room.

Next up was Gretta. She walked straight up to Liew.

"Are you coming, Ms. Von Strither?" he asked in German.

"*Nein,* Ambassador Liew."

"Are you sure?" he continued in fluent German. "You would be a powerful addition to this team. I specifically requested for *you* to join us."

"Yes, I am sure," she said with a heavy heart.

"Very well," answered Liew in English, gesturing behind him. "If you change your mind, please contact Director Xi. Best of luck to you, Ms. Von Strither."

She remorsefully gave Liew her unsigned paperwork. "It was a pleasure meeting you, Ambassador. Please know this decision had nothing to do with you. I just don't want to travel so far away from home." She calmly turned and left the room.

Behind her was Manny, wearing a long-sleeved silk shirt splashed with every color of the rainbow. He sauntered into the room and gracefully handed Liew his paperwork. "*Sí*, Mr. Ambassador, and I would like to thank you for this opportunity."

"You're welcome, *Señor* Suarez. Please be ready in one week."

Manny smiled, "*Sí, Señor*," and nodded, and left the room.

Next, in sashayed Stoke the Jam, using a very different stride. He was purposely putting each hand in front of him accentuating each cross step. As he approached Liew he squealed, "Oh, so *STOKED!*"

"I take that is a, yes, Mr. Townsend."

"Yup-duppy!" he said bowing, placing the folded paperwork in his hands onto the table.

"Oh good. You will need to be ready in one week."

"No probs. Ready now, Bro." He winked at Liew, then swaggered sideways, doing a form of the electric slide out of the room.

After he left, a slight chuckle could be heard from Director Xi behind Liew. He glanced back at her, and she cleared her throat trying to cover up the lapse of formality. "Should be an interesting group, Ambassador."

"Yes, indeed, Director Xi. The best Humanity has to offer."

Behind Stoke marched in Jenefer. "Thank you, Ambassador Liew, for this opportunity. My answer is a proud yes, praise the Lord."

"You're welcome, Mrs. Washington Lee. Please be ready in one week."

"Perfect. That's more than enough time to get my nails redone, my hair fixed-up, and all my equipment ready. You think it would be OK if I put bling on my fingernails? There's no rules against jewelry or long nails that I read in the contract."

"I think that will be fine, Mrs. Washington Lee. As long as it doesn't impede you during the competition."

Jenefer put down the contract and held up her inches long bedazzled nails painted with red and purple flames. "You kidding? These things? No problem. They have their own, Twitter, Insta, Torbillion, and Poyaint VR feeds. *They* have more followers than I do personally!"

"Even I follow them," interjected Director Xi.

"See!" said Jenefer, smiling and holding up her nails for the Director to get an up-close look.

"Very nice, Mrs. Washington Lee," said Director Xi, beaming.

"We will see you Monday, October 27," finished Liew.

"Yes, sir. I'll be ready." She exited the conference room.

Liew waited a moment for the next athlete to enter, but no one else was behind Jenefer. He surveyed the room, and the door, then the pile of contracts on the conference table. "Sixteen answers."

"One to go," said Director Xi, who never wavered from her position behind the Ambassador.

After waiting a few minutes in silence, a somber looking man ambled into the conference room; His head held down, he made no eye contact with Liew or Director Xi.

"And what about you, Mr. Al-Nair Shabbat?" asked Liew breaking the long silence.

"Ambassador, I'm afraid I must disappoint you. My answer is no."

"I'm very sorry to hear that. May I ask the reason why?"

"The publicity that will come after we return home will be too much for me to handle. There won't be a single place left on the Earth where I won't be recognized. These young ones don't understand. They don't realize the consequences of what they are about to do."

"Do *you* understand the consequences of what you are about to do, Mr. Al-Nair Shabbat?" questioned Liew, quite seriously.

Mo was taken aback. He wasn't expecting Liew to fight him on this decision, and he remained silent, contemplating.

"I have already lost one athlete," responded Liew after a good long moment. "I'd hate to lose two. Will you please reconsider?"

Mo stood still, just shaking his head no.

"Very well, Mr. Al-Nair Shabbat. This is your decision, but if you change your mind, please let Director Xi know. I still believe you could be an outstanding member of Earth's team. It's a shame to lose you."

Moses glanced at Liew only once, then sheepishly walked out of the conference room.

Director Xi followed Moses to the door then closed it sharply. "His answer gives us fifteen ayes," she said returning to Liew. "And two nos. It's better than I thought, Ambassador."

"That's two less than *I* thought," huffed Liew. "It's a shame. I wish they knew I picked each of them for a reason." He sighed heavily. "If either of them comes back to you and reconsiders for any reason, at any time, please let me know."

"Of course, Ambassador."

Liew stood up, and holding a small silver ball in his hand, projected a hologram of the athletes' faces above the conference table. He swooshed the images around, switching to the faces of Moses and Gretta, and touched their foreheads. Their holographic pictures turned red. Those who said yes, he touched one by one, turning them green. "The fifteen faces of the team from Earth."

"It's a good team," answered Xi.

"It will be, Director Xi."

Liew threw up three additional faces into the holographic mix. The red, green, and new faces revolved in a circle as he touched the air. As foreign writing projected from an invisible keyboard above each head, the hologram created a white highlight around each individual face. He swished his hand up to the sky, and all the holograms disappeared. "It will be."

Chapter 3

Olympic Flame

For the athletes, the week flew by in the blink of an eye. Between practice sessions, travel preparations, equipment selections, and meetings with coaches, the departure week was upon them, as well as the realization that soon all of them would be gone from planet Earth—home. They would be doing what no human had done since the 1960s—stepping into the unknown. They would go beyond our solar system to another one.

In truth, not a single member of the team knew what to expect from the games. There were many guesses. Amy wondered if the competition would take place on a single planet similar to Earth. Others, including Stoke and Jodie, speculated it would look like something from the latest Granger Island VR game—except for taking place in space, after all they were aliens. The majority of the chosen athletes didn't guess at all. They understood that it was important to wait and see what the games would bring—prepare as well as humanly possible and be open to anything happening. Because in life, as well as in sports, often what you don't expect to happen, too often does. The Universe Olympics were beyond what they, or any human being, had experienced before, but these competitors were chosen because they were the best the world had to offer. If they couldn't do it, no one could.

"Let's just hope we're good enough, to beat whatever or whichever 'beings' we're up against," said Pappie to his coach the day before the scheduled rendezvous.

Everyone was waiting silently and patiently at 6:10 a.m., Monday, October 27th, at the rendezvous point in the Brooklyn Navy Yard. The amount of luggage and equipment sitting around the athletes would make any bellhop cringe. These contestants had bags, boxes, containers, and piles and piles of luggage near diva level. Surprisingly, the person who had the most equipment wasn't the decathlete, the triathlete, the skier, or even the bobsledder; one would have thought the decathlete would have the most to bring—ten being the magic number. Shockingly, the person with the most gear was Ariel Foxx, the surfer.

In the early morning dew, the Olympians quietly waited patiently for whatever was supposed to happen. At 6:18 a.m. Jaysen strolled over to Ari, who was standing by a pile of boxes almost twenty feet high.

"So, I hate to ask the obvious question here," mused Jaysen in a hushed voice, eyeing her equipment. "But how many surfboards are you bringing?"

"Twenty-four."

"*Twenty-four*! And I thought I had a lot of baggage with the javelins and poles."

"I couldn't help it. And I think I'm being conservative. My coach wanted me to bring thirty-five, but we narrowed it down to the twenty-four most critical boards."

"Ok, *WOW!*" The irony of the word was not lost on a man named Pow-Wow Powell.

"I have a bunch of thruster boards, fish boards, long boards, and a few gun boards."

"Why so many?"

"Each board is for a different range of wave sizes. I'm not sure how big each of these sets are going to be. And each board can have a different number of fins, which changes its performance. You can have a single, twin, thruster, quad, and five-fin, as well as different board tail shapes and sizes."

"I had no idea it was that complicated."

"Yeah, then there's the multitude of waxes I need for different water temperatures. I don't know how warm or cold this water will be, wherever we're going."

"Yeah, we don't know much do we," stated Jaysen, realizing for all the contract had said about zero communication to and from Earth, strict rules of conduct, passports, and near perfect isolation from all the other members of the human race, it said practically nothing about what each of the games were going to be, what the rules were for each particular event, and how they could win it.

"But I'm covering every gravitational possibility," said Ari with a smile. "Gravity's the surfer's best friend, that and the moon. Bet you didn't think of that before?"

"No, in fact I didn't."

"So, no matter what the break, pipeline, or peanut, I'm ready. Ever surf, Jaysen?"

"Once in California around the San Diego area, but I wasn't very good."

"Don't give up! When this is over, I'll get you surfing again, if you like."

Then there was a sound that wasn't a sound, but an emptiness like a hollow pop that descended on them; it was the vast movement of air and the change in air pressure as the silver ship instantaneously and silently appeared over the top of the athletes. Ari and Jaysen looked up in the sky fifty feet above them. "I think that's our ride," he said.

"*Ehng,*" Ari said, looking up at the ship as it slowly creeped down to rest half on the ground, half over the river.

The triangular silver ship had no obvious windows or doors, and was the size of a New York City block, both vertically and horizontally. It finally landed without a sound next to the group of waiting athletes. The bottom tip of the triangle facing the athletes, opened and Liew walked out.

"Good morning, everyone," he said, sauntering over to the huddled group. It was quite an entrance. "I'm glad to see you all made it here, on time. Please, follow me," he said quickly turning around to go back into the ship.

Ramon and Ari hesitated for a moment next to their large boxes of piled equipment. Liew stopped and glanced back at the two as the rest of the group walked up to him. "Don't worry about your equipment, Ms. Foxx, Mr. Stead. I promise it will be loaded. Come on board. Hurry, please, we have a very tight schedule to meet." Liew was the most cheerful and happy they had ever seen him.

As all the athletes boarded, there was another surprise waiting just a few feet inside the ship. Where the small hallway met a long main passageway, there were three new human faces. Every one of the named athletes was surprised to see additional humans.

There was a man and a woman, both tall, lean, fair-skinned, and light-brown hair, and their close proximity to each other indicated a paired relationship. The third was a shorter muscular olive-skinned brunette woman standing by herself.

All eighteen humans stared, waiting in silence until Liew marched up to make the introductions.

"Oh yes, everyone, I'd like to introduce you to our three Alternates. This is Mark and Justine Hallperan, from Canada," said Liew gesturing toward the couple. "And this is, Onorina Di Mateo from Italy."

"Hello," said Mark and Justine, one after the other.

"*Buon giorno*," said Onorina. "Good morning," she repeated in English.

"This is Pappie Rapperhand," continued Liew pointing to the group crowded together across from the three alternates, "Jaysen Powell, Ariel Foxx, Dmitri Pedrovich, Josie and Jodie McQuenzy, Manny Suarez, 'Stoke the Jam' Townsend."

"Dude, just Stoke!" interrupted Stoke.

"Yes, and Amy Ride, Zhang Yosi Chen, Eric Verheinen, Yogitako Sito, Margit Housman, Jenefer Washington Lee, and Ramon Stead."

"Very nice to meet you all," said Justine with a smile on her face. Mark nodded to the group.

"Which of us needs alternates?" asked Manny, knowing full well who the Hallperans were. The entire planet knew who they were, but not *why* they were here.

"Mr. and Mrs. Hallperan are pairs figure skaters, and Ms. Di Mateo is a pentathlete."

"Oni, *per favore*," she said to the speechless group.

Amy looked shaken, which was odd, considering she knew Liew had promised her coach alternates. She stepped forward, "Wait! I thought you told my coach there would be alternate swimmers?" she said shocked, while the other athletes appeared just as stunned that *she* knew what Liew was talking about.

"Oh, she swims, Ms. Ride. It's one of the five events in the pentathlon."

"Yeah, I know that, Liew. I think my coach thought you'd get just a swimmer, like me, as an alternate?"

"Oh no, Ms. Ride. You are the only 'just swimmer' in the group. But don't worry, Ms. Di Mateo is one of the best athletes on your planet. All three of these athletes are Alternates for the *whole* team from Earth."

There was an awkward moment between Onorina and Amy before Liew announced, "It's time to show you all around the ship! The main door behind me goes to the shuttle bay. Hurry now, please, follow me. There's not much time."

*   *   *

First up on the tour, down a very long hallway and up a few flights of stairs—Liew assured them there was an elevator, but not one big enough to accommodate the entire group of nineteen comfortably— was a very large set of open doors. The group of athletes walked into a room the size of three football fields.

"I thought since this is the main area where most of you will be spending your time, we should start the tour here, first," said Liew heading into the room. "This is your gym, or workout arena, as I call it."

And it was the size of an arena, maybe three. The room in both size and scope looked like the inside of an airplane hangar—high ceilings, bright warm lights, and every type of exercise equipment imaginable (and unimagined) laid out in orderly rows in front of them.

"Please know," continued Liew, "I spoke with each of your coaches and every type of equipment, machine, or facility that every individual trains with for your sport is here. And I added in a few extras for variety. Ask me or the glass panels on the wall if you're not sure," said Liew, as he indicated the square glass panel next to the door. With a touch, words, categories, and maps appeared on the panel.

The group hushed in awed silence. It was, for an athlete, a spectacular site to behold, like a playroom for adults. They took a few steps into the arena, eyes filled with exhilaration at the rows and rows of different types of machines. Weights, ropes, rowing, bikes, balls, and apparatuses all sprawled across three football fields.

"Oh. Around the door here on the left, are your lockers and cubby holes to put your stuff—towels, clothes, bags, water bottles, equipment, energy food, etc.," said Liew pointing to a long row of wide conventional-looking lockers and oversized cubby holes like those used in a kindergarten class.

"Only the person whose name is on the front of the locker or cubby can take what's in it."

Stoke tried to reach into the nearest cubby which had Amy's name on it, but his hand couldn't go further than the opening. "Cool!" he said, jamming his hand into the invisible barrier.

The group scattered towards their respective lockers and cubbies.

"Lest I forget, men's restroom and locker rooms are to the left, and ladies' to the right, but there's more scattered throughout the arena, for your convenience."

Ramon walked up to his cubby, reached inside and pulled out a small two-by two-inch clear square that was as thin as a sticker. It looked like and felt like one, with a sticky adhesive back.

"Ambassador, what's this?" he asked.

"Oh yes, I know you weren't allowed to take any electronic devices with you on this trip, and I understand each of you listen to music while you're training, so I came up with this handy alternative."

Most people reached inside and pulled out the clear sticker.

"How does it work?" asked Sito, holding up the small clear square.

"It sticks to any surface; put it on your clothes, your swimsuit, even your skin," said Liew. "It's waterproof, actually it's practically indestructible."

Stoke immediately switched the patch from his arm to his face several times to test the adhesiveness.

"Touch or speak to the screen and the playlists each of you were listening to, as well as other music, are on each one. Your specific earbuds are in the cubby too," said Liew, pointing to the nearest hole.

Ari grabbed one of her earbuds, barely the size of her earhole, and put it in. "How much music is in the library, Ambassador?"

"All of it," said Liew matter-of-factly.

"You mean all of our digital music libraries?" questioned Ramon, playing with his small earbuds, which were tiny in his hands, and the same dark black color as his own skin.

"No, all recorded music."

"In history?" wondered Jodie.

"Up to this point, Ms. McQuenzy, yes. And I tossed in a few from my home world in case you all were curious."

Margit touched the small square screen and said, "Liew's music," very softly. His name popped up, and she pressed the first song titled, "Grape Jelly." She flinched at the name, figuring it was a mistranslation into Norwegian.

"The library is also categorized by decade and type of music, as well. Please listen to your playlists or try something new."

"This is rad, Liew," said Stoke, putting the clear square back on his arm. "I'm never taking it off."

"Trying to make you all feel more at home, Mr. Townsend. I know how hard it was to leave all your digital devices behind."

"It feels weird not to have my smartphone," said Amy remorsefully.

"Or the internet," added Jenefer, ruefully looking at her newly designed nails that no one would appreciate via social media.

"Which reminds me, for those of you whose base language isn't English, you can also use the earbud as an immediate translator."

Liew stepped up to Yosi, speaking in Chinese, "Touch the patch, and say, translate into Chinese, put the bud in your ear, and it will translate all conversations for you."

"*Shì, Xièxie.*"

"And that works the other way around for everyone else too. Just put in one earbud. Hit or say *translate* and let Yosi comfortably speak in Chinese to you." He looked around at the group, adding, "Or listen in Italian, Norwegian, Japanese, Russian, Spanish…"

"We get the picture, Ambassador," smiled Ari.

Liew walked into the arena. "If you have any questions, please ask anytime. Next, over here, this is our treadmill, Mr. Powell and Mrs. Washington Lee."

Jaysen stepped up beside Liew. He looked down at a patch on the floor that was slightly lighter in color than the silver-grey of the rest of the floor. "How does it work?"

"Go onto the designated area and begin running. The floor will move with you. Stop for two seconds when you're done."

Jaysen stepped on the slightly lighter part of the floor and began running. The three-foot square around him moved at the speed of his pace. "WOW," said Jaysen, who seemed to be stuck on only one descriptive adjective.

It made a few of the other athletes wonder if Jaysen purposely said that adjective since it was his nickname, or it was the reason why he got the nickname in the first place.

"Race, ya," retorted Jenefer, strutting over to the light-grey square next to Jaysen and she began running at a sprint. Jaysen tried to keep up with her pace, but it was impossible to keep up with the only woman to ever beat Florence Griffith Joyner's 100-meter and 200-meter 1988 Olympic world track records. Jenefer was the fastest woman alive.

"Call me Jen," she said to Jaysen, barely out of breath.

"To the left is your decathlete training facility, Mr. Powell," said Liew, pointing directly to the immediate left at a triangular area. "You can train with your discus, shotput, pole vault, long jump, even javelins too."

Jaysen half-nodded in response, as he sprinted in place. Sweating and losing steam next to Jen, he finally gave up the race, walking over to his decathlete area.

Liew continued further into the arena. "Over here are the bikes, Pappie," he said pointing out a long row of sleek cycles standing up straight without any stands. "For those of you who cross-train on the cycles, there are road bikes, mountain bikes, and BMX bikes to choose from."

Pappie immediately jumped on the road bike that was identical to his racing bike and began peddling. "Liew, this feels oddly similar to my race bike! Down to the weight."

"Yes, it is," answered Liew. "An exact copy."

Pappie was joined by Manny on a different BMX bike that was a few feet further down the low row of bikes.

"That's the gymnastics training area, Ms. Zhang," Liew said in Chinese, pointing far off to the middle-left where a balance beam, uneven bars, vault, and even a floor area waited for an athlete to occupy it.

"And Mr. Suarez," said Liew, nodding to a large open hallway past the gymnastics area. "This is for you."

Manny jumped off his bike and trotted over to Liew.

"Down this hallway is the diving room. Touch the glass panel by the door or tell it what you want to dive off of: springboard, platform, even cliff, and the height of the dive, then walk in."

"*Muchás, muchás gracias, Ambassador*," said Manny smiling then springing down the hallway.

"Some free weights, Dmitri," said Liew. Moving on, he pointed to a long row of hand weights in every size lined up perfectly. He and Ramon stopped and picked up a few heavy weights and began pumping. "And a few bench presses..."

Liew lost a few stragglers behind as they checked out their specific areas. "Mr. Townsend," he said, continuing further into the arena.

"Stoke! Dude please," said a voice from far away on the treadmill, trying to keep up with Jen and now Onorina running.

"In the back left is the snow room!"

"There's a snow room?" asked Stoke, darting up to Liew.

"Yes, for you and Margit to practice. You can change it to half-pipe or slopestyle from the glass panel beside the door."

"DUDE!" yelled Stoke, running up to the room.

"And Margit," said Liew. "Touch the panel and tell it which snow terrain you want and the distance, then walk in."

"Wonderful," she said, though Stoke almost pushed her out of the way.

"Shotgun!" shouted Stoke, touching the panel and sprinting into the snow room first.

"Stoke, we don't have our equipment yet," called out Margit, walking in after him.

"Don't care…" called a faint voice deep inside the room.

"And me, Ambassador?" questioned Eric, who stood behind him.

"Oh yes, I'm sorry, Mr. Verheinen. There's an inline-skate track for you to practice in the back left, as well as a small ice rink for you and the Hallperans to share on the opposite side of the arena, in the back right," Liew said pointing to both far off in the distance.

After most of the group left to play, the few athletes left behind finally reached the very back wall of the workout arena. "And this is for you, Sito-san," said Liew in Japanese, pointing to a long wall that had hundreds of sport climbing hand and foot holds up to the top of the fifty-five-foot ceiling. "If you'd like to change the course, the glass panel on the left will change it to any arrangement you want, touch or say your preference. You can even ask for a random alignment."

Sito bowed to Liew and touched the panel. The hand and footholds, as well as the small and large elevations running up and down the wall, moved into another zigzag formation. Without any ropes, proper clothes, or shoes, Sito climbed the first foothold to feel its strength.

As the remaining group circled back past the ice rink, Ari tugged on Liew sleeve. "Not that I expect anything, Mr. Ambassador..."

"Of course, we have something for you, Ms. Foxx. It's next to the twins' practice room."

Ari, Amy, Liew, and the twins walked over to another entranceway. "This is the wave room. Tell the glass panel what breaks you want, time of day and year, from where, and how many. It will give it to you."

Ari smiled and stepped inside. "Unbelievable. Thank you, Ambassador."

Liew raised his voice, "Ms. Di Mateo!"

In a few moments, Onorina jogged over to Liew. "*Sì, Ambassador*," she said, rushing up. "Oni, please."

"Oni, this is your training area," announced Liew, pointing to the large space between the weights and the wave room. "There is a shooting range for you and Ms. Housman to share, as well as a fencing practice area."

Oni smiled. "Thank you," she said.

Meandering into the shooting range, she grabbed an air pistol, checked it, and shot at a red dot target which swiftly turned green, after only a few rounds. She was an expert sharpshooter, as was any pentathlete.

A little further down the arena, past the shooting range, was another entranceway. "Girls, this is for you," said Liew, acknowledging the McQuenzy sisters. "The pool room."

The twins look at each other and smiled, "Cheers, Liew!" they said as they headed down the hallway.

Amy was about to follow them inside when Liew tapped her on the shoulder.

"Where are you going, Ms. Ride?"

"You said that was the pool room?"

"No, I said that was for the McQuenzy twins. It is a grid bottom pool specifically made for synchronized swimming."

Liew continued walking back toward the main entrance of the workout arena.

"This lap pool, Ms. Ride, is for you." Liew pointed down a long hallway. "Let's go see it."

Amy followed Liew down the hallway to a metal open-mesh gangway that hovered over an unbelievable sight—the most perfect infinity pool that ever existed. The water was in a perpetual 360° circle. It defied gravity. Amy's eyes slowly made a lap of the pool, starting at the right-side stairs, up and over their heads—the water somehow suspended in mid-air—and down to the left, making a perfect ring.

Amy gazed at the water directly over her head. "Will I fall down swimming in this?"

"No, you can't, Ms. Ride, once you're in the water. The full circle circumference measures half a lap of an Olympic-sized swimming pool."

"OK," said Amy, the incredulity present in her voice.

"Pappie and Onorina will also want some time to swim their laps," mentioned Liew.

"I'll coordinate with them," said Amy, crouching on the gangway to examine the water that circled down below, then flowed back up to the small stairs on the other side. "This is way cool, Liew," said Amy, standing back up. "But I have to admit, I'm a little afraid to swim in it."

"Don't be. Give it a few laps and you'll be fine. If you'd feel more comfortable, I'm happy to be here during your first training session, Amy."

She smiled a reassuring smile to the Ambassador. Her trust and faith in Liew, like her trust in Coach Sayers, seemed well placed. "I'd like that, thank you."

Amy got up and followed behind Liew, heading back into the arena. He touched the glass panel by the door, and his voice echoed over the whole room. "Everyone, please return to the main entrance. There will be time for your training later. We need to continue on to the next part of our tour. We have a very tight schedule to keep."

*   *   *

On board the ship everyone was taken up stairs to the main deck of the ship. Liew stopped at a very long, brightly lit hallway with doors every fifteen to twenty feet. "It's not a village," he said, gazing down the long corridor, "I know that's what you are used to, but this is the Athlete's Corridor. You'll find your name on the front door of your individual cabin. Please go see."

The curious athletes walked down the warm, earth toned carpet to their individual cabins.

As each person stepped inside their prospective room, something mysterious happened. Loud gasps, hollers, even a quiet scream, could be heard one by one in succession down the corridor as each athlete disappeared inside their rooms.

A head appeared out of a door halfway down the hall, "Liew, what the…?" yelled Josie at the top of her lungs.

A small voice, four doors down from hers, could be heard yelping, "*Dios mío!*"

Jodie, whose room was across the hall from her sister, leaned out her door, laughing hysterically, "Liew, Oi! Liew! This is sooooooo wicked!"

"And frightening!" replied Josie from deep inside her room.

"Girls, do you feel at home?" asked Liew, strolling down the corridor and ending in front of Jodie's door.

"Um, yeah Liew," Jodie stepped aside from the door, pointing at the contents of her cabin to Liew, "that's because this *IS HOME!*"

Inside, her room was a lovely blush shade of pink and soft lighting. A queen-sized bed, covered with pillows and a flower comforter, a wooden six-drawer dresser with a tall mirror on top, two small nightstands and cute lamps with odd-shaped shades took up half the room. On the opposite side, there was a large wall mirror with a ballet bar running down the middle of it, next to a door that opened into a bathroom. "This is an exact copy of my room in my house!" Jodie walked over to the nightstand with a paperback book half open lying on top. "This is *precisely* how I left my room, book and all."

"Yes, it is!" said Liew with an inch of pride in his voice.

Jaysen peaked his head out, five doors down, "Me too! This is an exact replica of my bedroom at home, Liew!" said Jaysen, looking at his familiar Japanese Zen-inspired bedroom. It had white walls, wood panels, lower futon bed, and hand carved wooden furnishings.

"Yes, for all of you! We didn't want you to feel uncomfortable, or out of place while you were here, so it was decided to literally make it home."

Another head popped out of a door at the end of the hall, "Dude, Liew! This is *crazypants!*" shrieked Stoke as his head disappeared out of sight. "And, kind of cool!" Not shockingly, he had left behind a very dirty room with clothes, papers, gear, hats, goggles, posters, paintings, and junk all strewn around the room.

"Oh good, Mr. Townsend," he called down the hall.

"Ambassador?" A small voice came from the room next to Josie's.

"Yes, Ms. Zhang," Liew said, stepping in front of her door.

"This makes me very homesick," she said, in Chinese, with a hint of regret in her voice, glancing at the small neat clean room that was sparsely furnished.

"Now each of you can change the atmosphere in your room." Liew announced loudly, leaning his head down the hall. "Touch the wall and say the place: your room, home, city, or any location on Earth, that will make you feel relaxed. It will appear on the walls."

Yosi got up and put her hand on the wall and said, "*Năinai de jiā*." A bigger house with nice antique wood furnishings, a wide-open door with green fields on the other side appeared on her walls. She turned to Liew. "My grandmother's house is my favorite."

"Perfect, Ms. Zhang," he said to her, in Chinese, then yelled loudly again, in English, down the hall. "And only each individual athlete can open their room door." He turned back to Yosi, returning to Chinese. "We put you, Amy, Ari, and the twin's rooms together."

He turned his head back toward the hallway, speaking in English, "The older ladies, Jenefer, Onorina, Margit, and the Hallperans are closer to the gentlemen's rooms, so they can keep an eye on you all."

"Happy to do it!" said Jenefer, who was just outside the door listening. Her watchful stance was already assumed.

"Doesn't anyone worry about me?" roared Stoke from way down the hall, clearly looking for attention the gentlemen didn't want to give.

"Nope," Jenefer yelled back, half-joking, half-serious, leering back at Stoke. But she knew in her heart she would keep an eye on Stoke, and *all* the little ones. It went with being the eldest of seven children.

"You'll be fine *way* down there, Mr. Townsend," replied Liew. "Mr. Rapperhand can help keep an eye on you."

"Yeah, right." Stoke said quietly to himself, looking across the hall into Pappie's room, whose walls were now showing the top of Big Ben and surrounding London scenery.

Liew stepped next door and looked inside to see Ari calmly sitting on her bed.

"And you, Ms. Foxx?"

"Oh, this is great, Liew," said Ari with a warmth to her voice. She pointed to the walls that displayed a beach and waves crashing on the sand. "This is my surfing beach in Micronesia. It's more home than my house."

"Good, Ms. Foxx, I want you to feel at home. Also, you can turn on the ambient sound if you wish to hear the waves."

Liew moved out of her room and called down the corridor. "If you need anything, please let me know. I am here for you." Liew looked down at his own clear patch on his sleeve. A clock ticked down. The athletes reluctantly meandered back into the hallway.

"Now, everyone, are we *all* ready to go up to the observation lounge? It's about time."

*   *   *

The whole group journeyed up five more flights of stairs—bypassing the small elevator, though Liew pointed it out—to the very top of the ship.

A wide set of wood-framed glass doors opened to an enormous semispherical lounge area. There were couches, seats, tables, chairs, plants, even what looked like a glass bar in back, all strategically placed around the large spacious room.

As the group walked in, a few sat down on the couches and chairs, while the rest explored the room.

"I thought this was an observation lounge," commented Jodie while plopping herself on a couch. "Where's the view, Liew?" she asked, looking around the room at the opaque walls and closed environment.

"Indeed, it is, Ms. McQuenzy." Liew pressed a glass panel on the wall by the door, a recognizable technological theme by now. "There is the option: view or not to view."

"*That* is the question," quipped Pappie, looking around the room at the others for a response to his quick Shakespearean wit.

No one flinched.

"Really? *NO ONE!*" called out Pappie.

But any retort was lost. Almost all of the 360° ceiling and the walls down to the floor suddenly became transparent. The change was immediate and jarring. There was nothing but the blackness of space and twinkling stars far off in the distance.

"WOW," said Jaysen.

"Really, dude. Get a new word!" replied Stoke as he practically pressed his face against the window.

"OK, *dude,*" countered Jaysen.

"*Touché,* man," laughed Stoke. "Peace."

"Wait," shrieked Amy, examining the stars and blinking lights in front of them. "Where's Earth?"

"Where's Brooklyn," dryly added Jenefer.

The whole group stood in wonder at the sight of endless space.

"Yes, we already left," said Liew enjoying the star view as much as the athletes.

"*Obviously,*" joked Josie.

"Are we there?" said Margit astonished, "Is this the 3rd galactic quadrant near the Dranthlin nebulae, in the Outer Arm?"

"Yes, Ms. Housman. We are here."

When asked later by the press how their ship traveled through space so quickly, not a single athlete had a definitive answer. "We aren't engineers or physicists," said Margit to the scrum of media, even though she once took a few Quantum Physics classes at the University of Oslo.

No athlete knew exactly how they arrived at the games, only that they did instantaneously in the ship. "Although," continued Margit at the Press Conference. "I did ask Liew later if Humanity was close to this type of space traveling technology. He smiled and said, yes, in 'theory' Humanity was. Our mathematicians already have the equations. It was just the matter of time before they put them into practical use with a quantum energy source."

"When did we leave?" asked Stoke, who seemed shocked, staring out into the vastness of space with stars blinking off in the distance.

"Probably while you were too busy fussing about your room," responded Jenefer quickly, shutting down any further inquiry.

"Where are we, Ambassador?" asked Dmitri.

"You are looking back into the Milky Way Galaxy. We are outside of the last spiral arm, sitting in interstellar space between our galaxy and the next.

"This is amazing," said Mark sweetly to his wife Justine. They were both in awe, stars reflected in their eyes. "Thank you for including us, Ambassador."

Everyone stood around for a few minutes soaking in the star view. Slowly, a few athletes began to find seats, but Liew didn't move. He gazed out to a specific point in space.

"What are you waiting for, Ambassador?" asked Yosi, who turned back to join Liew's side.

"For the games to begin."

Some of the athletes returned to his side, staring out the windows.

"In order for the Universe Olympics to begin, we have to light what you call the Olympic Flame."

"Light the Olympic Flame? With what? Where? There's nothing out there," announced Jenefer, gesturing toward the vast emptiness of interstellar space.

"Just wait," said Liew, glancing down at the translucent patch on his sleeve. "Any moment now. Everyone please, turn in this direction."

The stragglers on the couch joined the group. They stood still, waiting.

"In three, two—look out the window—one!"

It was hard to miss. No one could have, unless they were, literally, blind. A bright white-yellow sun exploded from seemingly nothing into existence. It was a yellow dwarf star, like our sun.

"The Olympic Flame has officially been lit," said Liew with elation in his voice. "The Games have begun. Welcome Humanity to your first Universe Olympics!"

It was amazing—the Olympic Flame was in fact a sun. There was no greater 'flame' in the universe.

Everyone continued staring out the observation window. The sun's shockwaves of heat and energy expanded in all directions into space. Suddenly, it was stopped by what looked like an invisible force field just shy of their next surprise, a small planet. The globe looked brownish red in color, like Mars.

"Oh my," observed Onorina, not looking at the sun or red planet, but closer to their ship. They were close to another planet. "Look!" she squealed. The light from the new sun—the Olympic Flame—made it possible.

This second planet was mostly green with a few patches of blue water, and white polar caps and clouds. It was a mini-Earth, only with more green land space than water.

There was a gasp. "*Oh my God!*" cried Amy, turning to her right and walking over to the other side of the observation lounge. There was another planet gleaming brightly in space. Everyone rushed over to the opposite side of the observation lounge. "It's all *WATER!*" Amy shrieked in pure exhilaration. She shed a few tears of joy. A bright blue pure ocean planet sat third.

"And, please, look over there," suggested Liew, pointing toward the back part of the lounge, near the doors.

A little further away but still in view was a fourth planet, and it glowed white.

"*SNOW!*" gasped Margit.

"YES!" howled Stoke. "I'm sooooo friggin' Stoked!"

"Good," answered Liew with a steadiness to his voice. "Ladies and gentlemen, boys and girls from Earth, this is your playing field, your Olympic arena. There is a rocky terrain planet, a mixed forest and plains planet, a water planet, and a snow planet."

Slowly it all came into view: the red, green, blue, and white orbs all revolving around the single yellow sun. It was the perfect replica of the miniature floating model Ambassador Liew had shown them at their first meeting in the UNOOSA. Only this time it was real—a whole solar system.

"Were these planets always here?" wondered Margit.

"This micro-solar-system, each of these planets, was created just for these games."

Everyone in the group was hushed for a moment. This was beyond anything the human race could do: creating planets and stars for the specific purpose of playing the Universe Olympics. It was humbling.

On Earth, human beings were only traveling in space to their nearest planet, Mars. The creation of an entire solar system was on a different scale. To construct planets and a sun was a technological and scientific sophistication that belonged in their dreams, or science fiction.

At that moment, every athlete understood that they were about to partake in something special, something life changing, both for themselves and for all humans on planet Earth.

"W-O-W," said Jaysen, pausing for a moment, glancing at Stoke. "Sorry, Buddy, I mean it for real this time."

"Totally agree, dude!" replied Stoke, staring longingly at the snow planet.

The other shock, and probably biggest surprise of all—yes, bigger than a sun and four planets—was when they realized they weren't alone.

They were so busy staring at the new sun and focusing on the planets before Ari loudly announced, "My, goodness!" she pointed out the top of the lounge, "There are other *ships!*"

Hundreds of spaceships floated all around the observation lounge. They joined the human ship in observing the newly lit Olympic Flame sun. The armada was of every shape, size, and color imaginable. Many ships were the expected square, rectangular, spherical, cylindrical, disc, triangular shapes. They were also in every color of the rainbow, most commonly a shade of silver. But off in the distance, were shapes and sizes only recently imagined by Humanity. The fractal spiral-shaped spaceships were the same pattern, over and over again, and in surprising color combinations. Another ship was a square within a square, a hypercube, and it was in constant motion, the ends of the square always moving and changing. There was even a spaceship that didn't have walls. All that was visible was the grid-like infrastructure and hundreds of decks, one on top of the other in a lattice work. But the most astounding of all, the ship closest to the green planet, was shaped in a perfect sphere, a globe. It had a hard-translucent surface like a giant crystal ball but inside was water. And if you stared long enough you could see massive black floating objects moving through the water.

Amy gazed at the water ship when she asked, "Is this everyone?"

"What do you mean, Ms. Ride?" wondered Liew.

"Is this all the intelligent life in the universe?"

"Oh no! These games are just for the Milky Way Galaxy."

"All these creatures…" said Eric.

"Are your neighbors, yes," Liew said towering over him at his seven-foot height.

"How many are there?" asked Mark.

"There are close to a million intelligent life forms in this galaxy, but many are like Humanity, only just now reaching beyond their own solar systems. In truth, we accepted Earth early."

Liew turned around, walked to the center of the room. He surveyed all of Earth's athletes. "Because of you."

Everyone paused for a moment, looking at each other and then Liew.

Margit asked, "Does a spaceship from your home world look like one of these," she said pointing to the nearest red quadrangle ship. "Or that," she said pointing to a dark green ship that was concentric circles within circles, like a chain link fence.

"Oh no! My home world doesn't have spaceships that look anything like those out there. We aren't participating in the games this year since I'm an Ambassador. And *this* ship was made for all of you."

Pappie turned around to face Liew. "Let me understand this correctly. What do you mean when you say? '*MADE* for us?' Meaning this ship was created for the sole purpose of taking athletes from Earth here or that this structural design is for *us*?"

"Both. This ship was built for this trip only, and it was structurally designed to match what human beings think a spaceship would be like."

"I don't understand," said Dmitri. "What humans *think* a spaceship would be?"

"Yes, what you've imagined. Humanity doesn't have interstellar spaceships yet, and to make you all feel comfortable with this ship, the builders used a mixture of all the images humans speculated a giant space ferrying vessel would look like. So, we built *this* ship to those specifications."

"*I KNEW IT!*" screamed Stoke. "I knew this ship reminded me of something! Everything! It's like a combo of the lounge of the Enterprise, the hallways of the Galactica, the Prometheus, the Andromeda exterior, the Millennium Falcon, Pleiadean, Adonis..." He kept naming off more science fiction spaceships which seemed to have a penchant for Greek star names.

"This ship isn't designed like other spaceships, is it?" continued Margit.

"No. This spaceship is *ALL* human," stated Liew.

"COOL!" shouted Stoke. "I love it even more," he said, lovingly stroking one of the walls. "We'll have to name her…"

"The observation lounge, the bridge, hallways, cabins, galley, game rooms, even the training facilities were all put together to give you a sense of familiarity and ease."

"I'll admit, it works, Liew," stated Eric.

"Good, Mr. Verheinen," said Liew. "The builders will be pleased. I will give them your feedback. Personally, I like it. No, I'm getting used to it."

"What are the other ships like?" asked Amy, though she specifically pointed at the one ship, which looked like a giant ocean filled globe.

"Much more efficient. Every section isn't separated off and defined like this one. It's more—together, cohesive, is the best word."

"Can we go over to another ship, Ambassador?" wondered Manny.

"No, I'm sorry Mr. Suarez. Not this trip. Not for Humanity's first time at the Universe Olympics. Strict rules. You remain here."

"Oh, that's too bad," sighed Manny.

"But don't worry," said Liew, patting Manny empathetically. "You'll get to enjoy all the comforts of this ship. It's new to you. You have yet to explore ninety-five percent of it. Adapt to this one first, then you'll be able to see the others, in time."

"We need to name her!" exclaimed Stoke, who was not using his inside voice.

"What would you like, Mr. Townsend?"

Stoke furrowed his brow for a few moments. "Not sure yet, let me meditate on it. I'm sure it will come to me! But I know it's a girl."

Liew smiled. "Very well, Mr..."

"Jam," Stoke interrupted, "or just Stoke is cool too!" He tried to high-five Liew but missed by a large margin since Liew was so tall. "Down low, man, down low," persisted Stoke, still trying to make something of the missed high-five. He was now also unsure if Liew actually had five or six fingers.

Liew waited a few minutes as the athletes gazed out the observation lounge panoramic windows taking in the spaceships, planets, and Olympic Flame sun around them. "OK," he finally said, raising his voice to the group, "Josie, Jodie, Amy, you're up first!"

All three girls abruptly turned around, with eyes about to bulge out of their heads.

"WHAT?" yelled Jodie.

"Together?" questioned Josie, looking over at a stunned Jodie.

"But Liew, we are in *totally* different sports than Amy," asserted Jodie.

"Yes, I know, Ms. McQuenzy. We need all three of you to participate in a simple qualifying round. We leave in one hour."

"One hour!" hollered the twins in perfect unison.

"But Liew," interrupted Jodie in a not-so-hushed voice. "It takes us almost an hour to prep our makeup, hair, suits. The gelatin alone takes a half-hour to set."

"And swim warm up," added Amy.

"Oh no, ladies! Don't worry about any of that now. This is just a quick qualifier. None of that is needed. Just throw on your practice swimsuits please."

"Oi, Liew!" yipped Jodie. "Maybe you could give us a schedule, or something so we are a little more prepared, next time."

"My apologies, ladies. I've been so busy preparing everything. Now, please go get ready."

"Our suits?" questioned Amy.

"All of your belongings are in either your rooms or the workout arena."

Chapter 4

Qualifications

A tiny shuttle approached what appeared to be three rivers of water. These rivers weren't next to each other, as one would imagine in a bucolic countryside setting. Nor were they attached to any of the four planets in the new Olympic arena. The three waterways were simply floating in the middle of space.

The small spacecraft was a carbon copy of a Space Shuttle from Earth, the black tip nose, white sides, black tipped wings, tail, and a black underbelly. It was a mini-Discovery.

The three girls, Amy, Josie and Jodie huddled together gaping at the Mini-D's viewscreen. The girls almost stopped breathing at the most disturbing sight; the three rivers were suspended, one on top of the other, with only a few empty feet of open space between them, anchored by metal platforms.

"Liew, not to ask a stupid question here, but will we be able to breathe out there in space?" inquired Jodie, never taking her eye off the water.

"Of course, Jodie. There is—your closest word is a force field, or shield, and inside the field is all the oxygen both you *and* I—all of us—need to breathe. Remember, I can't breathe in space, either."

"Are there people or creatures who can? Or live in space without a ship?" asked Amy curiously.

"Of course!"

"I'd like to see that!" she said eagerly.

"You already did. When the Olympic Flame was lit."

The idea was staggering to Amy. Which one could do that? And how would she know what she was seeing, if no one told her about it?

"Next time, Liew, will you point them out to me, please?" she asked eagerly.

"Of course, Ms. Ride—when you're not competing. I apologize. I need to remind myself that humans have never seen anything like this before. I forgot to mention it. I'm consumed with executing my duties for humanity; thinking about how this team is doing, thinking, and feeling, that I forget about the other contestants. I'll make more of an effort next time."

"Thank you, Liew," she said sincerely.

The Mini-D docked horizontally on the middle of the three platforms, pulling up beside it. The door near the front window opened.

Liew walked out first, while the three girls stood back, peeking their heads out for a quick look.

"See, it's alright girls. I'm breathing perfectly normally," said Liew, taking in a deep breath and letting it out slowly.

Amy was the first to step out followed by Jodie, and finally, a reluctant Josie, who seemed very nervous.

The long metal platform looked almost like every swimming deck at home. It was rectangular in shape, about twenty-five feet in length. On the long end, opposite the shuttle, was the water—a lot of it. It ran horizontally fifty feet in length, at least. On the edge where the water began, were three starting blocks, separated by only a few feet.

Amy looked directly above them. About twenty-five feet up was the bottom of another platform. The upper platform led to another lane of water that seemed to be suspended in the space above them.

"Geez, you all really seem to have perfected the science of suspending water," said Amy, glancing up at the first lane of water hovering over them. After seeing the lap pool in the ship, she was beginning to understand that defying gravity, even creating it, was no problem for their hosts.

"There's another one below," announced Jodie perched on the edge of their platform looking down at the other river. She turned to her sister. "I don't know how they are doing this, and I'm afraid to ask."

"I can't look," responded Josie, who was taking off her warm-up track suit.

Amy joined Jodie, and together they peered down at the lower platform that was suspended in the middle of space, like theirs. "It's wicked!" declared Jodie, glimpsing the green planet that shined on them from afar, much like the moon does on Earth.

The twins began their stretching as Amy took off her warm-up track suit. When ready, Amy walked up to Liew. "So, this qualifier, is it time based?"

"No," said Liew nonchalantly.

Amy looked very confused. "OK. Is it stroke based? Do you want me to use breaststroke, butterfly, or freestyle?"

"Nope."

Josie and Jodie joined Amy.

"Then what's this for, Liew?" questioned Jodie.

"For this qualifier you three need to swim in the water and touch the other platform. There is no time limit or specific stroke required. All you need to do is make it to the other side."

The three girls stared in disbelief at Liew, then each other.

"*THAT'S IT?!*" bellowed Jodie.

"I don't understand," interjected Amy, noting the twins' building frustration. "What's the point of *this* qualifier?"

"To make sure no one drowns."

The twins gasped in unison. "*WHAT!*" shrieked Josie. "*DROWN!*"

"You're kidding right," blurted Jodie.

"No, girls. I'm not," answered Liew.

"I was swimming before I could walk, Liew. I'm not going to drown!" declared Amy, forcefully.

"I know that, Amy, but the rules are the rules, ladies. And species that haven't evolved incrementally over the last twenty-thousand years have to qualify. End of story." Liew could see the devastated looks on their faces. "You aren't the only ones."

The idea of drowning was so ludicrous to Amy that it was borderline insulting to her and, by the looks on their faces, to the twins as well. "I've spent most of my life in water," insisted Amy.

"Yes, I know, so this will be very easy for you, and the twins."

"Wait a minute," interjected Josie. "Why isn't Manny…"

"Or Pappie," slipped in Jodie, knowing exactly where her sister was going because she was thinking the same thing.

"Here qualifying as well?" finished Josie.

"Oh, he doesn't have to worry about drowning with diving," said Liew.

"Last time I checked, Liew, diving ended in water," Jodie snarkily replied.

"And a triathlon starts in water," pleaded Josie, trying to rationalize their case to Liew.

"Don't forget about the pentathlete, Onorina. She swims in water too!" said Amy, catching the logic in the twin's argument. "That's one of the five."

"Yes. Yes, but they won't have the chance to drown here," replied Liew.

"And we do?" asked the twins almost in unison.

Though it's generally untrue that twins think and speak alike, on this matter, the McQuenzy twins were in perfect harmony.

"Please ladies, that's enough bickering over this qualifier. Go get on your blocks and get ready," said Liew with an inch of authority in his voice. "It's about to start."

"Fine," stated Jodie, seeing the futility of arguing in the middle of space.

"Thank you, girls. This will be an easy one-two-three," said Liew, following them to the three blocks.

"Oi, Jos. What are we doing?" asked Jodie from the left-most block.

"Sidestroke. Taking my sweeeeet time. Liew said there was no rush."

"Good idea, you turning right?" Jodie said with a little laugh.

"Ya."

"OK. I'll do left then... In synch?"

"Ya, ya!" said Josie smiling and laughing, getting over herself and the pointlessness of the qualifier. If Liew wanted them to prove they wouldn't drown, so be it. It would have been beneath her not to use this time in the water for some sort of practice. And oddly enough, it took away their anxiety about the venue.

Amy contemplated using the breaststroke, not that anyone asked her. She got on her block, which was nearest on the right. Adjusting her strategically placed goggles, Amy got in her start position. She didn't want to push herself too hard on a travel day (if that was what you could call traveling tens of thousands of light years in an instant). She did want to use this opportunity to get in a little workout, stretch her muscles. She considered doing her backstroke, but that would mean she would be staring up at the lane of water suspended above their heads, and that might have freaked her out. It was best to keep her eyes straight ahead on the water and the platform. She didn't want to swim out of the lane because, besides the two metal platforms at either end of the water, the lanes literally just stopped in mid-air, or rather space. She wasn't sure what happened if they went too far. Would she float away? Liew never mentioned how far that force field extended.

Jodie looked down and realized the water wasn't very deep. "Oi, Liew. What's the depth of this water?"

"About twenty feet, six meters. Oh ladies, do be careful. Don't fall through the water or you'll be disqualified."

"Disqualified from the qualifier. Got it," winked Josie.

"That might have been helpful to know before we got on the blocks," retorted Jodie.

"Anything else, Liew?" questioned Amy.

"Begin at the beep. Ready."

All three took their start positions at the ready.

"Set," said Liew, unable to keep the building excitement from his voice. He watched the patch on his sleeve.

They waited what felt like an eternity. When a very deep, loud, honking sound that reminded them of an elephant boomed, the girls weren't sure if this was the "beep" Liew mentioned. All three hesitated for a moment.

"GO!" shouted Liew, almost jumping up and down. He was clearly thrilled about their first qualifying round.

At Liew's shout, the girls dove in.

The twins did a perfect dive facing each other, and executed a little flare kick at the end in perfect unison—after all, they were synchronized swimmers.

Amy's dive was a little too forceful off the block. Before she knew it, she was only a few feet from the bottom. It was a scary sight. The water just ended, and all there was beneath her and the next lane of water was air. She immediately swam upwards to the surface of her lane.

The twins, true to their training, glided across the water in beautiful sidestrokes, obviously rehearsing a small portion of their routine. Their hands came up with a flare. The girls performed a perfect mirror image of arches, and lunges, and pretty pinwheels.

Amy started out with a fast freestyle rush, but realized there was no time constraint. Then it occurred to her that this might be her only opportunity to literally swim in space. She chuckled to herself, imagining Coach Sayers was there to see her. She had done it. She was swimming in outer space.

Deciding to make the most of it, she slowed her pace. Her heavy freestyle stroke changed to a leisurely breaststroke.

At racing speed, Amy would complete the distance in less than half a minute or so. She knew as long as she didn't drown, she was good, and she WASN'T going to drown.

About halfway to the other platform, Amy plucked up the courage, between strokes, and stared straight down to the lane below. She could faintly make out a very long, dark serpentine figure moving through the water.

Midway through her swim, Amy heard and felt a giant splash in the water behind her. Amy stopped mid-stroke and turned around. Treading water, she checked on Josie and Jodie. What she saw shocked her.

Between Amy and the twins thrashed a multi-colored octopus-like creature. About twenty thick, fleshy tentacles surrounded a massive blue blob core with no discernible head.

Both Josie and Jodie halted their routine, watching the thing in front of them flail in the water. They were astonished both to see the dog-sized creature itself, but also to realize that it was sinking under the water, drowning. After a few seconds floundering, the octopus creature submerged, sinking to the bottom of the lane, fast.

"Jos..."

"Got it," said Josie, who was the Flyer of the duet. She quickly plunged in the water after the creature.

Amy watched underwater through her goggles as Josie swam deep underneath the surface and snatched one of the thick fleshy legs of the creature. Then Jodie, who was the Base of the duet, went under too, grabbing Josie's legs by the ankles. She pulled both Josie and the octopus up before they reached the bottom of the lane and were disqualified.

Josie and Jodie surfaced with the creature in tow. "There you go," said Josie lifting the "octopus thing" above the water.

The girls quickly held out their arms in a crisscross formation. This position made a tight square for the creature to rest on above the water. The octopus didn't move from their arms and was heaving what looked like heavy breaths. It seemed to be pumping with blood, or fluid, as its skin flashed colors.

"You're lighter than I thought," Jodie said to the creature. Her legs did their eggbeater kick with due diligence, treading water without a hint of her arms going under. Both Josie and Jodie's leg and arm strength were apparent, and one of the many reasons they won gold in their event.

Within a few moments of letting the poor creature rest without worry of drowning, a giant tentacle suddenly emerged from the side. It pulled the smaller version of the creature out of the girls' hands, and onto a floating platform beside the water lane.

Amy immediately swam up to Josie and Jodie, and all three treaded water. They silently caught their breath while watching the floating platform with the octopuses travel back up to the lane of water above them.

"You guys, OK?" Amy finally said.

"Oh yeah, great," answered Jodie. "But that was the weirdest thing I've ever seen."

"I was so stunned I couldn't move," said Amy. "I'm sorry I didn't come over sooner to help."

"No time, mate. We're closer," said Josie happily to Amy. "Also, we barely had time to snatch it ourselves, before its mommy came and got it." All three girls started laughing. They floated in a triangle formation in the middle of the lane.

"Did its skin bother you?" wondered Amy.

"Nah, only my internal disco beat." howled Jodie.

"Maybe these qualifiers make sense, after all," finished Josie.

"Yeah," giggled Jodie. "Speaking of... let's go. We've got to show Liew *we* won't drown too."

At an easy pace, all three made their way across the remaining fifty yards to the opposite platform. As soon as they touched the wall, Liew—who had arrived on the other side without the girls noticing how he did it—reached down and helped them out of the water onto the firm deck.

"See, I *KNEW* it!" said Liew chortling out loud and smiling at the three girls. He handed them their towels. "I *knew* you all were ready!"

"Ready for what, Liew? Our swimming qualifier?" wondered Amy.

"Or not drowning," sassed Jodie.

"No, no! Humanity. I knew human beings were ready," said Liew jovially.

"So, *we* qualified?" asked Amy.

"Yes! Yes, Amy. You, Josie, and Jodie, all qualified to compete, congratulations!"

"With extra points for the super-cool save," said Josie, high fiving her sister. She offered one to Amy, who at first felt a little reluctant to take any credit, even if it was just a high five.

"Poor thing, he was much too young to swim," said Liew, handing the girls their warm-up track suits. "Needs a few more years to master buoyancy."

"How old was it," asked Amy while putting on her clothes.

"Two."

"Two years? I could swim at two," stated Amy.

"No. Two hundred."

"Oh yeah right, Liew. Total baby," cackled Jodie, and all three girls started laughing uncontrollably.

Chapter 5

Welcome

Only a few stragglers were left in the observation lounge after the lighting of the Olympic Flame. Ramon stood alone by the window, staring past the myriad of spaceships, which were loaded with untold life forms. He gazed silently at the far-off white snow planet. It was a sight of pure beauty for Ramon. The planet meant so many things to him.

He marveled at the technological sophistication—the probable Kardashev Scale Type 2 civilization—necessary to create a planet just for one particular sporting environment: frozen water. Excitement filled his heart at the very idea of bobsledding on that snow planet; the runs that could exist on an ice world were beyond human imagination, even his. Then an icy pain stabbed the core of his soul, for an unfortunate realization dawned on him—a bobsled couldn't be driven by a single man.

After a few minutes, Jenefer walked up beside him, staring out into space.

He quickly glanced at her. "They get off to the qualifier, all right?"

"Yup, shuttle should be taking off any second. I asked the girls if they wanted me to go with them, but they said they would be OK."

"You believe them?"

"Yeah. They are old enough to speak up for themselves."

"How old is Amy?" wondered Ramon.

"Seventeen or eighteen, I think, but she's old enough. I think the twins are a little bit younger. She'll watch out for them."

"But those McQuenzy twins seem like they don't take nothin' from no one."

Jenefer laughed a little bit. "You're right. Heaven help anyone or anything that crosses those two spitfires. Ramon…" She trailed off. "It just occurred to me we haven't been properly introduced. I'm Jenefer Washington Lee," she said holding out her hand.

"I'm Ramon Stead. Nice to meet you, Mrs. Washington Lee."

"Ramon, please call me, Jenefer. It's nice to meet you."

The two shook hands.

"I wanted to tell you," she said hesitantly, "I meant you no offence when I asked about everyone being gold medalists back at the UN last week. I understand to even qualify for the Olympics takes years of hard work and dedication."

"No offence taken." He smiled a wide gracious smile. "I know you weren't the only one in there thinking about that. Why else would everyone laugh? But I take it all in stride. A Jamaican bobsledder is no different than an Antarctician beach volley baller." He said with a wink in his eye. "And I hear they make some great digs too!" He laughed at himself.

"I do truly admire you and your team, Ramon."

He turned and gave a whole-hearted smile. "I appreciate that, Jen. We put everything we got into that sled. We call her Bessie, after my mom."

Jenefer smiled. "And I was also thinking, when any of the little ones: Stoke, Ari, Yosi, Amy, Josie, and Jodie, go to a competition on one of those planets, a human adult really should accompany them."

"Agreed." He looked at her. "Do you trust Liew?"

"It's hard to say. He seems nice, but we know hardly anything about him. All we know is from the news reports. I don't know the individual person; like does he have kids or like kids?"

"And does he know how much trouble little humans can be?" asked Ramon, and they both laughed for a second at the truth.

"Probably not. Speaking of..." Jenefer surveyed the observation lounge. "Where's Stoke?"

"Last I saw him was when he left with you and the others to go see the girls off."

"I lost him," scoffed Jenefer. "That one's gotten in trouble. I've got to keep an eye on him. I should go look for him before he breaks something."

"Or gets into someplace he shouldn't. Hopefully, Liew locked all the doors." Ramon caught sight of the tiny white shuttle as it sped away from their ship to an unknown destination. "There they go!" he shouted as a mini-D space shuttle shot off like a bullet.

"You see them?" inquired Margit, who gravitated towards Jenefer and Ramon at the window.

Jenefer pointed to the speeding shuttle as the yellow light from the Olympic Flame sun shimmered off its surface. "Where are they going, you think?"

"I would imagine the water planet," answered Margit.

"But they are flying to the middle of space, not toward any planet," observed Onorina, as she and Pappie joined the group of congregating athletes.

For a moment they lost sight of the white shuttle as it passed behind another spinning pinwheel spaceship.

"Ah, I see it," yelled Justine, who approached with her husband Mark. "It's docking at..." she paused, stared at Mark for a moment. "Well, it looks like suspended rivers of water. Three of them. In Space."

Both Yosi and Ari, who were lounging on a couch, rushed up to the window.

"Coolio!" cheered Ari. "I wish *I* had to qualify."

"You may yet, Ari. We *ALL* may have to. Who knows?" speculated Margit to the petite surfer by her side.

It was a tight fit as Dmitri, Sito, Eric, Manny, and eventually Jaysen strolled into the lounge, and up to the spectators.

"What's up?" asked Jaysen as he headed into the huddle.

"Watching the girls qualify," stated Jenefer. "Kind of…"

"Or at least trying to," said Ramon. "Is it my eyes or are they out of the shuttle?"

"Yup, and on the platform," added Justine, "in the middle of space."

"WOW!" said Mark, not Jaysen, who turned and smiled at the decathlete.

"See, it's catchy," retorted Jaysen to the group. "Well said, my man," slapping Mark on his shoulder. "Well said."

"Justine has amazing eyes," commented Onorina. "I can barely see the girls. They look like black dots."

Pappie squinted his eyes to catch sight of them. "These games are going to be tremendous! I mean, a qualifier—in the middle of space."

"I can't see them on the platforms," complained Ari.

"That's because they're in the water now, off the middle platform," pointed out Justine.

The lounge door opened. "DUDE! Is *this* where everyone has been?"

"Where you been, Stoke?" questioned Jenefer, without taking her eyes off the action in front of her.

"I've been looking everywhere."

"For what, Bro?" wondered Jaysen, who turned around to see a very distraught Stoke.

"To try and find some food. I'm starving!"

Stoke sauntered over, "What's everyone staring at? Some cool spaceship?"

"No. We're watching the girls at their qualifier in the middle of space," stated Sito.

"DUDE!" Stoke pushed his way past Sito, and Jaysen, to the front of the window next to Ari.

"You find any?" Jaysen finally asked after a few moments.

"What?" answered Stoke, confused.

"Food, Bro! You find any food?"

"Oh, yeah!" Stoke pulled out a candy bar from his pocket that looked an awful lot like a Butterfinger, and he began munching on it.

Almost everyone in the group turned to the sound of the crunching candy bar. It was loud and flaky, crumbling down the front of Stoke's loosely fitting baggy shirt that read "It Aight, He Bite." with an inexplicable picture of an overturned tortoise biting a tiny human doll.

"You have anything else stashed in there?" wondered Jaysen, who stepped up behind him.

"Yeah. Tons! Want some?"

"Yes, please. My stomach is rumbling."

Stoke reached deep into his jacket pockets, creating a cacophony of wrapper sounds. He pulled out bags of gummies in every shape, size, and color, as well as candy bars, Twizzlers, Skittles, and Reese's Peanut Butter Cups. He started passing out candy like it was Halloween. "They really did a good job of replicating my bedroom. I had a stash of candy in there."

"Um, this is more than a stash, Stoke. This is a store," replied Jenefer, who took a bag of peanut M&Ms. "Thank you," she said half-smiling, wondering what other stashes he had hidden in his room. She made a mental note to check on it later with Liew.

"Dude, word," said Stoke as he passed out chocolate covered malt balls, jellybeans, sour-thingies, and Hi-Chew.

"How many pockets you got in there, Bud?" asked Mark, taking a Kit-Kat, opening it, splitting it in two, and offering half to his wife.

"I have a ton in my pants pockets, too," answered Stoke. Digging deep, he handed out more candy to Yosi, Ari, Manny, Dmitri, Pappie, and finally a chocolate Hershey bar to Oronina.

"*Grazie*, Stoke," she said, biting into the bar.

Everyone chewed and nibbled as they stared out the window, awaiting any movement from the shuttle.

Sito munched as he stared at the wrapper of his chocolate bar. "I have never heard of anything like this... What... cha... ma..." He struggled to finish the name.

"Whatchamacallit! It's old school man, but it's great! Nice crunchy surprise."

Sito chewed a bite. "*Hai*, old school is good school. *Arigato*, Stoke."

"All good!" Stoke was barely able to get the words out because he was shoving another handful of neon sour cherry gummies in his mouth.

"At least eating will keep you busy for a while," said Jenefer, finishing her bag of M&Ms. She felt sure it must be time for lunch or dinner. Her stomach was grumbling too, but there was no clock anywhere. Who knew what time it was, and what time zone these Games were on. They were well beyond the Earth's twenty-four hour time cycle. Most importantly, the human body clock was telling everyone it was time for food.

"LOOK!" shouted Ramon, pointing out the window, candy wrapper in hand "They're coming back to the ship!"

Like a herd of zebra when they see a lion, the group of professional athletes ran in a pack, out of the lounge, down the long hall, and descending flights of stairs toward the shuttle bay door, following Jen.

The whole group: Yosi, Dmitri, Pappie, Jaysen, Jenefer, Ramon, Margit, Stoke, Eric, Onorina, Manny, Sito, Ari, Mark, and Justine waited patiently in the main passage for what seemed like an eternity until the door opened.

"How'd it go?" shouted Pappie, always the first, at the sight of Josie, Jodie, Amy, and Liew, who seemed a little startled by the fifteen expectant faces in the hallway.

"We didn't drown!" hollered Jodie jubilantly.

"I didn't think you would," Pappie happily retorted.

Liew stepped into the passage, followed by the girls. "And most importantly, *we* qualified," he said proudly.

"Yay!" said Josie, holding up her hands in a half-hearted cheer.

"And we saw our first alien," stated Amy.

"Cool!" shouted Stoke. "I want to hear ALL about it."

"Actually, you have already seen your first alien, Amy," announced Margit, nodding at Ambassador Liew. "This would be your second."

"Oh yeah, sorry Liew. You look so much like us, I forgot. You're always my number one."

"That is a great compliment, Amy," said Liew. "Thank you. I do my best to be considered a part of this team."

"This being looked nothing like us," said Amy "It was squishy, and flashed rainbow colors with, like, thirty octopus kind-of arms."

"Their species is called a Ciapor, Amy, and they are very advanced beings."

"Not in the water," nudged Jodie to Josie.

"No, not that one. You're correct Ms. McQuenzy."

The whole team stood in a large circle around Liew, waiting.

"Dude, Liew. I'm starving. Is it time to eat yet?" wondered Stoke.

Eric held up his empty bag of gummies. "Stoke's been feeding us all from his 'stash' of candy."

"That's why you're all here," said Liew, like he found the answer to a long-lost puzzle.

"We're all hungry," laughed Ari.

Amy reached up and snatched the empty candy bag from Eric with a sullen look on her face. Yosi stepped up and handed her a half-filled box of chocolate Snow Caps. "Thank you," Amy smiled.

"You're welcome," said Yosi, after adjusting her ear bud.

"Translator functioning properly, Ms. Zhang?" asked Liew.

Yosi listened for half a second. "Yes," she happily answered in English.

Amy immediately started eating Yosi's Snow Caps, shaking the box like maracas. She also offered the contents to the twins, who graciously accepted a few.

"Ah, yes. The candy drawer," said Liew. "There was a great debate about that."

"Really?" asked Manny. "What about it?"

"To keep all food in one designated area or not. But it was decided to replicate your rooms down to the very last detail. So, the candy drawer stayed."

"Good! I would have starved to death," said Stoke defiantly.

"I doubt that, Mr. Townsend," answered Liew. "But it is about lunch time. Let's go see your cafeteria."

"*FINALLY*, FOOD!" howled Stoke.

*   *   *

Liew's understanding of human languages was phenomenal. He seemed to jump with ease from language to language without a second thought. But it occurred to most of the athletes that his understanding of the human word *cafeteria*, no matter which language, was completely wrong. When two large wood doors opened, there wasn't a cafeteria; the better word was *jungle*.

The group of humans, hesitantly, stepped inside a giant room. There was a green jungle laid out before them: green grassy floor, green bushes, plants, vines, tall green trees whose canopy made up the high ceiling, and dead center in the middle of the room was a light green path. It felt like a combination of an African and Asian jungle.

Up to that moment, Liew, or whomever put this ship together, had done a beautiful job of making the athletes feel comfortable and at home. Every person on the team handled the surprises and unexpected occurrences with grace and ease. But huddled at the doorway, knee deep in green grass, every human being stopped dead in their tracks.

"Liew… This isn't right," announced Jenefer, looking up at the trees. For someone who spent much of her life outdoors, the track was as close to nature as she dared to get.

"What do you mean, Mrs. Washington Lee?" answered Liew, confused.

"This," she pointed to the grassy ground and surrounding jungle, "is no 'cafeteria.' You've got your words wrong."

"*Si*," said Manny. "It's a jungle."

"No, this is your cafeteria," said Liew, as the sound of a loud howler monkey overtook his voice.

"What's next? A tiger's roar?" asked Pappie, who seemed just as perturbed as everyone else.

"Would that make you feel more at home, Mr. Rapperhand?" questioned Liew, even more confused.

"*No!*" Pappie answered very loudly.

"I'm afraid to go," said Yosi, pointing down the trail of light green grass that was shorter than the rest.

Liew took a moment and noticed the entire team's hesitation and how they had managed to cluster together in a large group, like a prey defense mechanism.

"I'm sorry, everyone." He stepped up in front of the group, addressing them very formally. "This did not have its intended effect."

"What were you expecting?" wondered Jaysen.

"The intention was for humans to feel relaxed around nature, and enjoy the calming effect of the color green."

Liew stared briefly at the McQuenzy twins, who cowered together in the middle of the group.

"I see now that research was wrong. Unfortunately, it is too late to change this, so I will reassure you all, this place, this ship, will not harm you. There is nothing to be frightened of in here. You are *safe* in my charge."

Another kookaburra-like bird wailed loudly from up in the canopy. The sudden sound made everyone jump.

"How about turning down the sound, Liew?" suggested Ramon who stood tall in the middle of the group. "May help a bit."

"Of course." Liew touched the display patch on his sleeve and the "jungle" noises quieted to a hum. "Now please, follow me into the cafeteria."

Liew started walking down the grassy path Yosi had pointed out earlier. It was S–shaped and when he passed a very large tree, the group lost sight of him. For a moment, no one moved.

Pappie, always first, always wanting to set the best example, courageously stepped forward behind Liew and gingerly walked around the curve.

Everyone waited for a scream or any sound.

A few seconds later, Pappie popped his head back around the corner. "All clear! You have to come see this. It's brilliant." Pappie returned behind the tree.

Slowly, with Jenefer leading the way for the "little ones," the whole team ambled down the path together, and turned the S-shaped corner to find a large clearing. The light green grass still made up the ground area, and standing in the middle of the clearing was Liew. He had a food tray in hand and cutlery already on top of it.

"As you can see, please take your tray and silverware as you walk in."

There was a carved-out opening in the middle of the large tree that made up the S-curve. Inside were piles of trays, along with forks, knives, spoons, chopsticks, and napkins.

"Once you have your tray, the clearing is divided up according to meals. It is organized like the face of a clock. First at nine o'clock is breakfast, then lunch at twelve, dinner at five with the dessert and snack area here," said Liew pointing out the two o'clock area, imitating the hands of a clock. "And beverages are at the six."

For the first time it looked like a cafeteria, albeit a weird one. Each station had both hot and cold sections, glass coverings and an enormous selection of food waiting to be eaten.

"All of your coaches gave me explicit meal plans. Everything you need to eat, and more, is here at your disposal, at any time, day or night." Liew's face showed a hint of disappointment, and his voice had a contrite tone.

"When you have chosen your meal, on the other side of the clearing at one o'clock is a short path that leads to the seating area. Please feel free to begin and help yourselves to whatever you want," said Liew, indicating each station.

Margit, Ramon, and Jenefer stepped aside and watched as the younger ones helped themselves first to their meals. Stoke immediately went over to the dessert section before Jenefer spotted him.

"No, lunch first, then you can come back here for dessert," called out Jenefer, watching him.

"Oh, come on!" finished Stoke.

"You've had enough candy from your stash. Meal first, then sweets." Jenefer didn't move a muscle, just stood there.

"Man," griped Stoke. He grudgingly reversed direction and headed toward the breakfast section.

"*LUNCH*, Mr. Jam. Lunch," declared Jenefer, watching him like a hawk.

Stoke grudgingly reversed direction again and headed to the "lunch" section of the clearing with everyone else.

"This isn't going to be any fun," he said talking, not so quietly, to himself.

Jenefer never wavered. Only once Stoke began taking a few plates from the lunch section did she finally stop her vigil, shaking her head "no" the whole time, in answer to him.

Ramon walked up to Jenefer, tray in hand, and gave a quiet smile. "Little humans."

"Mmmm… hmmm…" answered Jenefer, still shaking her head no.

"Mrs. Washington Lee, please go help yourself," said Liew, watching the watcher.

"Don't worry, Ambassador, I will."

Amy walked up to Liew with Ari, Josie, Jodie, and Yosi by her side. They had trays piled with food, drinks, and goodies.

"Where do we go again?" wondered Amy.

"Down the path, Ms. Ride," said Liew pointing the way down the grassy path that was on the opposite side of the clearing. "You can't miss the seating. Do you want me to come with you?"

"No, thank you. I think we got this," said Amy. She nodded in the direction of the path and the girls were off.

Liew watched his team eagerly helped themselves to much needed sustenance. Finally, the last athlete filled their plate and walked to the seating area. Only then, did Liew head over to the lunch section of the meadow and pick up a plate of food for himself.

He made his way down the path into another clearing. Everyone found a seat around a long, polished wood table finished with a high lacquer; creating a shiny smooth surface of light and dark browns. It wasn't a rectangular cafeteria table. It had curves and bumps, and was more S-shaped, like the path. The team was still in the middle of a jungle, with tree branches and leaves high above. There were hushed sounds of birds whooping, and insects buzzing, and a slight breeze blew through the leaves.

Liew sat down at one of the three vacant seats. He surveyed the plates of fried chicken, spaghetti, pickled herring, crab cakes, plantains, sandwiches, sausage and mash, macaroni and cheese, bammy, cheeseburgers, bitterballen, chicken nuggets, breadfruit, pelmeni, meat and veggies, sushi, udon, and what looked like Peking duck. It proved to him the old adage was indeed true: When stressed, human beings longed for the comforts of home, especially in space.

"Ambassador?"

"Yes, Mr. Suarez," answered Liew, to the diver digging into the plantains and crab cakes.

"*Que hora est?*"

"Oh yes, that's a good point. Everyone..."

The table of athletes stopped eating for a moment.

"The time is now 12:30 a.m."

"A.M.?" interjected Stoke.

"It feels later," whispered Pappie to Ramon, who was sitting next to him.

"That's because we are no longer on the twenty-four hour clock from Earth."

"How long is a day here?" asked Onorina.

"We have a fourteen-hour day and a fourteen-hour night. It is standard time for the Universe Olympics. We call it U.T."

"That's a long day," commented Margit.

"It won't change to p.m. until 14:00. We use a twenty-eight hour clock. If you like, I can put the time on each of your patches. It will go up to 14:00 p.m. then switch back to 1 a.m., for ease of familiarity for you all. But you can change it to a continuous twenty-eight hour clock, if you'd like. Just tap the patch and ask for it."

"Thank you, Ambassador, I think that would help," said Jenefer.

"More sleep for us," winked Josie across the table to Jodie.

"Yes, and a little longer daytime than you are used to. I recommend you take advantage of the extra sleep time. The twenty-eight-hour day will take a toll on the human natural circadian rhythms, and take a while to get used to."

Liew touched the patch on his sleeve, and a fourteen-hour digital clock appeared on the tree across the table. "There, so you can visualize it better. And just say "time" to your patch and it will appear."

Liew started eating the food on his plate. It was clumps of green, white, and blackish food that looked like it had a bone or two in it.

"What is that, Ambassador?" asked Eric, pointing to his plate.

"It's a version of what you call, meatloaf. It's one of my favorite foods. I thought it appropriate, since you all seemed to have chosen yours. I figured it would be a good meal to celebrate. This is our first meal together as a team."

Every athlete stopped eating for a moment and stared at Liew.

"It's like our first Thanksgiving!" announced Amy, smiling. She turned to Yosi who was seated beside her. "It's an American thing."

"Yes, Amy it is like your Thanksgiving," answered Liew. "And in light of that, let me say how thankful I am that you all are here. We are about to begin the Universe Olympics together, and I admire your courage for coming with me to this extraordinary event. I do not take your trust in me lightly. I consider it a great honor and privilege—one of the greatest in my lifetime. I know we are very far away from Earth, but together as a team, I believe we shall put in a good representation for Humanity."

"Here, here!" said Pappie raising his glass.

The rest of the team followed suit. "Here, here!"

Liew finally raised his glass to complete the impromptu toast. Everyone returned to enjoying their lunch. Liew leisurely ate while watching his team interact with one another. There was a lot of talking and laughing, even with the introverted members of the team. The twins were regaling everyone with their adventure of the qualification round. While surveying them all together, Liew knew it was perhaps too premature to boast, but he was oddly proud of what they'd accomplished so far. Everyone was handling the transition to space reasonably well, and the natural leaders of the group had already taken steps to oversee the well-being of the other members of the team. And when the events started, he knew he would grow to appreciate each person individually, as well as a group.

Liew felt so privileged and humbled to be given the opportunity to introduce a new planet into the greater Universe through these Olympics. It was the first time that anyone from his home planet had been asked to be an Ambassador, and it was a great responsibility. To this day, he wasn't sure why the Universe Olympic Committee had picked him. He wasn't famous or well-known on his world. He was just one of seventeen billion individuals.

Liew had graciously accepted the position and spent the last twenty years getting ready to interact with beings from a planet called Earth. His business, his family, and his children all understood this great accolade and were supportive of the decision to devote his life to Humanity. The study of their customs, languages, governments, history, sports, science, anatomy, as well as food, were all-consuming.

There were many stories about Beiahisa's first Ambassador, Kelnda, many millennia ago, when his home world first competed. Her legend created a high standard for any Ambassador. He only hoped he was able to give the humans as much of himself. They were such a dynamic species. His life's everlasting legacy will be guiding the people from Earth through the Universe Olympics, which will lead to...

"Ambassador," said Jenefer.

Liew looked at her, then turned his head. "Everyone." The jungle got quiet when he spoke.

"I think I would prefer it if you would just call me Liew."

*　　　*　　　*

Later that afternoon, most of the athletes were in the workout arena getting in some much-needed training and exercise, when an announcement came over a loudspeaker, as well as from their patches and earbuds.

"Excuse me, would everyone please come up to the observation lounge, immediately. We have a guest who would like to speak to you all." The voice was obviously Liew's. No one else knew how to use the intercom system on the ship.

Ramon and Pappie, who were on different racing cycles, looked at each other, and stopped mid-workout.

"This should be interesting," commented Pappie, jumping off his triathlon bike and grabbing his towel and container of water.

"Human?" questioned Ramon, jumping off his BMX training bike. The two began walking toward the arena entrance and stragglers emerged from their respective workout rooms.

"I'd venture not. We all are about to meet our first sentient life form," said Pappie.

"Second," winked Ramon, as they both dropped their belongings in their cubbies by the door.

"True, true, Ramon. I should have specified, an alien who isn't anthropomorphic in appearance," retorted Pappie.

"Why do you say that?" questioned Ramon as they headed toward the stairs.

"They said Ambassador Liew was specifically chosen because he looked human," answered Pappie. "So logically most of the other life forms in the universe *DON'T* look like us. I'll make a bet with you, Ramon. Beings who look like us aren't the norm in the universe."

"I'll take that bet," answered Ramon, "I think the opposite. The human form must be the norm because it is what wins the evolutionary advantage: forward facing eyes, bipedalism, opposable thumbs; it's what got us to the top of the food chain." Ramon held out his hand for a shake, wiggling his thumbs, to complete the formal bet with Pappie.

They opened the observation lounge door and walked in. Pappie thought he'd won the bet. Well, sort of. They would eventually call it a draw because standing next to Liew was another life form. But it wasn't what either imagined.

The alien was indeed upright on two legs. Wearing clothes made of linked hard shells, like a samurai warrior's armor, the material made a crinkling sound when it moved. The visitor had claw-like fingers and toes, a long torso, and a squared head with a shiny rounded beak for a mouth. Like a long lean turtle without any shell, large black eyes were sunken in leathery worn skin of a darker shade of green.

The other athletes assembled in the seats around the guest.

Ari ran into the room, still drenched in her wetsuit, "I'm sorry I'm late." She froze halfway to the others at the sight of the stranger in their midst.

"Ari, please come in," encouraged Liew, who guided her to a vacant seat.

She looked up at Liew. "I'm still wet. Shouldn't I stand back here?"

"No, it's alright, Ms. Foxx. Please sit down."

Ari plopped down and realized how thankful she was for Liew. They had been correct in sending an Ambassador who resembled a human being. Instinctually, she had to admit, she wouldn't have trusted another life form. She sat, staring at the turtle.

Liew made his way up to the front of the crowd and then turned to their guest. "She is the last human on the team, Madam. We can begin when you are ready."

The turtle pressed a button on her sleeve and began speaking. "Welcome," she roared, the volume of her voice shaking the room. Her mouth moved, squeaks came out, and then human language was heard all around the room.

Yosi covered her ears at the deafening sound.

"Madam," interrupted Liew, "Their hearing is very good at this frequency."

"Very well," said the turtle, touching another button on her sleeve.

In a hushed voice she started again. "Is this better?"

The group of athletes nodded.

"Yes, Madam," acknowledged Liew.

"Welcome Humanity," she started again, claws open.

Amy smiled at the twins, who beamed back at her.

"I am Sypsen, the President of the Universe Olympic Committee. I am here today to say hello before the official events begin tomorrow morning, and to express how pleased we are to have Earth joining us for the first time this year. It is a privilege and honor that Earth is here at Liew's early request."

The athletes turned and peeked at Liew. He was standing just beside them, smiling.

"This is the 100,121st Universe Olympic Games. It has commenced for this galaxy you call the Milky Way. These events are meant to test you as a species: to see what you are made of, not just physically, but mentally, emotionally, and spiritually. The games will push you to the limits of what humans are capable of doing, but don't let that deter you. It is difficult for every new planetary civilization the first time they enter the competition."

Pappie looked over at Ramon, raising his eyebrows high on his forehead.

"Ambassador Liew from Beiahisa was specifically chosen to help steward Humanity through this process. He has trust in you. He requested that Humanity enter the games a hundred of your solar years early. He believes Earth is ready. I hope he is correct."

Margit turned to Jenefer, eyes bulging.

"Humans will be seeing and entering contests that are a first for your planet. This is an exciting moment for Earth, and I look forward to watching Humanity during the games. It is now your chance to make your world proud. Good luck and thank you."

The athletes began clapping loudly, which startled Sypsen a little.

Liew stepped forward and said, "It's their way of thanking you for the speech, Madam."

"Oh yes, very good, Ambassador," finished Sypsen, inspecting the team from planet Earth. She stopped and stared at Stoke's T-shirt of a turtle crunching a human doll.

Chapter 6

DAY 1

Beep. Beep. Beep. The day started as almost every day begins for most human beings on planet Earth: with an alarm sounding. The clock on the nightstand repeated the consistent rhythm. Amy was still half-asleep and couldn't remember setting it the night before. In fact, for a few seconds, her mind was in a fog. She quickly tried to figure out what day of the week it was, and what that meant on her training schedule, trying to account for the alarm. Was it a Tuesday or Wednesday? It felt like a Sunday because something seemed peculiar, not normal. The time on the clock shined a bright red 5:45, in the *ante meridiem*.

Amy reached over and tapped the snooze button. She took another few seconds surveying her room. Her blue furniture, blue rug, and desk had a slight pinkish-yellow glow from the rising sun's light. She turned, expecting to see Coach Sayers in the opened door as the usual morning indicator to get up and *in* the pool. But her door was closed. It must have been a Sunday.

As she slowly rolled out of bed, she spotted something on the wall across from her bed. The wall should have been painted an ocean blue. Instead, it had a digital display with a single word in large print. She read the word, "motivation," aloud with confusion in her voice. She always had a word of the day, to help her focus on her goals for each training session. This must be today's word.

The entire wall immediately changed into a screen. It was Coach Sayers, sitting in a chair in his living room. The living room that was supposed to be right down the hall. That's when she remembered. She wasn't home. This wasn't her room. And before she could complete the thought, the video of her Coach began speaking.

"Hello, Amy." Coach Sayers looked a little uncomfortable talking directly to the camera.

Amy sat back in bed and watched, still a little dazed in the haze of sleep.

"Ambassador Liew asked me to make a few videos, about twenty or so, which logically leads me to think you'll be gone about a month, assuming one per day. This is video number one." Her coach adjusted his seat and started to appear a little calmer.

"How are you? I know you can't answer me, but I think it's important for someone to ask, and for you to know—I'm thinking about you and worried sick about the team. Was it a crazy trip?" Coach Sayers ran his hands slowly through his hair, "I can't even imagine. Hopefully you don't have any fatigue or motion sickness, or jet lag…" He laughed at himself. "Or space lag."

Amy smiled.

"Or anything. But let's assume you do. Please double up on your energy drink and protein shakes for a few days, to compensate for any damage done to your body during the trip. That brings us to today's topic. Number one is your training routine. I think it makes sense, if you can, to try and keep the same schedule so you don't throw your body off kilter and you keep your muscle tone and endurance. At your meals today, add in an additional five ounces of protein and an extra 'greens' shake at snack breaks. Ambassador Liew has all your meal specifications."

"Yeah, he told us," responded Amy to the screen, but she got no response in return.

"As for your workout, let's do as usual, your two-hour morning swim, break, cross-train on ropes or rowing, break, add in weights, for the next few days, then back into the pool for our usual five-four-five."

Amy huffed at the screen. "Man…"

"I know it's tough for the first day, but I'm afraid you will lose muscle mass in space, if any of the stuff I've read about the human body and long-term effects in zero gravity, assuming you're in zero gravity…" He trailed off, thinking to himself, and was quiet for a moment.

He continued, "Number two is motivation. I'm praying this isn't the case, but just in case I want you to be prepared."

Amy began to look nervous, sitting on the edge of her bed.

"I don't know the order of events for the games. Or which day is your competition. So, God forbid, if *today* is your competition day, I want you to, please go do our usual warm-up. Add in just a few sprints, if you can. And when it's your turn, I want you to get out there and be the best Humanity has ever seen. Because if today is your day, Amy, you will be the *first*. Think about that for a moment," Coach Sayers paused himself at the thought.

"You will be the first human being to compete off world and with aliens. Just as Ambassador Liew is the face for other worlds here, you too will become the first face for Humanity there."

Amy remembered the previous day's qualification round. She didn't put her best foot or face forward, the twins did. At the shocking sight of an alien, she treaded water and didn't move a muscle to help—not what Coach Sayers would have wanted.

"This is an important responsibility," continued Coach Sayers. "You have to go out there today and show the other aliens about human beings—what we are capable of doing. To represent planet Earth, I need you to go and be the athlete I saw in the Nairobi Olympic Games, and also the dedicated person I see every day in the pool. If today is your event, it is time to take a leap for mankind."

Amy knew he was right. Yesterday, she had felt like a bumbling idiot. The twins had pulled most of the weight, literally and figuratively, in the water. She needed to step up her game.

"I want you to know that you can be the best athlete on this team. And by being the first, you will become an example for the other team members. It's time to raise the bar for your bravery, your commitment, your strength, your spirit, and your integrity to your sport, wherever it is in the universe you are swimming. Take heart."

Coach Sayers breathed deep. "Please know I miss you, and pray daily for your well-being, and for the entire team. Also, you need to know…" He paused for a moment before he continued. "I admire you tremendously. I would have been too scared to go across the galaxy by myself and compete with aliens. You are doing something that I could never do. And remember, you are the one who knew deep down in your heart that you had to go to these games. You knew. Keep that knowledge; let it motivate you, be the secret spark in your heart. You are meant to be there, Amy. And if you are stuck in any deep, dark place by yourself, use that light to find your way home. Also remember, Ambassador Liew picked you for a reason. Show him that reason today. Be the girl, no, the *tremendous* human being I know you to be. Get out there and swim the hell out of it."

Amy was a little teary-eyed and now fully awake in her room filled with morning sunlight.

Coach Sayers got up from his chair, reaching for something beyond the frame, when he suddenly stopped. "One more thing—watch out for that Stoke, kid. I've been internet stalking him, and he's crazy wild. Got into some trouble."

He paused for a moment, taking another breath, and he looked steely at Amy, eye to eye. "Make me proud, Amy Patricia Ride. Make your mom and dad proud. Make all of us on Earth proud. *Let's Ride!*" he said, his raspy voice growling like a car engine revving up. The video ended and Amy's bedroom wall returned to normal.

Amy stood up, now composed and fierce as any warrior before battle. "Let's Ride," she repeated aloud.

*   *   *

As Amy entered the workout arena, she wasn't surprised to see her teammates on bikes, running on the treadmill squares, and she could hear Onorina shooting across the way. Sito was halfway up the bouldering wall, and Yosi was on the uneven bars circling away. Amy kindly waved at Jenefer, who smiled back without breaking stride. Most of the team had already begun their morning training. It was barely six o'clock in the morning, but she was running a little late because of the coaching video.

The only team members who weren't directly in sight were the ones with special workout rooms, although Amy guessed the twins might be sleeping in a little bit, since it was such a tough day yesterday.

Amy smiled to herself. She was glad to have some companions her age during the games.

She put her gym bag in her cubby, tapping the patch to listen to some music for her morning workout. Strolling over towards the entrance of the 360° infinity lap pool, she noticed the passageway was blocked by a very tall person.

"What's up?" she asked.

"Good morning, Amy," said Liew. "I wanted to ask you not to do your usual workout today please."

"Why not?"

"Because after our team breakfast it is time for your event."

Amy's heart jumped for a second. Her coach had been right. "Today is my day?" she gingerly asked.

"Yes, today is your day, Ms. Ride," answered Liew. "Only do whatever warm-up is necessary. Please be ready to leave on the shuttle at 9 a.m. U.T."

Amy's attention drifted off for a second. She thought of her mom and dad, and her best friend Lucy. They weren't going to get the opportunity to watch her at this competition. It would be the first time ever that they weren't going to be at a major competition of hers. She felt a slight pang in her heart she never felt before. Their support, their encouragement, besides Coach Sayers, was what got her in and out of the pool. And now they weren't going to be there on the biggest swim day of her life. She suddenly felt homesick.

"Don't worry, Amy. You will do a wonderful job today. I will be there with you. And I have every confidence in you."

"Thank you, Liew. I better get in my warm-up."

She started heading down the passage when Pappie, still wet from his own morning swim, stopped to listen to the exchange.

"Good morning, Amy," he said with a forceful cheer in his voice, "Today is *YOUR* day!" Only another athlete could comprehend how his emphasis was a combination of encouragement and fight.

*   *   *

By the time breakfast rolled around, Pappie had told everyone that Amy was first up on the schedule. She was taken off guard when she walked into the jungle seating area of the cafeteria, and every other athlete stood clapping and cheering.

"You can do this!" shouted Josie.

"Let's go, Amy," hailed Margit with a smile on her face.

"Time to W-O-W the galaxy," yelled Jaysen, who was still having a hard time letting go of the word "wow."

"Huzzah!" yelled Pappie, who was standing on his chair, hands held up.

"You get them, mate," hollered Jodie.

And then there was Liew. He wasn't cheering, he wasn't joining in; he was standing back in pure elation, watching the team encourage one of its youngest members. It made him proud—proud of their encouragement, proud to be representing them in the Universe

Olympics. If this show of team spirit and unity was so high at the very beginning of the games, he couldn't imagine what it would be like at the end.

Amy stopped, tray in hand, overwhelmed by the show of support. She had a tear in her eye as she walked over to an empty seat, "Thank you, thank you."

The clapping didn't stop for a few more minutes as both Ramon and Jaysen whooped up a little more frenzy. Amy finally stood up. The bellowing only got louder.

"I'm very nervous to be the first. I appreciate your support and I hope I make the team, and all of planet Earth proud today at my swimming event. Thank you, everyone."

"Want us to go?" Josie and Jodie said in almost perfect unison.

"I don't know what the rules are. Can they go, Liew?" questioned Amy.

"I think it would be best for Ms. Ride if it was just the two of us for the start of the first event, girls. That way Amy can concentrate on her competition and the task at hand."

The twins looked visibly bummed out.

"Liew, Ramon and I would also like to volunteer to be present at the start, to be her human representatives from the team," offered Jenefer.

"I will leave that up to Amy, if she feels she needs that," answered Liew.

Amy contemplated for a moment. "No, thank you, Jen. I think I'll be, OK. If Liew feels it's best to start out the event alone, I'll stick by that."

"Amy, are you sure? Jenefer and I are happy to accompany you down to the water planet," added Ramon. "No hassle."

"Thank you, I think I'll be fine."

"You will," said Liew with certainty. "We leave in one hour, Ms. Ride."

*   *   *

The same mini-D shuttle took off with two solitary individuals inside. Amy paced the small interior of the transport shuttle doing some warm-up exercises, as Liew piloted, which was more like overseeing a self-propelled vehicle than actual piloting.

"Amy, please come and see your arena."

She stopped her lunges and gazed out of the viewscreen. They approached one of the most beautiful sights Amy had ever seen—a water planet. The color variations of the blue water changed from pole to pole, but it was all one ocean. From space, there were no visible signs of any land masses.

"I've never seen an all water planet before," mentioned Amy.

"Yes, it is very beautiful, if you can swim."

"Can you, Liew?" wondered Amy for the first time.

"Of course, Ms. Ride. I wouldn't be allowed to be your Ambassador unless I was proficient in your sports."

"All of them?"

"Yes, all of them."

"So, you are the coach of coaches then," she laughed a little.

"What do humans say? 'A jack of all trades is a master of none.' But don't worry, Amy. I can swim," he winked at her.

She noted the truly human gesture and idiosyncrasy. Amy wondered if they winked on his home world. Did Liew have to take human gesture courses to be their Ambassador?

The mini-D shuttle easily passed through the atmosphere. Amy braced for impact, having watched all the old videos of the Apollo missions re-entering Earth's atmosphere. She was expecting a bump or bounce, but it was perfectly smooth.

Down they traveled toward the ocean surface; it was water as far as the eye could see, and then some. Amy guessed that this is what it must have felt like to be in the middle of the Pacific Ocean—no land, all water. Like a shipwrecked sailor.

"Liew, where is my start?"

He pointed. "There." Far off in the distance, barely visible to the human eye against the blue of the water, was a small rectangular platform, much like the platform for the qualifications. It was hard to see because it was silver, like a mirror.

"That's it?" questioned Amy with some shock in her voice.

"Yes, there."

The shuttle slowly descended to the floating platform that was no bigger than ten by twenty feet wide.

"Were you expecting something else?" asked Liew.

"Yeah, something bigger."

"No, this is your starting point."

The shuttle opened directly onto the small silver platform in the middle of the ocean. As soon as Amy and Liew exited the shuttle, it abruptly flew away. Leaving them quite alone in the middle of an ocean.

"Thank God, I didn't leave my bag in there," said Amy watching as the shuttle disappeared into the wispy clouds.

"Then, I wouldn't have let it leave," answered Liew.

Amy blinked twice, staring out. The platform gently bobbed up and down with the tiny ripple of waves. The water was magnificent and daunting at the same time. Surprisingly, at that moment she missed Earth. Not the planet itself, but dirt, land. She never appreciated how much she took the comfort of land for granted—the safe harbor the Earth provided in the sea of the planet. Maybe she wasn't the "water baby" she always thought she was. Maybe she was more an Earth baby after all.

She took in a deep breath and realized she was able to breathe on this foreign world. Come to think of it, she was the first human being to ever set foot on another planet, outside of our solar system. And she hadn't even stepped on any land yet.

"Please prepare yourself, Amy."

Amy suddenly remembered that she had a competition ahead of her and this wasn't a time for gawking. Her hair was already under blue double swim caps that read "Let's Ride" on the side. Amy took off her warm-up suit, and stretched her arms by swinging them around.

"You ready?" asked Liew, standing next to her on the solitary platform.

"Yeah. But, Liew. I'm really nervous."

"I can see that you are, and it's perfectly normal and natural to be so. Please keep your mind on the competition ahead of you and I know you will be OK."

Amy stared at the blue waves and the cloudless sky. She had expected the gravity to be slightly off, as this planet was only one-fourth the size of Earth, but she felt fine. "It's quiet out here. I'm surprised I'm the only contestant in this event."

"You aren't," said Liew with a confused look on his face. "It would hardly be a competition if there were only one contestant."

"Oh," said Amy, looking for any other signs of life on the water. There was no other platform, there wasn't anyone else, just them.

"How far do I have to swim?"

"The goal of this event is to reach the other platform first."

"How far away is it? I can't see it?"

"It's a few miles away."

"A few miles! Liew, I'm not an open water swimmer. We have marathon swimmers on Earth for that."

"I know, Ms. Ride, this isn't a marathon swim. Let me ask you. During your usual workouts and practices, how far do you actually swim?"

Amy understood his meaning right away. She would spend hours in the pool everyday, building up her endurance and muscles. Her sprint for the 1500-meters was the icing on the distance cake. She usually spent a minimum of three to four hours a day training in the pool.

"I'd like you to swim, whatever stroke you feel is your best, to the other platform," said Liew, pointing straight ahead. It could have been North, South, East or West—Amy had no real navigational bearings on this tiny water planet.

The Olympic Flame sun was to her left. But she was afraid to make it her visual marker, because she wasn't sure how fast such a small planet rotated. In an hour, the Olympic Flame sun could be halfway across the sky. It wasn't a reliable point of reference.

"I'll be waiting on the other platform when you are done." Liew handed her goggles. "If you feel you're drifting or off course, your goggles will navigate and show you what direction to swim in. We put a clear display film on them, like the patch. Are you wearing the patch?"

"No." She held up her arm.

Liew peeled it off her warm-up suit and put it on her skin. "Please, from now on, keep the patch on at all times and check your goggles."

Amy examined her goggles. They seemed the same as before. If there was a "film" on them, it was indecipherable to her eye. "What are my chances of winning this event, Liew?"

Liew smiled at her. "Just be as good as any being in the Universe, Ms. Ride," he said with confidence, touching her shoulder encouragingly. He caught sight of the countdown clock on his patch. "Please, get ready."

Amy stretched her arms, her legs, and moved around briskly. She tightened her goggles into place on her face. On the inside, as if in 3-D stereo view, a display showed an outlined green path with arrows pointing straight in front of her. "This is cool!"

"Just follow the arrows, Amy. No matter *where* they go. And make sure you swim through the rectangular markers; they'll be in red. If you miss one, you're disqualified. Swim as fast as you can, and I will see you on the other platform." Liew glanced at his display again. "Get ready."

Amy put in her earplugs.

"And Amy," Liew said loudly so she could hear him through the earplugs.

She turned her head.

"Let's Ride!"

Amy smiled, then leaned over the side of the platform in her "start" position.

"Also," he shouted even louder "ignore the other…"

Before he could finish his sentence, the same elephant honking sound she heard during the qualification round, blared deafeningly, as if from the sky.

"GO!" screamed Liew.

Amy dove in, did her best dolphin kick, and she was off in an ocean as wide as the world.

The salty water felt warm and comfortable to her. There was a brief moment of thankfulness, because it never occurred to her to ask what temperature the water might be; if it was too cold, she would have certainly needed a wetsuit. The ocean had a little current; it was calm as a pool.

Amy wondered what *others* Liew was referring to, as she surveyed the water that seemed empty both above and below. Who, or what was she competing against? And how did Liew expect her to ignore them?

She started out strong with the freestyle stroke and soon she began pacing herself. With every lift of her head, she watched the green arrows in her goggles. If she had a few miles ahead of her, she needed enough kick at the end to provide the extra boost to win. She quickly glanced back for both Liew and the platform, but they had already disappeared off the water. It was just her and the sea, and the green arrows to guide her along the way.

After a few minutes of swimming, she saw what Liew was talking about. In the middle of the water, half in the ocean, half in the air, only visible through the film of her goggles, were two parallel red lines about ten to fifteen feet apart. As she approached, the bright green arrows pointed directly between them. When she swam past the first markers, the two red lines were quickly gone in a bright flash of green. Markers completed.

She estimated that at her pace and distance she usually swam, she was about 200 yards from where she started. But without any land or other visual clues, it was a bit disorienting to figure out where she started.

She continued forward for a few more minutes, swimming through another set of red markers, when something odd happened. The green arrows in her goggles were no longer pointing straight ahead along the waters' surface, but they curved down into the water. Amy took a shallow breath and plunged, following the arrows as they went into the sea. She was beginning to get a little nervous; her breath wasn't very deep when she spotted the two red markers floating about twenty feet below the surface of the water.

As soon as she swam through the markers, to her relief, the green arrows pointed straight up to the surface again. When she finally made it back up to the air, she took a deep breath and continued on with her usual freestyle long swim.

That's when it occurred to her. What if this wasn't just a quick swim straight across the surface of the water to the other platform? What if this event was something more? The turtle had said these games were different from Earth's. She never did ask Liew for specifics. She assumed, now it seemed incorrectly, that her event would be a carbon copy of her 1500-meter race at home.

After a few more yards along the surface, the green arrows again pointed down into the water. This time she took a deep breath, understanding she was wrong. This swimming event *was* something more and she was a little frightened.

Amy dove down deep, using her best dolphin kick. The water was a pretty clear blue, and at about twenty-five feet below the surface, she spotted the two red markers floating in the sea. As she swam closer, an underwater rip-current grabbed her and quickly spun her around the markers. She managed, with great difficulty, to swim her way out of the rip-current and turn around, only to realize she was on the opposite side. The green arrows in her goggles directed her back through the red markers in the middle of the water. She tried again to swim toward the markers from the opposite side, but the rip current grabbed her and pushed her around the markers to almost the same position where she started. In frustration, she went back to the surface to catch her breath.

As she breached the surface, she took in a huge breath and then treaded water for a moment, thinking. The green arrows in her goggles were ever vigilant, pointing back down to the intended target. Amy knew she couldn't skip this portion of the race or she'd be disqualified. There was only one way to go, that was back down and through the markers. After a few more seconds at the surface, she inhaled a deep breath and dove back in.

Quickly, she tried to make up for lost time and swim back to the swirling vortex of water surrounding the red markers. She hesitated, observing the waters movement for a moment; she realized all of the previous markers were placed up and down, top to bottom, for her to swim through, but *these* markers were different. Instead of pointing up and down they were placed left to right. In order for her to swim through them, she couldn't approach from a horizontal angle.

She was thinking about this all wrong. She was reasoning like a human being who lived on the ground, only having control and living on one plane of existence; the *x–y axis*, like in geometry. Her tenth-grade teacher, Mrs. Blacker, always spoke about how people lived mainly on the *x-y axis* along the surface of the Earth, but people weren't birds who flew in the air, or fish in water. Amy knew what she needed to do. What she needed was a little "z" axis.

Amy submerged, diving deeper than she had ever gone before, all the while thanking Mrs. Blacker. Down through the water she swam, until she thought she was safely underneath the surrounding circumference of the rip current. She slowly made her way parallel, swimming directly underneath the red markers. Amy looked up, and only when the markers were directly above her, did she ascend straight up the *z-axis*. There was no current or riptide up along the *z-axis*, so she guessed correctly—the underwater current circled the markers like a donut. Up, up she swam, along the *z-axis,* through the red markers, and then finally the green flash of accomplishment she'd been striving for. She continued straight on up to the surface.

When she finally breached the water she yowled, "Yes! *Z rocks!"* and then swiftly continued swimming along the surface, as delineated by the green arrows. Feeling thankful, she remained along the surface of the sea for what felt like a few minutes, making a good pace with her freestyle stroke.

Amy began to wonder if the rest of the competition was going to be along the surface of the water when the green arrows changed again. For a moment, she dreaded what she saw. The arrows pointed down, straight down. Where were they going? What was she going to have to figure out next? It was one thing to swim as hard as she could for 1500-meters, giving everything, she had physically. But these puzzles were pushing her mind, her heart, and her soul to the limit. The turtle was right. These games were more, and she prayed she had it in her to do it.

She followed the arrows, diving down deep as they pointed the way until she saw the top of something. It was hard to see at first, but as she swam closer, she recognized the peak of a very large sand dune, only it was underwater. The arrows continued to indicate her downward swim along the side and around the dune, until it was suddenly joined by another on the left.

Amy found herself zigzagging around these colossal underwater sand dunes, praying that the red markers were soon in sight. Left, then right, hard turn left, then back right again. She pondered how useful fins might have been to help her easily glide around these underwater obstacles. As she finally made it past another dune the red markers were floating along the side, slightly askew.

Amy rapidly swam through the markers, and regardless of the arrows, she made her way straight up to the surface, dying for breath. Once she surfaced, she stopped for a moment to catch her breath. She had been underwater, she guessed, for almost a minute and a half. This had pushed the limit of what she was capable of doing. After a few more very deep breaths, she continued forward, seeing the arrows point along the surface, for which she was very thankful.

Her pace had slowed; being underwater for so long took some life out of her kick. She wondered if Liew should have brought a scuba diver to this event. The depths she was swimming were almost to free-dive levels. She had once read of a woman who could go a couple hundred feet on a single breath, but that was with years of training and pulse control. Amy had never even thought of getting her scuba certification, and now she was borderline diving to those depths. The average pool was only twenty feet deep.

After five more minutes swimming along the surface the green arrows pointed down. This time Amy wasn't going to be caught off guard. She paused for a moment, pushed out all the air from her lungs with a few exhales, then inhaled the deepest breath humanly possible and dove in.

Down…

Down…

Down.

The color of the water changed from a light sky blue to a darker, deeper blue as she followed the arrows through the depths. She couldn't believe where the arrows were pointing. Just a few feet ahead of her was a very dark cave with an opening just big enough for a human to squeeze in. It took all of Amy's fortitude to continue swimming forward into the blackened tunnel. When she entered, unexpectedly, a light emanated from her goggles, illuminating the few feet in front of her. The only other light was from the ever-present green arrows beckoning her deeper into the cave.

As she swam down the narrow furrow filled with water, she began to wonder about Liew and her unquestionable trust in him. Did he know how long she could hold her breath? Did he know she couldn't last much longer than one minute forty-five seconds without oxygen? It was an act of faith and courage that she continued onward into the dark night of that cave.

Deeper into the dark hole, she persisted with dim light and no air available. Amy began to wonder if she was swimming to her death. Could her naïve trust in Liew be her end? On and on, she swam deeper into the cave that didn't seem to have an end in sight. She tried to swim as fast as she could, but her muscles began to burn from oxygen deprivation; her eyes were losing colors, seeing stars. There wasn't much time left for her in the cave. She wondered if they would find her body and when? Would it be an embarrassment that the first human being from Earth to compete at the Universe Olympic Games drowned? The qualification round that she and the twins made fun of, now didn't seem so foolish. She was being pushed to the brink of death. At that instant, the green arrows pointed up, and there was a color change in the water above. Amy followed and surfaced into a small air-filled cave. She coughed for a moment, taking in as much air as her lungs allowed.

The air pocket was tiny, only a few feet around. A small blue light turned on inside the cave when her head surfaced. The purpose of this cave was obviously just for air. There was no ledge for her to rest on. She had to tread water, having just enough room to move her hands and feet around. This pocket of air in the cave was the small miracle she needed. Had she stayed under any longer, she would have lost consciousness.

That's when she felt it: Loneliness. It was just her alone in a cave, deep under water, on a planet at the edge of the Milky Way galaxy, all by herself. She had never felt further from Humanity, from Earth, from home, and from loved ones. Her eyes teared up, but she stopped herself; filling her goggles up with salty tears would be detrimental to her competition.

She inhaled a few more deep calming breaths, holding back the sob, and she talked to herself. "You're OK. You can do this. You're not alone." She thought of her mom and dad, her best friend Lucy, and Coach Sayers, the people closest to her heart. "You're *not* alone." Even though she was tens of millions of miles away, their love filled her heart—their love for her and her love for them.

Then she remembered what Coach Sayers said in his video this morning. His motivation. She was meant to be there. "*YOU* are supposed to be here," she repeated loudly to herself, trying not to wail, and it echoed in the small cave. She knew deep down in her heart that she was meant to be in this place, this cave, this swim; it was why she was always reading on exoplanets. Why in astronomy class she wondered and wished for a planet made of one ocean. Why in her nightly dreams, she dreamt of this place, this planet. And why she was here now. Something—God, the Universe, her subconscious, or all of them, had been preparing her for this exact moment. She knew. And that knowledge, that acknowledgement filled her heart with confidence, and with certainty. She could do this. She was going to be all right. Everything was going to be OK.

"OK," she finally said quietly to herself, "*Let's Ride!*" The true meaning of the phrase resonating in her heart for the first time. She took her last full breath and dove back in the water and into the tunnel.

Continuing through the dark channel, Amy followed the green arrows until she finally caught sight of a twinkle of light. She swam faster down the shaft, traversing its crags, further and further, as the twinkle turned into the full sunlight, at the end of the cave, and floating just past its opening were the bright red markers.

With great satisfaction, she burst out of the cave as the markers flashed. She swam forward, through what looked like piles of pink coral, under an outcropping, around a ridge, deeper into the water following the green arrows, almost blindly forward. After a particularly challenging turn, she was again on the brink of needing air. She looked up but the surface of the water was at least forty to fifty feet away, if not more, and the arrows in her goggles weren't pointing up but straight, through the water.

The question was: Did she follow her instincts and immediately ascend topside, or trust in the games, or at least trust Liew? She silently prayed that, like before, she would get air when she really needed it. Amy took the proverbial leap and continued swimming through the deep water, ignoring her instincts. She swam straight through a hollowed-out circle, like an upright basketball ring, that had been created out of holey coral. Her muscles began to burn, she was starting to feel a little light-headed, and her sight was growing hazy from lack of oxygen.

The green arrows beckoned her on forward through her foggy mental state. It took her a moment before she could properly process what she saw directly in front of her. After she cleared the coral, it was all open water, but for a distant object. It was hard to guess what it was at first. It looked like a spherical silver underwater spaceship lying in wait, but as she swam closer, following the green arrows pointing straight to it, she realized what it was: a giant air bubble.

Joyfully, she pushed and pulled with every last bit of strength to make it to the air bubble. It was massive; at least thirty feet in diameter. There was enough air in there for her to camp out for a week. As she broke through the surface, she coughed and sputtered taking in lungs full of air. She treaded water to keep her head in the bubble while her body bobbed at the bottom of it.

Red-faced and gulping in deep breaths, she looked up around the inside of the shimmering air bubble in the middle of the sea. What an incredible and welcome sight. She took off her goggles for a second, wanting to see it with her own two eyes. The bubble was like being in the middle of a large spherical magnifying glass. She could see the ocean's surface far above her head, when she suddenly felt a forceful stream of water, like a fire hose. The water splashed her with such intensity that she was knocked back into the sea. She swiftly popped back up into the bubble to take a breath when she heard a deafening noise. It was the sound of rushing air, like a jet engine intake. She quickly turned around and saw on the opposite side of the bubble an astonishing sight—the competition.

The behemoth form was floating halfway up the bubble, a greyish mass with a large air hole that was breathing in air. Obviously, this air bubble wasn't only meant for her. For a second, she was stunned silent by the splashing water and the intake of massive amounts of air from the creature, whose size must have been amplified through the convex lens of the air bubble. It was long, about four school buses long, with fins, and a huge tail; it resembled a blue whale. It turned its head from the top, where the air hole was, to the side with the giant eye. They both stared at each other for a minute, eye to eye, sizing each other up. The competitor in Amy kicked in. She had just seen her competition; there was no ignoring a whale-like being despite Liew's directions. It was time to get her head back into the game. She put her goggles back on and took in as much air as humanly possible, then dove back into the water, leaving the air bubble behind. In a flurry of movement, she followed the green arrows.

She swam hard and fast through the ocean, trying to put some distance between her and her competitor. Faster and faster she pushed through the water, not able to use her freestyle stroke, her backstroke, or butterfly to get her moving. Surrounded 360° by water, she chose a version of the breaststroke with a dolphin kick as her best option. She noted the irony that she needed to mirror a marine mammal to beat one. Grasping gallons of water and pushing them around her body, the red markers appeared mid-way to the surface. Amy gave it everything she had to get there.

A few feet after the flash of the completed markers, the arrows began pointing back to the ocean's surface. Amy quickly complied. She glanced back and saw the full length and enormity of her competition.

It was a grey whale; only the eyes were larger, the fins longer, and the smaller teeth filled mouth resembled a killer whale. Killer whales frightened Amy to the core, more than sharks. Because whales were a highly intelligent species.

If she thought she was swimming fast before, with a giant creature reminiscent of an apex predator from planet Earth behind her, she was now swimming at lightning speed!

Amy surfaced and started her sprint freestyle stroke. Faster and faster, she picked up her pace and managed to get a little distance between her and the whale. It was still hanging out in the giant air bubble, but she wasn't sure why. Maybe it was taunting her, or the creature legitimately needed to rest and breathe. Perhaps it felt a little sorry for her and wanted to give her a little head start. It seemed, by all visual examination, to be a "marine" animal. She didn't see any legs or feet to walk on land, only fins. Given its hydrodynamic advantage, it would soon be upon her.

She quickly glanced back to the bubble. The whale was gone. She truly doubled her pace and only breathed every other stroke, to try and gain some more distance. Her aching body was dragging.

Only a minute or so later, there was no need to look back and check out where the whale was. She felt it closing in on her. Or rather, the hydrodynamics of the water made it quite evident where it was. She felt her stroke, not gaining, but pulling her backwards. It was directly behind her. Amy looked back at its long snout. All it needed to do was open its large mouth and she was inside—a little crunch—and she would be whale dinner.

It was like swimming next to a submarine as the whale overtook her. She then remembered another important rule of fluid mechanics that every sailor, fisherman, and swimmer knew all too well—drag force. With her competitor so close, so large, and so fast, she began to get pulled under in its wake. As it pushed past her, she took a large gulp of air as the drag pulled her under, behind the large mouth—she wasn't sure if it was open or not—toward the belly of the whale.

She was no longer swimming to win the game at this point, she was swimming to *live*. The drag continued to pull her under. As she made her way down the underside of the belly, she realized it was much larger and longer than what she had guessed through the air bubble.

Amy tried desperately to get out of the drag, and out from underneath the creature, but her little hands and hurting feet were no competition next to fins the size of a truck. She knew what she needed to do, but it was against every fiber of her being and training as a swimmer. She finally stopped fighting the water, stopped swimming, and let the drag force swiftly carry her behind the creature. As she made her way down the long flapping tail, luckily it didn't flap down and crush her. Even after it was gone, the swirling wake of the whale made it a struggle for Amy to get back up to the surface. As soon as she did, she gulped in air, thankful she had survived.

Amy continued swimming half-heartedly along the surface of the water, slowly watching the whale underwater as it disappeared in the deep blue sea. Her competition had bested her, it had steamrolled past her, and was gone.

Then she heard a muffled, echoing sound underwater. It wasn't the giant blue whale-like creature. She surveyed underneath the water, only to see empty, deep, blue ocean. Amy finally picked her head up fully out of the water and the noise amplified. She saw where the noise was coming from. About a hundred yards away, on her finishing platform was every member of Team Earth cheering her on!

Both twins had their hands in the water, splashing, hitting the side of the platform, screaming, and making a ruckus. On top of the platform itself, Jenefer and Ramon jumped up and down cheering at the top of their lungs, "Come on, Amy!" Stoke, Jaysen, Sito, and Pappie were whistling at a high pitch, hooting and hollering. Onorina was crouched down next to the twins screeching, splashing, smiling, and hollering expressively in Italian.

It was a tight fit for eighteen people on the twenty by ten-foot rectangular platform. How no one was knocked off into the water during the uproar remained a mystery.

Amy had almost no energy left, but when she heard all the cheering, she dug deep for a final burst of strength. The shouting only amplified as she approached the platform.

Ari howled louder with Yosi, Eric screeched and yammered, and Manny waved his hands high above his head, shrieking. Mark and Justine were jumping up and down, wobbling the platform itself, and even Dmitri was clapping his hands. The only person on the platform who kept his calm, standing as the beacon of quiet strength and dignity, representing the solemnity of the finish, was Liew. He waited amid the chaos for the first Olympian to complete the initial event of the Universe Olympics. It was a truly momentous occasion.

Amy just barely had enough steam to make it to the platform. She placed her hand squarely on the mirrored surface, and as soon as she touched it, Liew reached his hand down and pulled her easily out of the water.

"*You did it!*" yelled Josie and Jodie, surrounding her on each side.

"Awesomepants!" wailed Stoke.

"Yee-ha!" roared Jaysen.

"You *ROCKED!*" shrieked Ari, still slightly jumping up and down in excitement.

"Well done, Amy," said Liew gently in her ear, amongst the yelling.

"I didn't win," said Amy quietly, with a tinge of sorrow in her voice.

"But you put in a wonderful showing for Earth, Amy. And you completed your event and that is something to be proud of," said Liew handing her a towel and something to drink.

Every team member squeezed in and took turns congratulating her on the completion of the event and being the first human to compete in the Universe Olympic Games.

"Well done *FIRST!*" said Pappie, with a twinkle in his eye.

"Congratulations, Amy," said Sito as he bowed in front of her.

"I'm so happy you finished," said Margit. "This ocean planet is formidable! You are a great swimmer."

It took Amy a few seconds to get her bearings and think about what just happened between all the congratulating. She would go down in history as the first human being to compete with an extraterrestrial being, on an alien planet, and complete her event. She didn't win, but she had given it everything she had, and for any athlete that should be enough.

"How did you all get here?" asked Amy, breathless.

"Liew announced on the ship after you left, that if anyone wanted to be at the finish, 'to please go to the shuttle.' As you can see, everyone showed up," exclaimed Ramon.

"You rounded us up a little," teased Mark to Ramon, who shrugged off the acknowledgement.

"Dude, Liew, do we have a bigger shuttle?" questioned Stoke. "It was a pretty tight fit in there."

"I'm sorry, Stoke, I had no idea *all* of you wanted to come."

"Heck, yeah," snorted Jodie, "I'm shocked you thought we wouldn't, Liew!" She gave him a wink as a medium sized mini-D shuttle descended from the sky to the mirror platform in the middle of the sea.

"Thank you all for coming down and cheering me on," said Amy who was battered, out of breath, a little shaky, had a slight redness to her cheeks, and shakily walking at a glacial pace. "It felt good seeing everyone on the platform. You *all* helped me finish."

"Of course!" cried Josie, "We wanted to be here," she said giving Amy a gentle hug. "You did amazing."

"We are so proud of you, Amy," cheerfully declared Jenefer.

"Good job," said Jaysen. "Saw your competitor come up for air. It was ginormous, Amy! Thing looked like a whale."

"And its belly looked like one too," said Amy, who again thanked God that she didn't drown underneath the alien.

"There is *nada* out here but *agua*!" said Manny, gazing across at the barren sea.

"Too much water!" joked Amy, as the shuttle door opened, "A little solid ground would be nice."

"I want to hear ALL about it," announced Stoke.

Jodie squeezed Amy gently and rubbed to warm her up through the towel. "You did great, mate!"

"Go Team Earth!" yelled Pappie to the sky, and then repeated it to the water as he boarded the shuttle. Pappie was yelling to no one in particular—perhaps the water, more probably the whale.

"G.T.E.," echoed Jodie as she boarded. "We should have T-shirts made that say that!"

"With a little outline of a human in front," finished Josie, striking a "running man" pose. She trailed into the shuttle behind her sister.

Liew smiled to himself as he was about to embark. He glanced over to see half the team helping a drained Amy into the shuttle. "Yes, indeed," Liew said, stepping inside. "Go Team Earth."

Chapter 7

The Call

When the shuttle returned to their spaceship, the entire team exited down the hallway to the left, but Liew began walking to the right. "Amy, please come with me," he kindly asked of his very slow-moving athlete.

"Can we come?" asked Josie, who kept a protective hand on Amy's back.

"I'm not sure I could stop you two," joked Liew, as he headed further down the passageway.

"Probably not, mate," retorted Jodie, who also remained by Amy's side.

Jenefer and Ramon led the other team members down the hall and upstairs to the Jungle Cafeteria, since it was almost lunch time. Adding the four extra hours of the Universe Olympic clock made mealtime that much further away, so when it was finally at 13:59 a.m., usually everyone was ravenous.

Liew guided the girls down a long, empty hallway to a distant door.

"Where are we going, Liew?" asked one of the twins, since Amy had neither the strength, nor the breath, to ask.

"The Recovery Room," he answered, walking up to the door in the long hall that seemed to go on forever.

As they walked in, lights came on, but they were very dim. It was hard to see inside the mostly empty room. A bright spotlight revealed a large, elevated lounge chair that slightly resembled a hospital bed, but without sheets or discernable pillow.

"*This* is it?" announced Jodie, looking around the room at the plain black walls and spotting only two stools in the corner.

"Yes, Ms. McQuenzy. Now, Amy, please head into the restroom, right there," said Liew, pointing to one of the black panels. Had Liew not said that it was a restroom, no one would have guessed the panel was actually a door. "You can get out of your swimsuit, change into your sweats, and put on the fresh pair of pants in there. Please, use the facilities if need be. When you come out, we need to get you in the Recovery Chair. Immediately."

Amy slowly drifted over to the bathroom while Josie pushed open the door. "Need any help, mate?" inquired Jodie

"No, thank you," she whispered softly.

"If you're not out in five, I'm coming in to get you," proclaimed Jodie nodding to Josie, who also intended to do the same.

As soon as Amy closed the door, the twins turned around to see what Liew was doing. He was busy at work on a large glass panel that took up most of the opposite wall. He touched it again, and the Recovery Chair descended closer to the ground.

"She doesn't sound good, Liew," said Josie, very concerned. Both twins kept a vigilant watch by the bathroom, one on either side of the door.

"Yes, that's why she is here," answered Liew. As he touched the panel again, brightly illuminated words, in an alien language, appeared on it.

"Is this like an infirmary?" asked Jodie.

"An infirmary is where you go if you're sick. This is where you go to recover."

"What is wrong, do you think?" continued Jodie.

"We will soon find out."

The girls overheard the sound of a flushing toilet.

"That's good," winked Jodie to Josie.

"Things are flowing," replied Josie with a rotten potty pun.

The door opened, and Amy hobbled out in a fresh pair of sweatpants, socks, sport flip-flops, and a new "Let's Ride" hoody.

"We were worried the flush took you down with it," joked Jodie.

"Even after you passed the qualification drowning test," finished Josie, as they helped Amy into the lowered Recovery Chair.

Amy didn't have the heart to laugh. The flows of water she had just completed nearly took the life out of her. She knew the twins were trying to brighten her spirits, and she appreciated that fact, but there was not a single smile left in her. She felt as though, by losing, she hadn't only let herself down—she had also let down her coach, her team, Liew—and, most importantly, her home planet, Earth. She was the first human being in the Universe Olympics. Instead of shining a bright path through the competition, she came in dead last. The loss was devastating.

Amy managed to lay down, her head elevated.

"Girls, please step back," cautioned Liew.

Liew touched the screen. The Recovery Chair began to rise up quietly, and the soft spotlight turned into warm yellow sunlight. It felt comforting and warm on Amy's skin, like sitting in Earth's sunlight. It felt like home.

The twins immediately walked over to Liew's side, as a giant 3-D holographic scan of a human body appeared on the panel. It was Amy, inside and out. Bones, veins, heart, lungs, every muscle, every cell beating with life. Liew gazed deeply, zooming in and out of certain sections of the image. The twins remained silent, watching intently as Liew investigated.

"It is just as I feared, Amy," he said, just loudly enough for her to hear. "I'm afraid you have bursitis in your shoulder, again. Bruised a rib, too. There's a micro-tear in your meniscus, and expectedly, there is both a build-up of lactic acid in the muscles, and dehydration."

"Yeah, I don't feel great," she said faintly.

Liew tapped on the wall, and the holographic image magnified in on her lungs. "And you have slight pulmonary barotrauma from the deep free diving."

"English, Liew," chided Jodie.

"Her lungs got damaged in the final portion of her race." He quickly zoomed on towards her feet. "And you tore a few tendons in your ankle," he said, turning toward Amy.

"Probably did that while kicking my way out from under the whale," answered Amy with a hint of regret in her breathless voice.

"*Under* it?" howled Josie.

"Girls, please," said Liew, looking worried. "And Amy, no more talking. Please. Not until we can heal your lungs."

Amy nodded and took in a shallow breath.

A slight humming sound could be heard around the room. Liew walked up to Amy, but never touched her. He remained outside the spotlight encompassing the chair. "This light allows your body to heal, regenerate cells, as well as get rid of any toxins."

"Wicked!" said Jodie, curiously walking over to Amy.

"Do *NOT* touch her, girls! Never go within the lighted area."

"Yes, sir," both twins said in unison. They meant it. Amy's health and recovery were no laughing matter.

"Amy, needs at least four hours to recover, maybe more. We will do one two-hour session. Then we will get you some lunch, followed by another session later this afternoon, if necessary." Liew walked back to the Holo-scan on the wall. "And we will probably need to," he said zooming in further—this time along the spine.

Amy nodded her head yes and mouthed a word.

"I think she said water, Liew," stated Josie, keeping one eye on her friend.

Liew touched the panel. "Oh, yes," he said, as a super fine needle came out from underneath the chair, and without a second's warning, swiftly slid into one of the veins in Amy's arm.

Surprise, not fear, made Amy flinch for a second. She could see clear liquid in the IV, running from the tubing which originated somewhere underneath the chair.

"This will help," said Liew.

"What is that? Saline?" Josie wondered. Crouching down to examine the line, she carefully avoided going within the lighted portion.

"Yes, among other things. All of it will help her hydrate and heal."

Josie turned her attention to the intricate scan on the wall. The full color image used all the colors of the rainbow. Whatever was flowing through the IV tubes took on a bright red color in the 3-D holo-scan.

"All of this works best if you rest while you recover, Amy." Liew turned to the twins. "Girls, I'm heading up to the team lunch. Please give Amy some quiet time to sleep and heal."

"Can we stay, for just a few minutes, to keep her company?" wondered Jodie.

"Only a few, then she must sleep." Liew touched the panel on the wall. "And to help you relax, Amy, I've programmed a scenic view."

The formerly dark walls instantly changed to a bright view of rolling hills covered with green grass and trees.

"Wow!" stated Jodie, "This is great!"

Liew headed toward the door. "Five minutes girls, please, at the most." He spoke to Jodie in particular. She seemed to be the leader of this pack.

"We promise, Liew," she answered. "See you in the Jungle!"

"I'll be monitoring you the whole time, Amy. Don't worry." He motioned to the patch on the arm of his clothing. "Thank you, girls. I'll be back in about an hour. Call me if you need me, Amy—and by that, I mean, just say my name out loud."

Amy nodded briefly, and then turned to the scene on the walls, watching the wind blowing through the tall grass on the hills. The smell of bluegrass and honeysuckle filled the room. As in the cafeteria, the sound of the wind and atmosphere took over once the view was on the walls. And it wasn't just one wall. It was a full 360° view from the top of the ceiling to the floor itself. The beautiful perch on the top of the hill overlooked endless pastures and lush trees.

After Liew left, the twins grabbed the two stools and placed them on either side of Amy, never venturing too close to the spotlight encompassing the chair.

"Wonder where this is?" questioned Josie, looking at the trees off in the distance and the clouds gathering in the sky. A herd of horses ambled up from the bottom of the hill.

"Kentucky," answered Amy in a whisper.

"Really? How do you know that?" inquired Jodie.

"It's my family's horse farm," said Amy, just faintly audible.

"Nice. It's a beautiful place, Amy."

"Wait? I thought you lived in California?" asked Josie.

Amy nodded her head yes. "I do, with my coach's family. My parents live here." She motioned to the horses still coming up the hill.

"It's a very peaceful place," said Jodie, mesmerized by one horse, who got so close that he almost took up an entire wall.

"Isn't it amazing how Liew knows all this stuff about us," commented Josie to Jodie.

"A little, but I think that's part of his job," answered Jodie, staring at the horse who began eating grass.

"That's my favorite horse," drowsily muttered Amy, also staring at the beautiful brown beast. "He's Strider."

Strider lifted his head with the white blaze and long light-brown mane blowing in the wind.

"You know, we had a 'horse' theme once," declared Josie.

Amy furrowed her brow, "Theme, for what?"

"Our routines. Every synch swim routine has to have an artistic theme to it." Josie said, making air quotes at the words "artistic theme."

"Really?" said Amy, just barely audible.

"When we were in the Junior Australian Championships, our gold medal routine theme was horses," said Jodie.

"More like the history of the horse," inserted Josie, leaning away from the light.

"Across North America," grandly finished Jodie, making a big sweeping gesture with her arms that probably looked more at home in the water than in the air.

"That's a big theme," squeaked Amy.

"Yeah, it started with about forty Ibizan horses brought over from Europe in 1493, and the program illustrated how 'the horse' spread across the continent and were adopted by Native American tribes."

"Wow," mouthed Amy.

"It was cool. We had horse neighing, bucking, and galloping gestures—all while swimming across the pool to represent the spread of the herds from the islands to across the American Great Plains."

"Are the themes always an animal?" asked Amy, highly curious at this point.

"No, you can choose whatever you want," answered Josie. "As long as it creates a story."

"Within reason." Jodie interjected. Both girls snickered for a moment. "A very long time ago, in 1996, a synch swim team from France chose a *very* controversial theme for their Olympic routine."

"What?" inquired Amy, curiosity giving her a slight hint of energy.

The twins looked at each other. "The Holocaust!" They said in horrified unison.

"No!" reacted Amy. "Really?"

"Yeah, and it didn't go over too well," answered Josie. "The routine started with Nazi goose-stepping and ended with the final march to a gas chamber!"

"Oh, my God. That's horrible," stated Amy.

"Yeah, they were told to change it before the Atlanta Games," said Josie.

"Well," quipped Jodie, very dryly. "It *could* have been worse."

"Worse?" wondered Amy, "How?" she said, astonished by the statement.

"The team could have been from Germany," responded Josie.

There was awkward silence for a moment, then the girls laughed slightly at the truth, which was always at the heart of any good joke.

"That's true," acknowledged Amy, not sure what else to say.

"But now FINA—the International Federation controlling aquatic events—uses it as an example of what themes not to choose," finished Jodie.

"Quite right," stated Josie.

"What was your theme for the Nairobi Summer Olympics?" wondered Amy.

Josie glanced at Jodie. "We can't tell you."

"Not because we don't want to," declared Jodie. "But because we are going to do a variation of it for the Universe Olympic Games. We want it to be a surprise when you watch."

"But we can give you a hint," said Josie.

"It's big. Really, REALLY, *REALLY BIG!*" countered Jodie, holding up her hands wide.

Amy's eyes were slowly closing, and sleep was taking hold of her healing body.

"Come on Jos, the Jungle calls."

The twins got up and left the Recovery Room, leaving Amy alone in the chair.

After they left, Amy turned her head slightly as she was about to fall asleep, watching her favorite horse peacefully eat the grass. A tear fell from her eye and rolled down her cheek as sleep took hold.

*   *   *

Amy woke up with a start. Liew was standing right in front of her. She was in such a deep sleep that she didn't hear him come in.

"Hello, Amy. I thought it would be easier if we brought lunch to you." Liew lifted up a tray filled with her favorite lunch foods: a ham and cheese sandwich, chips, pickle, and extra fries, among other things.

As soon as Amy lifted her head, the entire Recovery Chair followed her movement to an upright position. "Yeah, I don't think I could have made it to the cafeteria." A desk popped out of the side of the Recovery Chair and settled over Amy's lap. Liew gently slid the tray across the desk, never touching Amy or reaching inside the lighted area. Amy pulled the tray fully over on the desk and then noticed another person standing quietly in the corner of the room.

"Oh, hi, Jen!" said Amy, her voice had a little strength.

"Hey, girl," said Jen who was busy studying the room and the scenery that was still on display. "Just checkin' in on you."

Liew touched the panel on the one wall, and Amy's 3-D holo-scan took over the backdrop. He stared at it intently, zooming in and out of the image.

"Lactic acid buildup in the muscles has dissipated."

Jenefer stood next to Liew. "How are her lungs? She was whispering earlier."

He magnified the upper lobe of the lungs. The inflamed air sacs were visible, contracting with every breath. "Better, but not fully healed. A few more hours, I think."

"Where are the twins?" asked Amy, taking a hefty bite of the ham and cheese sandwich.

"They wanted to come, but it's their training time. Don't worry, you'll see them later." Liew touched the wall. "You're hungry," he said, examining the stomach area which was emitting a light green color.

"I AM!" exclaimed Amy, with a mouth full of chips. Looking down, Amy saw a box of Snow Caps on her plate, and she merrily shook them like maracas.

Jen turned around at the noise. "Compliments of Stoke, from his stash."

"Ooooo! My favorite," answered Amy. Abandoning her meal, she eagerly opened the snow caps box. She figured it was OK, after everything she had been through, to indulge in a little treat first.

"Speaking of," Jen returned her attention to Liew, "Are there any other 'stashes' in Stoke's room I should know about? Anything illegal?"

Liew laughed a little, never taking his eyes off the diagnostic panel in front of him. "No, Mrs. Washington Lee, that would be in violation of your signed athlete contract. No illegal substances allowed on this ship. Only sugar."

"Good!" she said with relief. "I don't have to ransack his room then."

Liew grinned at Jen and turned around. "Amy, I'd like you to spend at least three more hours in the Recovery Chair, if you would."

"If you think it's best," answered Amy, gulping down her green protein shake.

"Do you want me to stay here and keep you company?" inquired Jenefer. "I'm happy to stay," she smiled kindly.

"No, thanks, Jen. I'll probably sleep most of the time, anyway, but thanks for offering," responded Amy smiling. It was her first heartfelt smile all day. She was feeling a little better, and her spirits were lightening, despite the devastation of her first competition loss in years.

"Good. I'll be back later this afternoon." Liew walked to the door with Jen right beside him. "Again, say my name aloud if you need me," he told her.

As Liew was about to leave, he touched the panel on the wall, the 3-D holo-scan disappeared, and the scenic rolling hills returned. Jen caught sight of the green grass floor illumination as they headed out the door. "That's so beautiful, Liew. Where is that place..." she asked, her voice trailing off as the door closed behind them.

Amy smiled, pushed her empty tray and desk out of the way, and promptly fell back asleep.

*   *   *

Later that afternoon, Liew and Amy walked side by side down a long corridor, and then entered a part of the ship that she had yet to explore. The room's only illumination inside came from the lighting around a few long U-shaped couches, which were scattered around the large dark space.

"What is this room, Liew?" asked Amy, scanning the abyss.

"This is the entertainment center," replied Liew.

"Really? What's the entertainment?"

"Movies, TV shows, video games, and virtual reality games."

"Oh, wow!" said Amy, shocked. "Why didn't you show us this before?"

"Truthfully, no one has mentioned they've been bored," laughed Liew, walking up to what looked like a giant single sheet of glass hanging in mid-air.

"You're right. We've been so busy training and everything, up until you mentioned it, I never thought of being 'entertained.'" Amy stopped next to Liew and waited by the empty, translucent, piece of glass. "Are we watching a movie?"

"No, Amy. Someone would like to speak with you."

"OK?" Amy trailed off, looking even more confused.

Liew touched the corner of the glass, and it filled with bright light.

Amy was surprised by what appeared inside the frame, which was apparently a holographic viewscreen, not glass. The screen was filled with a glowing bluish light. A single giant eye took up most of the 3-D frame. The iris focused in and out rapidly.

"What the...?" said Amy loudly.

"I'm sorry, Ms. Ride. Let me change the aspect view." Liew touched the corner of the glass again. The extreme close-up of an eye zoomed out to show a whale floating in the middle of water.

"Wait," said Amy trailing off incredulously, "is that?"

A sound, much like a whale song, emanated from the screen, and then words appeared at the bottom of the holoscreen in English. A deep voice spoke to them aloud. "Earth contestant, Amy Ride."

Amy turned to Liew, puzzled.

"You can answer, Amy. He can hear you."

"What is this, like FaceTime? Can he see me?"

"Let's call it SpaceTime," said Liew smiling. "Yes, he can see and hear you."

Amy turned back to the whale, and waited a moment, not sure what to say. "Hello," she finally answered.

The whale floated in the water, just barely moving. Behind him, there was a hint of a current, flowing like underwater rivers in a vast ocean. The whale song started again, and the translator started reading the words that appeared along the bottom of the holoscreen. "I am Auel, and I wanted to congratulate you on your swim today."

"Thank you, Auel. You also had a very good swim and let me congratulate you on your win today."

"Amy Ride, I may have won our heat overall and finished first because of the physical portion of our race, but I wanted to commend you on your exemplary performance in the intellectual, emotional, and spiritual portions of our race," conveyed the whale.

For a moment, Amy was taken aback. She didn't know what to say. The victor of their race was congratulating *her*. "Thank you, Auel," finally came out of her mouth; it seemed like the polite thing to say.

Auel continued, "I am very impressed with human beings from planet Earth. If you had fins, and evolved a few hundred thousand more years in water, you would have won our entire competition today."

Amy paused for a moment. A sentient alien—who looked like a blue whale, lived underwater, and beat her in today's marine competition—was praising her swimming. It was all too weird to process.

"I would like to extend a formal invitation to you. After the Universe Olympic Games are over, you are welcome to visit our home world, Salini, and to travel there on our ocean ship."

"That's yours?" asked Amy enthusiastically. "I spotted it when they lit the Olympic Flame sun. Your spaceship is extraordinary."

Auel moved around. He swam up into one of the flowing streams of water, all with the viewscreen following behind him. He glided through two different fast water flows, each a different concentration of blue. Finally, ended in the stationary water, next to a clear wall. Beyond it, was a vast dry deck. "Thank you. Unfortunately, since this is Earth's first official time at the Games, you can't visit now. But if you choose to visit Salini, we will house you in our dry dock, here." Auel swam around the area; it had white technological instruments, places to sit and sleep, and vast empty rooms. It would be like watching the world from the inside of an aquarium.

"*COOL!* I'd love that! I truly appreciate the offer, Auel. Thank you for the invitation."

"Congratulations, Amy Ride and thank you for the exciting race today. I look forward to seeing what the people of Earth have to offer during the rest of the games."

Amy smiled at the screen, and it went dark.

"Holy, je-lly!" said Amy turning to Liew.

"I thought it was important for you to know how well you did today. So, I set up the call."

"What did Auel mean by winning the mental portion of the race?"

Liew began walking back toward the entrance of the room. "When you swam into the cave today, not knowing where or when you would receive air, that mental leap you took, was an act of faith. And that leap was hard for Auel. It took him a very long time to pluck up the courage to enter his cave that only had enough room for his tail to move. But you went directly in, like a bullet."

Liew stopped for a moment. "You see, Amy, there are four portions to every competition here. While you won the spiritual, emotional, and mental portions of your heat, he won overall because of the last physical portion of the race."

"Why didn't you tell us this before?" asked Amy.

"I didn't think I needed to. Sypsen already did, during her welcome to the games."

"Oh, yeah. Probably should have taken that more to heart."

"But no matter," Liew continued. "You did a wonderful job today for Earth. Be proud of it."

Amy gazed up at Liew for a few seconds. "Thanks. It does help take a little of the sting out of losing."

"Oh, you won, Amy. Truly, you won." Liew put his hand over his hearts in the middle of his chest.

"I'm glad I took the call. Can I really go to their home world, Salini, after the games are over, Liew?"

"Amy, right now, I need you to help your teammates prepare for their individual events, and I promise we will discuss this after the Olympics are over."

"Fair enough," she said cheerfully.

"And I need you to keep up *your* training as well."

"Yes, sir," said Amy, confused since her event was already over. Then she remembered that Liew probably had his reasons for the request. It was her duty to honor it.

"Any thoughts on what to name the ocean planet?"

"Oh, am I the one who gets to do that?"

"I believe if you start the nomenclature, since you were the first down there, it will stick with the team."

Amy thought for a second. "How about Triton? My Ancient Mythology teacher would really love that."

"Triton it is," responded Liew.

"Hey, can we tell the twins, Ari, and Yosi about the entertainment room?"

"Yes. I was going to tell everyone at dinner. It's team movie night tonight."

"It is! What are we watching?" asked Amy, giddy as a kid wanting to play outside. She had a little more pep in her step, and it was apparent her hours of healing helped put it there.

"Only the *best* Olympic movie ever made," answered Liew, very seriously.

"What's that?" wondered Amy. *Chariots of Fire?*"

"Nope. *The Cutting Edge.*"

Amy howled, "That's one of my favorite movies!"

"Yes, I know," commented Liew, who never seemed to stop displaying his in-depth knowledge about each of the athletes on the team.

"D.B. Sweeney is the best! Toepick! Oh, Stoke's going to *LOVE* that one," retorted Amy, laughing to herself at the idea of Stoke watching an ice-skating romantic comedy, unwittingly.

"And so will Mark and Justine."

"Oh, yeah! It's right up their alley."

"I'd say rink, versus alley, Ms. Ride. But yes, you have the right idea," finished Liew as they continued down the long hallway toward the athlete's corridor and Amy's room.

Chapter 8

The Alternate

The next morning in the Jungle, Liew waited until every member of Team Earth had sat down with their mélange of breakfasts at the table. He stood up and began speaking. "Good morning, everyone."

Every athlete, but for Stoke, stopped eating because at this point, they figured out what was coming: It was announcement time.

"There has been a slight change of plans," proclaimed Liew.

"Not like we knew *what* the plans were in the first place," whispered Ramon to Pappie, who was sitting next to him, his plate filled with sausage and mash.

Pappie grinned and nodded in response, his mouth full.

"During your sleep cycle, we have moved the ship."

"Where?" asked Jaysen.

"Home?" interrupted Stoke, who was shoving pancakes in his mouth. Unlike Pappie, Stoke spoke with his mouth full of food. Stoke was again wearing a T-shirt with an inexplicable message—this one adorned with asteroids flying through space like the 1980s game, proclaiming, "Look Pout!" in blocky red letters.

"No, not yet, Mr. Townsend. We've moved closer to the Olympic Flame sun, to its southern pole, past the first planet."

"Why?" questioned Jodie, who sat next to Josie and Amy. All three were fresh-faced and bright this morning.

"We have added another event to the schedule."

"Which?" inquired the twins in perfect unison, expectant hope written all over their faces. "Ours? We're ready!"

"No, girls. Not just yet."

The twins had a crestfallen look on their faces.

"Don't worry girls, you will be up soon enough. This morning, it's time for our alternate, Onorina Di Mateo."

The whole table looked stunned. Even Oni, staring back, was shocked.

"The alternate, for the second event? *WOW!*" exclaimed Jaysen, leaning back in his chair. Finally, his "wow" sentiment was shared by the entire group of athletes assembled, including the alternate.

"Really?" said Oni surprised. "I thought I was only the alternate if someone got hurt."

"No, Ms. Di Mateo, those were never the terms of you being the alternate on this team."

Oni immediately stood up straight and at attention, speaking in Italian. "Pardon me, Ambassador, I am very happy and proud to participate in any event for Team Earth."

"Good." He returned in Italian. "My apologies, Ms. Di Mateo, I would have told you earlier, but I needed to put everything together for your event. This is the first time I've been able to see you."

Most of the team looked at each other, having no idea what was being said. The only person with their ear bud in and in translation mode was Yosi.

"Of course, Liew. I am ready to go when you tell me," Oni finished in Italian.

"Thank you, Oni," Liew returned to speaking in English. "Which brings us to the point of my announcing it to the entire team. You *all* will be able to be spectators at her event!"

"Wooo hoo!" shouted Stoke a little too loudly. "Shotgun!"

"Shotgun?" wondered Margit. "I'm unfamiliar with that American idiom."

"Oh, it means up first, front," answered Stoke.

"A.K.A. Stoke wants to be the first, and in front of all of us, watching Oni," deciphered Jenefer.

"And you can be," said Liew, happily. "Now let's finish eating. Oni, we must leave immediately after the meal."

"But I need to warm-up." Oni stopped eating, looking a little nervous.

"You will, on the way."

"On the way, *where*?" whispered Pappie to Ramon, devilishly smiling.

"Who knows, but at least we get to watch this one," Ramon winked back. He immediately stood up and began clapping loudly, "Good Luck, Oni! Come on everyone," said Ramon, gesturing for the group to rise.

The rest of the team instantaneously followed, standing and cheering for Onorina.

"You can do this, Oni," shouted the twins.

"You'll rock, Oni!" said Stoke.

"Bravo, Onorina," stated Margit.

"Kick butt, take names!"

"*Grazie, grazie!*" responded Oni, to dozens of never-ending encouragements, a tear in her eye. It warmed her heart that even the alternate—to be used only in case of emergency—could get such an enthusiastic send-off.

"*Va bene,*" said Liew to Oni, and they both left the breakfast table immediately after her last bite. "*Andiamo!*"

*   *   *

Without even knowing why, or how, Oni was hastily following behind Liew down the passageway that led to the shuttle bay. Liew set a brisk pace.

He turned to her, speaking in Italian. "Forgive the rush, but we are late." He said looking at the readout on his arm patch. "And we still have a lot to do before you begin your heat."

Oni gave up the pretense of walking briskly and started jogging to keep up with Liew's long stride. She figured it would do as a good warm-up, uncertain what lay ahead for her. Perhaps, it was another swimming event on the water planet, like Amy's. She was ready for water. Or maybe it was a shooting event on the green planet? But Liew had said they were close to the first red rocky planet. She wondered what type of horses, or horse-like creatures, they had down there that she could ride for her event. But no matter what, she was willing to go. A pentathlete prided herself on being a master of all: swimming in water, running on land, shooting in the air, fencing against an opponent, or riding a horse—and not just her own horse, but a horse chosen at random.

All of these complications were given to prove one simple fact: adaptation. No matter what lay ahead of her, she could adapt to any terrain, atmosphere, tool, or animal. To Oni's mind, being a pentathlete personified what it meant to be human. Human beings were masters of adaptation; she, the pentathlete, was supposed to be the master of the masters. She had to adapt or perish—well, hopefully not perish, and win. Losing wasn't an option for this gold medalist.

Liew scurried into the small shuttle with Oni close behind. As soon as the door closed, they shot off into space.

Immediately, Oni could tell that their spaceship had moved during the night. The Olympic Flame sun—a bright dot in the distance before—now loomed large in the viewscreen. Up close, the star was much bigger than she thought, and the light hurt her eyes. She saw the first red planet shining off in the distance, and she stood there confused for a moment. Instead of flying closer to the rocky planet for her event, the mini-D shuttle just kept racing closer and closer to the sun.

Liew spoke, still in formal Italian, as he pulled out a giant sack from a storage unit in the wall. "You know, humans weren't supposed to be in this event, but I officially protested."

"You did?"

"Yes, I couldn't justify Earth's non-participation in this event just because you couldn't breathe in space."

Oni wasn't sure how to take this pronouncement. For the first time, she scanned the interior of the shuttle, wondering where her equipment, her saddle, air pistol, running shoes, swimsuit, foil, or any of her bags, were located. The shuttle was empty but for the one bag Liew was pulling out, and it had white hard plastic peeking out of it.

"Ambassador, I can't breathe in space," she said a little nervously.

"Hence my appeal to allow you to use," he said as he revealed the contents of the bag, "a spacesuit."

Oni's eyes were as wide as the sun in the viewscreen. "A spacesuit?"

Liew meticulously removed the gloves, the shoes, and the helmet from the assembled suit. "I had this 3-D printed especially for you," he said proudly. "Technically,'—or at least according to the official Universe Olympic rules—humans can't use any technology that isn't already a part of their civilization," he pulled off the last glove, "but fortuitously, humans have been using spacesuits since the 1960s."

Oni never moved; she stood astonished.

"They saw the validity of my argument, and the Committee acquiesced." Liew stood ready for Oni to get into her new shiny-white spacesuit. She didn't budge as Liew waited patiently.

"Liew, I've never been in a spacesuit before. I've never been on a space walk before. Only a few thousand people ever have, in all of human history."

He smiled at her, motioning to the suit in his hands. "Don't worry, you soon will be!"

This spacesuit wasn't the puffy oversized spacesuit common in space travel in the 2030s. It was sleek, tiny—exactly the size of Onorina herself—and made of a white hard plastic-looking material, but for the elbows, knees, waist, neck, and hands. The helmet's gold reflective mirror visor gave the entire suit a futuristic look that Humanity's *actual* technology had yet to catch up to.

They both stood motionless for a moment, each waiting for the other to move when a beeping sound came from the main control panel on the viewscreen. "Please, Ms. Di Mateo, it is almost time for the start of your heat."

Oni remained motionless.

"You are the pentathlete, capable of traversing any environment, and considered the most skilled athlete on Earth."

"Yes, on *EARTH!*" shrieked Oni, realizing the gravity of the situation. The Ambassador to Earth was asking her to compete in space. She wasn't an astronaut. She had never even taken one of those new tourist rides outside Earth's atmosphere, where you could experience weightlessness. And she didn't know the first thing about using a spacesuit, let alone winning her heat in one.

"I have every faith in you, Oni. You will be as glorious in space as you are on earth," stated Liew, almost reading her mind. He held up the spacesuit with a giant smile on his face. It appeared tiny, like a doll's costume, in his hands.

Oni closed her eyes and took a deep breath. She knew it was time to 'put her money where her mouth was.' Her pride in winning the gold medal made her think of herself as the master of all terrains. It was now time to put that to the test by adapting to a new one.

"Yes, Ambassador, I will do it. For you, the team, for *Italia,* and for Earth!" she declared in English, as she grabbed the helmet.

"No, no, no, the body first, then the feet and hands," Liew said, snatching the helmet back from her. "This is the last to go on."

As Liew assembled the spacesuit around Onorina, he explained the rules, "Now, usually, we aren't allowed to divulge the different levels of the individual events."

"Why?"

"That is *part* of the challenge in the Universe Olympics—testing the adaptive skills of each species. But I *can* tell you there are four distinct parts to this heat, Oni. The helmet viewscreen has a display; please follow *ALL* the instructions when they appear."

"Or," she wondered, fright in her eyes.

"Or, things are going to get very, very hot, fast." Liew finished attaching her boots and the gloves to the suit.

He pointed to what resembled very small rockets on the back of the pack. "These are your mini-boosters that will help you move around. There are four in the pack."

"Here is a version of your air pistol," Liew clicked a long metallic object, that looked nothing like a pistol onto the lower part of her right arm. "You'll know when to use it." He quickly scooped up the helmet and put it over her head. It clicked into place. As soon as it did, he touched the patch on his arm and his voice could be heard inside her helmet.

"Can you hear me, Oni?"

She nodded yes and began shaking a bit, and not because she was cold.

"You can do this, Ms. Di Mateo." He touched the arm of her spacesuit. "I would *never* have picked you for this event without complete trust and perfect knowledge of your abilities. I know you can do this!"

She thought for a moment. In her heart of hearts, she never expected Liew to need her for these games. It was very rare for an alternate to have the opportunity to step up and become a contributing member of the team. Alternates were only necessary when there was an injury, and no one on Team Earth was injured. Not expecting this chance, she hadn't psychologically prepared herself to compete in this event, or any event. Her success could play a part in the victory of Team Earth in the Universe Olympic Games.

"Where do I begin?"

Liew walked over to the shuttle doors. "When they open, all you have to do is jump out."

Oni nodded and walked over to the doors. The spacesuit wasn't too heavy, like she had expected. It was surprisingly light. She moved her legs and arms around to see how much flexibility she had in the suit. As soon as she raised her right hand in front of her helmet, a target range for the air pistol appeared on her screen.

"Your finish line will be back on our ship."

Oni again answered yes, without a word, nodding slightly.

"And everything in the suit is controlled by voice command only. There are no buttons for you to worry about. Please remember that. Voice command only!"

She glared at Liew then nodded. She took in a few deep breaths, "*Madonna mia,*" she said, with a silent prayer. After a quiet contemplative moment, the fearful look on her face changed to stern focus—the appearance of any professional athlete about to perform the task ahead.

"And Oni..."

Oni turned, glancing at Liew. "Just remember this one important fact." The shuttle control panel began a beeping countdown.

"*Si?*"

"Gravity is your friend."

The loud honking sound blared. The shuttle doors opened.

"*Andare!*" shouted Liew.

With a tug of the spacesuit, Oni ran to the doors. She dove through the net-like force field over the opening and plunged headfirst into space.

To the end of her days, Onorina wasn't exactly sure how she found herself in the middle of space, floating in a spacesuit, hurtling toward the Olympic Flame sun in front of her. As soon as she jumped out of the shuttle, the screen in her helmet displayed an outline of her projected route toward the sun and an uncertain future. The bottom left-hand corner of the viewscreen showed vitals: oxygen, her temperature, space temperature, her velocity, (and a bunch of other numbers she wasn't sure about except for the distance to the sun in kilometers). She tried to turn around and glimpse the shuttle, but the helmet visor only went so far.

For the time being, her trajectory was at the whim of natural forces. She was being pulled closer to the sun. But soon Liew's advice became obvious—the Olympic Flame sun's gravity was drawing her closer. To Oni, this sun looked about a quarter of the size of the Earth's sun. Now she, like trillions of other heavenly bodies in space, was being pulled in by the gravity of their nearest star.

Oni picked up speed, moving faster and faster. The sun loomed too largely in her viewscreen.

She had often wondered what it would be like to float in space, and experience what all astronauts and space tourists raved about: the majesty and the beauty of seeing your planet from high up in the heavens. Staring at the red rocky planet glowing far away to her right, Oni could finally agree with their assessment. No picture could ever do it justice. No video or VR could replicate the distance, the emptiness, and the vastness of space. It had to be felt. And Oni felt it, deep in her core, and it made her feel like a very, very, very small human.

And just as she was about to wonder what the point was to her particular event (besides floating in space) she realized that the glare from the sun had prevented her from seeing the first part of her race. Onorina prepared herself as best as she knew how. Her eyes were open to what revolved around the sun. It was unthinkable. She wished that she had paid attention in science class—or even more helpful—that she had read up on the latest commercial space mining ventures. The next event seemed daunting. Her fleeting hope of an easy space heat dissipated. There was no mistaking it. She was headed into a swiftly moving asteroid belt.

She braced for impact with the stream, made up of rocks of all shapes and sizes—thousands and thousands of them, flowing like a deep river from right to left. There was no escaping the belt, which was as deep as it was wide. When she entered the asteroid stream, it was like stepping into a moving hailstorm. The tiny asteroids pushed her off course, in the direction of the belt's orbit.

Her viewscreen offered her no specific instructions. All it showed was the projected path forward toward the sun. As Oni got caught in the flow of asteroids, she could think of only one way out. She lifted her right hand and the air pistol targeting range appeared on her viewscreen. Liew did say that she would know when to use it. Perhaps the time was now? She wasn't sure. She presumed that the only way to stop the pelting was to blast her way forward out of the belt.

"Fire," she yelled, aiming at a group of asteroids off to her right.

Unfortunately, the shot didn't have its intended effect. Instead of creating a hole in the stream like Oni imagined, the kickback from the air pistol immediately started her on a backward spin, rotating in 360° circles. Around and around, she went, having forgotten an important lesson. The kickback force from the pistol had nothing to push back on in space except Oni herself, and a swirling death spiral ensued.

Head over feet she flipped, again and again, unable to stop. And without some way of ceasing this rotation, she could continue on forever. It was hard with the endless rolling for her to catch her bearings. She was circling so fast that she wasn't sure which way to instruct the suit to go. Unfortunately, the asteroid belt made the decision for her. She hit something pretty hard from the back. Her hands flailing, Oni flipped. She smashed into a medium-size asteroid. She reached out and grabbed on to it for dear life, finding grooves in the rock for her hands and then feet. The rock stopped her spin.

Oni was panting heavily. "OK, probably not the right time to use the pistol," she said out loud to herself in Italian. She glanced down and checked the oxygen levels, hoping there was enough for her deep breathing, and the rest of the race. The gauge had barely squeaked past ninety-nine-point nine percent. She exhaled a sigh of relief.

She held on to the asteroid for a minute and calmed herself down. It stopped her spinning, but it was still traveling in its swift orbit from right to left in the revolving river of rocks around the sun.

She glanced at the viewscreen. The projected trajectory still pointed toward the sun, not toward revolving around it in the asteroid belt. She realized she had to get off of this merry go round, somehow.

Once she collected herself, Oni had an idea. Maybe she could use these larger asteroids like skipping stones on the water, and "jump" her way out of there.

Oni searched the belt until she found what she was looking for not too far away. She leaped, pushing with all her strength away from the asteroid that saved her life, hurdling through the river of asteroids. She landed on another larger asteroid which was located just a hair closer to the sun. She grasped hold of it with all her might. Once she was secure, she climbed up over it, and then began surveying the field for the next one.

She continued on like this: skip and jump, skip and jump, through dozens of medium sized asteroids. Each one bringing her slightly closer to the sun. Sometimes her aim was decent, and the landings were good. But more often than not, she barely made it, even missed a few. She felt like the living embodiment of the retro game, Frogger. It had recently been released in VR game form, and it felt a little like this. Skipping, jumping, and flying in real life through the asteroids was very challenging; Frogger was *much* easier to win.

It was hard to tell where she was in the stream; finding the next asteroid was grueling at times, because the sun glared in her eyes. Every skip and jump took a lot of effort, but time and tide, remained against her. The river of asteroids in the belt carried her very rapidly around the sun.

The small pelting asteroids were the worst part. They were about a centimeter or two in size. She could hear them deflecting off her suit, like hail off a windshield. It took all of her target practice training to sight the next rock, swiftly duck, move, and turn, performing almost a summersault and twist around all the rocks. It was more like swimming, or diving, than anything else. This event was a combination of target practice, gymnastics, diving, and climbing. She thought perhaps Yosi the gymnast, Manny the diver, or Sito the rock climber, would have been better suited for this part. But now wasn't the time to allow doubts to creep into her brain.

She spotted the next medium asteroid, which was about the size of a large truck. And there was something weird about this piece of rock; the coloring was off, and it was headed in the same direction as her. All the other asteroids were headed in the same general clockwise direction, orbiting around the sun. But this one was headed directly for the sun.

Oni immediately had another idea. It was a little crazy, but a good one. And if this worked, the continuous dodging of asteroids from all sides would stop. Using a bit of exertion, she climbed over her current asteroid, and as soon as it was near enough, she lunged for the new lighter colored one.

She drifted in the stream, and almost missed her intended target. Fingertips barely holding on, Oni landed on the intended target. She crawled up the surface that was covered in small pits, making perfect hand holds. Then to outdo herself, she maneuvered up and over to the left side of the lighter asteroid, providing cover from the multitude of mini-asteroids that were bombarding her from the opposite direction. The asteroid became a shield and a piggyback ride.

A red light flashed in her helmet for the first time and a loud beeping blared in her ears. She turned to her right; her viewscreen told her what was wrong. Coming in from three o'clock was a huge asteroid, about twice the size of the one she was riding. It was headed straight for her.

"Uh-oh!"

Instinctually, Oni knew what she had to do. It was finally time to use her pistol, and because she was anchored onto the asteroid, she wasn't going anywhere from the kickback. She raised her hand. The target appeared on the viewscreen in her helmet. She lined up the target, and as she had done a thousand times before with her air pistols at home she yelled, "Fire!" It was weird not having a physical trigger to pull. But with her hands in the spacesuit's gloves, she wasn't sure the trigger motion was possible anyway.

She was shocked at what came out of her pistol. It wasn't a bullet or a blank as she was expecting, but a shower of what appeared to be waves of heat energy. The blast was practically invisible, but for the light distortion rippling through space. Oni had never seen anything like it before, whatever her ammunition was in that bizarre pistol, it worked. And the heat wave's energy spread was wide.

The incoming asteroid burst into a thousand pieces and dispersed in every direction, with only a dust cloud of residue coming over her and the asteroid as it passed. Her white space suit was getting dirtier by the minute. But with her tight grip on the rock, she had hardly any kickback from the pistol.

The alarm sounded again, this time from the other side of the asteroid. She rolled over and looked up. It was coming fast. So fast, she barely had the time to lift up her hand and shoot.

"Fire, fire, fire," she said thrice to cover her bases (figuring one shot might not have been enough).

The pistol shot annihilated the speeding asteroid.

The warning sounded again, but this time not for an approaching small asteroid.

Oni glanced back toward the sun and gasped. "*Madonna Mia.*"

She and her piggyback ride were headed straight for the mother of all asteroids, and there was no way to stop. They were going to crash into the enormous city-size oblong asteroid, and it wasn't going to be pretty. At the speed she was traveling, it would be like the splat of an egg dropped from a twenty-story building.

She realized her best option for survival was to ditch this smaller asteroid and potentially try to land on the large city-asteroid, using her micro-boosters to slow her down. But Liew's words reverberated in her mind. "Gravity is your friend." She knew she somehow had to use this momentum to her advantage, but how?

With a great effort, Oni jettisoned off her piggyback ride, which was still gaining speed. She watched as it passed her, dashing toward the large asteroid, but soon lost sight of it in the shadow of the new rock. Floating in the debris, Oni returned her attention to the problem in front of her. She kept checking the viewscreen for emergency instructions, but there were none. Whatever she needed to do, she had to think, quickly.

Her eye caught sight of a flash. For a moment, she thought she was seeing things. But as she got closer to the large asteroid, she saw it again. There was a shimmer of sunlight coming through the Manhattan-sized rock, and if she kept on her current trajectory, she was headed toward a small hole in the asteroid. She didn't have to stop, lose momentum, or climb up and over the giant asteroid. She just had to go through it.

Oni breathed a momentary sigh of relief, letting the sun's gravity pull her along as she finally entered the tunnel in the asteroid. There were some close shaves inside as she plunged through the middle of the towering asteroid. The interior was very dark and rough. A few of the outcroppings would have caught her by the leg if she hadn't tucked herself into a ball a few times.

When she cleared the last asteroid, she soon realized it wasn't the sun shining through the tunnel, but a bright, shimmering, red-yellow cloud nebula. And the cloud was dense, like a storm rolling in. In a matter of minutes, Oni was having a hard time seeing more than a few meters in front of her. The particles all around her glowed brightly.

For a very long time, Oni was left floating in the disorienting fog. Eventually, she wasn't sure which way was up, down, left, or right. She knew the gravity of the sun would keep pulling her forward; she felt as if she was being dragged behind a boat, only she couldn't see the towline or the boat. And it made her anxious.

There was a sudden break in density, allowing Oni to see more than a meter ahead of her. She quickly scanned the cloud, preparing for what might lie ahead, pop out, or catch her off guard. But nothing happened as she continued through the unending cloud of dust particles.

The worst part was the expectation. What was going to happen next? How large was the cloud? It was impossible to guess. On and on it went. She felt like she was floating in the cloud for hours. And the longer she waited, the more anxiety she built up inside. Her nervousness worked against her as she waited, and waited, and waited. She kept surveying to her right and left for what surprises lie ahead. It was mentally and physically exhausting having your muscles taut, skin sweating, and nerves tingling in anticipation.

A light caught her eye, and she winced inside her suit. "Ah!" she yelled, her nerves shooting off like a gun. She looked down at her hands and legs; everything was glowing with light. She was lit up like a Christmas tree. The further she flew into the nebula, the brighter she got. She tried to brush it away, but to no avail.

When she entered another break in the cloud, something dark passed by her. She raised her right arm, and the target appeared on her viewscreen. For a second, she thought she saw an asteroid. Perhaps it was the same asteroid she was riding earlier; it did seem to be on the same trajectory as her. Oni moved her arm around, searching for the rogue asteroid. What was, just a moment ago, a few hundred-meter range of sight instantaneously became zero visibility. She again lost sight of the phantom asteroid in the thick cloud nebula.

Oni waited for a long time for another break in the density, but there was none. Her nerves were shot. Without any warning, the nebula ended. It just stopped mid-space like an invisible wall was put up. The ending was abrupt, as surprising as the beginning. She never saw it coming.

She looked around, trying to assess where she was, and the invisible wall that seemed to hold back the nebula, but she was moving too fast. She soon realized what was directly in front of her. It was crystal clear and impossible to misconstrue. Between her and the Olympic Flame sun was a celestial body Oni had only seen in pictures. She was coming in hot, along the side of a comet.

The spectacular sight was one of the most beautiful celestial bodies Oni had ever seen. It was more spectacular than the sun, or the planets, or the spaceships. It was a work of art, and it took her breath away. The comet appeared to be a living-breathing thing, not a cold lifeless body in the heavens. It had motion. It had energy. It had life. She teared up for a minute, caught in the magnificence. She knew she would remember this moment for the rest of her life, and nothing else would ever compare—*nothing*.

There wasn't just one, but two tails trailing its nucleus. One bluish tint tail shot directly behind the head of the comet. The other tail, nearest to Oni, was white and curved in an arch. This comet was an awe-inspiring sight. The head that made up the nucleus of the comet was fuzzy. Oni could barely see the core of the comet through the misty fuzz surrounding the head. She wasn't directly on the tail but was coming in alongside, in a hyperbolic arc. Without realizing it, she had gained even more speed in the nebula. She didn't have the nerve to assess her velocity in real terms. She was worried it might make her sick.

Up first was the white tail. Whatever it was, she was about to get a full dose of comet tail and eat it for lunch.

"Here we go," she said, as she made her way through the white substance. She knew immediately what it was—dust. It began collecting on the front of her helmet, and the viewscreen was getting dirty. There was a moment when she wished she had a windshield wiper on her helmet, but it wouldn't have made any difference. She quickly passed through the long tail, heading straight into the fuzzy coma cloud surrounding the comet's head.

She wasn't sure what to expect. Part of her thought it would be a hard rock that made up the core of the comet, the other part wasn't sure if it would be all ice. As she ascended through the fuzz, water droplets landed on her helmet, and she made a somewhat rough touchdown on a very hard surface. The nucleus was much harder than she thought. The piggyback asteroid she rode earlier felt hollow compared to this. The comet was solid.

The surface of the comet appeared dark, very dark, almost black in appearance. She began the hard work of trudging up the nucleus. The comet didn't have the gravity of Earth, or even the ship, but it wasn't easy floating up the side either. She ran along the exterior, climbed up and down hills, made her way around rocks and boulders, and jumped over a few open pits containing water. It was a hard slog. She continued on, running over the rock, jumping over gas blows venting out water that helped create the fuzzy cloud around the comet's head. Luckily, the comet wasn't as big as Haley's. It was actually quite small, but the view once Oni made it to the top of the nucleus, was unlike any in the world. It was truly extraordinary.

Through a mist of the fuzz, she was staring out at the blazing Olympic Flame sun. As soon as she looked directly at the corona, a tint on her helmet visor became darker to accommodate her human eyes and the sun's intensity. It was bright, the brightest visible light that can exist in the Universe.

Her space suit was covered in dust, dirt, droplets of icy water, and God only knows what other particles; an astrophysicist and geologist would have had a field day taking samples of the debris. For a second, she paused, staring at the sun and surveying the comet. She had an epiphany. There was no place else in the universe that she would rather be than right here. If she could, she would build a country home on this spot (granted it would be a little hot). But for the first time in her life, she was living in the present, not wanting to go or be anywhere else. She felt at peace. Oni caught her breath on a partial sob. The release was spiritual. She was thankful to be a part of Team Earth, a part of this Universe Olympic experience, and to be alive.

After a few moments, her heart sank. She realized she couldn't stay here forever—in fact, she needed to get out of there soon. But she wasn't sure where to go from there. It was hard to imagine how to overcome the bright hot Olympic Flame sun beyond the end of the comet. There was no way she could survive in her tiny space suit that, up until now, miraculously, hadn't been demolished, overheated, cracked, ripped, or broken. Honestly, she was slightly shocked, but Liew had said that the suit was made for her. Maybe it was from some superior material—otherwise she would never be standing on the head of a comet.

Oni quickly made a deal with the Virgin Mary. If Oni somehow survived this race, she promised in her heart to do whatever she could for the betterment of Humanity by helping people reach beyond their star, into the greater galaxy. She prayed silently that her goodwill promise to the Lord, Mary Mother of God, and the Universe was enough to see her through this challenge.

"Madonna Mia. How do I get off this thing?" she said out loud in Italian, caught between a comet and the star.

"Sun slingshot burn maneuver ready." The words appeared on the viewscreen, and a woman's voice confirmed in her ears, in Italian.

Oni flinched at the voice.

"Wait, you could speak the whole time?"

"Yes," confirmed the melodious voice. "You only had to ask a question," answered the spacesuit.

"Are you kidding me!" she hollered. Oni was not sure if she was angrier with herself or with Liew.

"No. I am voice controlled to answer any verbal query."

Oni asked, a little disgusted, "What is a sun slingshot burn maneuver?"

"Your rocket boosters will give an initial thrust, enough so the gravity from the sun will slingshot you around to the north-pole side of the star."

"Will I burn up?"

"If you get too close to the sun, the statistical probability of that outcome increases one hundred-fold."

"When should I start this slingshot maneuver?"

"The best window would have been twenty seconds ago when you started asking questions about voice control. If you continue on this current trajectory, you will be outside the slingshot booster capability window in five, four, three."

"GO, for sun slingshot burn!" yelled Oni at the top of her lungs, making sure there was no mistaking her command.

"Slingshot maneuver initiated," responded the spacesuit.

Oni could feel the heavy pressure from the boosters attached to the back of her pack as she lifted off the face of the comet and moved closer to the sun. It felt like the worst rollercoaster on Earth. Only this ride could plunge into the sun.

"What's the statistical likelihood this works?" posed Oni.

"Note: there is a nineteen percent probability that you will be burnt to death, if the sun has a corona flare during the slingshot maneuver," stated the spacesuit.

"Greeeat," said Oni, as she rocketed toward the sun.

It was a sight to behold, just little Onorina Di Mateo and the Olympic Flame sun, together. She was a dark speck in front of the flaming sun. She was so close, she felt she could touch it. Oni wanted to touch the corona, play with it, without searing her hands off. She wished she could witness all the rainbow colors with her own eyes, not through the sunscreen filter. The flames were more dynamic then she ever imagined a sun would be. The flow and liveliness of the flames. It looked alive. But the possibility of burning to death was real.

"*È bellissimo.*"

The rocket boosters kept up their power at full, as she watched the viewscreen in her helmet map out the slingshot around the sun. She knew if this sun felt in any way persnickety, and spit out or flared up, she would be dead.

Oni could feel, about halfway around the sun, when the boosters ended their burn. The viewscreen spelled it out in red letters "Main Rocket Boosters Empty." Now it was just her against the sun and gravity. A giant corona flare went up way over her head, missing her by perhaps a thousand kilometers, though it was hard to tell distance in space.

A glint caught her eye; she turned her head and saw *something* she could not comprehend. It made no sense to her, but she had to accept the fact that it was there. A few hundred meters away, on roughly the same slingshot trajectory, and only a little bit ahead of her as she raced around the sun, was an asteroid. Not just *any* asteroid, it looked exactly like the asteroid she had ridden earlier to escape the rocky belt, and the one that she thought peeked out in the nebula. Only that would be impossible. Why would an asteroid be on the same course as her?

It took her a minute. She felt so foolish, so unimaginative, and so *human* for not thinking of it before. The prospect had never occurred to her. She was so busy skipping on asteroids in the belt, nervous in the nebula, and too preoccupied catching the comet that she had completely forgotten the point of why she was here. She was in a race.

She looked back at the asteroid. "And this, this rock thing, is my competitor," she stated matter-of-factly. It was the only logical explanation. She was expecting a creature, a monster, or an animal, or some crazy alien with five heads, eight feet, and a tail, like she imagined an alien life form would be. She never dreamed it would be a simple rock. Or what looked like a rock from the outside. Then she blushed; not because she was overheated by her proximity to a star. She blushed because she had used her competition as a piggyback ride. With her embarrassment, went dread. What if it was against the rules to ride a fellow competitor? What if everything she went through was for naught because she broke a rule and was going to be disqualified? The flash of that thought dug deep into her heart. It was more than a mere knife; it was a samurai sword of regret.

But there was nothing she could do to change it now. She was in the middle of space, sling-shooting around a sun. What was done was done. The consequences of her actions would be felt *after* the finish. And she needed to focus on that and complete this race, give it her best, disqualification be damned.

Her temperature and speed only increased after she made it more than halfway around the sun. She prayed that this spacesuit was no normal suit. It had withstood everything so far, but with the combination of extreme heat from the star and the increased speed it might tear apart. Her spacesuit was taking temperatures and velocities that any human spaceship would have a hard time holding together. And there was no escape pod. The side of her spacesuit that faced the sun felt warmer, but none of the hard exterior had melted away. This spacesuit was indeed extraordinary. It was made of no material known to man, which couldn't stand being so close to a star without being burnt to a crisp. Besides a slight increase in body temperature, her suit had thankfully maintained its stability.

She gazed at the sun as she completed the slingshot around to the other side. It was glorious. The star shown white hot, burnished with yellow, orange, and red. Gold flecks sparkled in spots, though that was possibly from the filter on her helmet. It was just bright enough for her eyes to see. This sun was a marvel of nature, created just for these games. And Oni was pretty sure that no human being had ever been so in danger of consumption by an Olympic Flame. She had never truly appreciated the sun, her sun, before—how it made life possible on Earth. These stars were the lifeblood of the universe; the sun was its heartbeat. And this star made the Universe Olympic Games possible. She would have liked somehow to take a souvenir of this sun home, but that capability was beyond human imagination.

As she completed the slingshot rotation on the other side of the sun, open space lay before her. Far off in the distance, she could see the planetary Olympic arenas from a new perspective—the rocky planet, green planet, water, and snow planets. Her direct heading was out from the north pole of the sun, into space. The nearest star was at her back—vast empty blackness was in front of her.

Then she hit the wall. The slingshot around the sun had increased her velocity exponentially—but to where? The green arrows were gone from her viewscreen. She gazed around in every direction that her helmet permitted, and there was nowhere to go. All the planets were in opposite orbits; she had completed what she thought was the third portion of the race. What could possibly be next?

She waited for a few minutes, traveling further and further away from the sun. Oni glimpsed the asteroid competition that was ahead of her. The rock had gained speed, probably because *IT* maneuvered at the correct moment. How could an asteroid not know when to maneuver in space? After her slingshot, she had felt an astonishing momentum, but it wasn't fast enough to beat whatever rock-being was racing her.

She glanced over at the asteroid; it didn't look like it had any particular mode of propulsion. There were no rocket boosters, or any type of propulsion known to man or woman, coming out the back. Yet, it had the jump on her. At their current rate, it was going to beat her. There was no way, playing the good old-fashioned game of physics, that she could win. Maybe if she used her pistol to shoot behind her, it would help give her the extra boost. But shooting, without something to hold on to, risked putting her into a never-ending tailspin again. Her rocket boosters were emptied by the slingshot maneuver. There was nothing left but inertia.

"How can I get the wind back in my sails," she said aloud, more as a statement to herself than a question.

"You could deploy the solar sail," answered the spacesuit.

"What the?" she stopped herself from finishing the question. Instead of asking first, like the last time, she decided to act first, *THEN* ask questions later.

"Deploy solar sail," she stated firmly. It was not a time for questioning. It was a time to trust. The suit had seen her through almost being burnt by the Olympic Flame sun. Perhaps she should trust the suit, even though she had no idea what a solar sail was or how it worked.

"Deploying the solar sail," the spacesuit returned in the kindly woman's voice, still speaking in Italian.

She glanced down and saw, starting at the underside of her arms, a very thin golden foil unfurled out of nowhere from inside her suit. It slowly expanded. Centimeter by centimeter, it unfolded itself to the edge of her fingers and then attached to the tip of her boots. At the same time, the other arm had an exact replica unfolding and attaching to her other boot. Once the arms were in place, a third portion of foil deployed from her left to right foot. All in all, the foil-like material had attached to every appendage except her head. She looked like she was in a base-jumping suit, only in space. When the feet were locked in place and the foil became taut, she started to move, fast.

It didn't take her too long to figure out what it did; she grew up on the Amalfi coast in Italy and had enjoyed sailing on the Tyrrhenian Sea. Somehow, this particular sail was taking the energy from the sun and propelling her forward, quickly along her current vector.

She was gaining distance on the asteroid. But if she moved her hands or legs in the slightest way, if every millimeter of sail wasn't catching the light from the Olympic Flame sun, she would slow down just a smidgen.

Onorina realized what was happening. This last part, part four, was a foot race, as it were, but in space. And the rules of this game were as old as time: *Ye who is fastest, wins.* She had trained hours and hours for it, she only hoped she could win this one.

She glanced down at the solar sail's golden foil. It was as thin as tissue paper. A good sneeze could probably tear it apart. She was a little worried that the wrong move would rip it in two. She checked her velocity on the viewscreen. It was slowly increasing. Once she unfurled the sail, she went from the very back of the asteroid, to the middle, and now she was gaining on the rock. She turned back to stare out in space, and she saw the danger for the first time. Up ahead, on a direct collision course with her current course, was the ship. Her spaceship. Her home. The finish line. It was hard to see against the blackness of space. The sun caught the edge of its silver exterior.

All this time, she thought the ship would appear before the sun slingshot, before the comet, or before the nebula. In that moment, the spaceship was as beautiful as every other celestial body she'd encountered in space. The triangle portion of the ship facing her wasn't as smooth as she thought, with patterns of bumps and windows along the silvery surface. The ship—her finish line—had only appeared once she had forgotten about it. But there was one problem, she had no idea how she was going to stop. At her current speed on her current course, she was going to smash into the very center of the triangular spaceship.

*   *   *

The door opened and there was a loud cry from the back of the room. "What are you all doing in *HERE*?" pounced a surprised Liew. He stared at the team, who gathered around the lounge window, watching the speck that was Onorina.

"Watching Oni," said Ramon Stead with a confused look on his face. "You did say we could be spectators for this event, Liew."

The whole team, sans the alternate, was huddled together on the far side of the room.

"YES, YES!" snapped Liew.

"It is called the observation lounge, Ambassador," retorted Jenefer.

"I didn't mean for you all to watch it from up here!" Liew said with a rush in his voice.

"Where do we need to go?" yelled Stoke.

"We have to go downstairs," Liew checked the patch on his arm. "NOW!" he yelled and started out the door. "Follow me," he screamed from down the hall. "Hurry!" he said running.

The team, without a moment's hesitation, immediately broke into a sprint behind the Ambassador. They were barely able to keep him in sight. Liew had to stop or slow down at each turn, to make sure they knew where he was headed. The only one who was able to keep up was Jenefer.

"Where are we going?" asked Yosi, unable to keep up with the front runners.

"Beats me!" answered Amy, who was closest and still not at her top form from yesterday's race and recovery. It was also equally true that Amy held back to keep an eye on the smallest teammate.

Jenefer kept looking back and yelling the directions as Liew made each turn. "Heading down Stair five," she relayed. Pappie, Jaysen, and Margit were not far behind her. Ramon, at the back of the pack, repeated each aloud in a deep voice the directions from the leader. "Down stair five, everyone!"

The sound of a hundred pounding steps could be heard as they scampered down at least twenty flights of steps.

"Won't need to cross-train today," remarked Josie to Jodie.

"Yaaa!" she laughed back. "Or the week!"

"Turning left onto Level forty-five," boomed Jenefer, her voice echoed down the stairs. She rushed to catch up with Liew, who was able to keep a swifter pace since she was relaying his location.

They continued through a maze of halls and stairs the team had yet to see. But it wasn't a surprise, their spaceship was the size of a New York City skyscraper.

Running down yet another flight of steps and down another hall, Jenefer finally stopped at large wide-open doors. Liew was standing at the threshold of a room.

"Wouldn't an elevator have been easier?" she asked with a smile on her sweaty face.

"Actually, this was better, Mrs. Washington-Lee, for all of you."

Jen peeked down the hallway as Pappie, Jaysen, and Margit sprinted towards her. "In here," she shouted when the far stairwell door opened, hoping Ramon could hear her latest and last bit of instruction.

The team, with much huffing and puffing, slowly assembled at the large doors.

"Dude, Liew, next time, take the scenic route, please," interjected Stoke, wiping the sweat from his forehead, and bending over to take in deep breaths.

"You all were at the top corner of the ship, but we needed to be here," said Liew, counting the remaining heads.

"Ari, Amy, Yosi, the twins, Manny, Dmitri, Eric, Sito San, the Hallperans," he calculated. They were followed up by Ramon, playing caboose.

"All here!" Ramon hollered happily.

The group gathered at the entrance of an enormous cargo bay. It was at least eight stories tall on the inside. In the far corner, Ari's twenty-four surfboards were still boxed up alongside Ramon's bobsled, Pappie's bikes, Oni's saddles, Jaysen's javelins, and every other bulky piece of equipment belonging to the team. But even their equipment only took up a small five percent corner of the vast bay.

They trailed behind Liew as he crossed the large empty floor, surprised to find that Liew had an even larger shuttle hidden in another corner.

Stoke froze in his tracks. "Holy jelly!" he yelled, "This looks exactly like the cargo bay in Star Trek, on the Enterprise – X Class."

"Yes, Mr. Townsend, as I said…" Liew walked up to a panel and began touching it. "This ship is an amalgam of *ALL* ships which Humanity has ever built or imagined. Designed to make you feel more comfortable and at home." He pressed a final button and the cargo bay doors cracked open directly to space.

"*COOOOOL!*" shrieked Stoke.

"AHHH!" screamed Margit, getting a direct view of the Olympic Flame sun blazing through the stretching opening which reached floor to ceiling.

"Don't worry, Ms. Housman, there is a force field in place. You're going nowhere."

"Liew, why are we in here?" she marveled, as the team watched the cargo bay doors slowly roll open across the entire side of the bay.

"This is where Onorina is finishing her race."

*   *   *

The moment she saw it, Oni knew. It started as a slit of light in the middle of the ship, which slowly got bigger and bigger, becoming a square in the middle of the triangular ship. The square gradually expanded into a large rectangle of light that beckoned Oni home. Her finish line wasn't alone. Positioned directly next to Team Earth's spaceship was a large asteroid—as big as her ship, if not bigger. She guessed it was a larger version of the smaller one she was racing.

She turned to her left. The smaller asteroid was only slightly ahead of her. "That," she said, realizing what she was seeing, "is your spaceship, isn't it?" But she had the answer to her own question at this point. There was no doubt in her mind. Her competitor was a rock, and the rock was beating her, and at her current velocity it would be at its ship before she got to hers.

Oni moved slightly, trying to catch as much sunlight as possible on her sail. She could feel her speed gaining with each passing second, but was it enough? If she had the space and time, she could (with the help of the solar sail) beat her competitor and win this heat. For a moment, her heart jumped. If an asteroid-nebula-comet-sun event was just the first heat for this space race, she could hardly imagine what the final would look like: beating a black hole?

She examined the surface of the asteroid, wondering what the inside looked like. Was it made of rock to its core? Or was it, like her, floating inside a controlled environment? Perhaps their species only used the safety of an asteroid rock as their spacecraft? She wasn't sure.

Faster and faster, they raced, approaching their ships. The rock was closer to its giant asteroid than she was to her ship. But what was once a small triangle in the distance was almost within reach. The light around the edges of the rectangular opening in the center of the ship flashed white in sequence, like landing lights on an airplane runway. She knew where to go. There was no need to elaborate. She knew "home" when she saw it.

The sail may have worked. The competitors were nose to nose. Well, more helmet to tip of rock, actually, but she and the rock were, heading to the finish line together. She needed to do something to gain that extra edge. What was she to do? The sail was pushed to its limit, and her boosters were empty. There was nothing but light and gravity…

"Gravity is my friend!" she shouted out loud, knowing her competitor couldn't hear, but it felt good to yell it, anyway.

"Gravity is your friend," repeated the spacesuit back to Oni. "Do you want to eject the booster pack?"

"Yes, eject the booster pack," said Oni. She had the key the whole time. Liew gave it to her in the shuttle. She wondered if he knew the exact moment when she would say it aloud.

The suit repeated back in Italian. "Ejecting booster pack."

And with a thump, the booster pack popped off her back. She was light, and with her sail, that much lighter.

Her speed increased without the weight of the pack. What was nose-to-nose now put her ahead by a hair.

"Yesssssss!" she screamed, pulling ahead of the asteroid by just a yard.

But there was a problem: A major, major, *MAJOR* problem. The closer she got to the ship; her trajectory became clear on the viewscreen. She was not aligned with the rectangular opening. In fact, she was off by just a few degrees. On her current course, she would smash into the ship just shy of the upper left side of the rectangular opening.

"Can you move the ship?" Oni asked the spacesuit.

"Unable to comply with this request." The suit answered. "Access only to the spacesuit and its controls."

"Damn," she said out loud.

"Liew, Liew. Please could you move the ship? I'm coming in at the wrong vector."

She waited a moment; she got closer to the opening and the ship.

"Ambassador Liew. *Please* could you move the ship three degrees to port."

There was no answer to her query. It was not surprising. Would any race have allowed the finish line to be moved just a little closer to suit a competitor's needs? No, they wouldn't. The finish line was a fixed location. To move it to benefit her would have been cheating.

"Damn it!" she yelled again even louder. "What can I do to move right?"

"Emergency thrusters available," answered the suit voice in the helmet.

"Where is it? I dropped my booster pack." She forgot to *not* ask questions. It was a bad personal habit to question everything said.

"Small emergency thrusters located in the helmet. There is enough for a 3 second burn."

"That would have been nice to know a while ago!" she yelled at the spacesuit. "Can you direct the thrusters to point me toward the finish line in the ship?"

"Coordinates confirmed. Solar Sail seventy-nine percent tearing potential."

"I'll just have to take that chance," said Oni, with a grim tone. It was now or never. She was getting so close to the ship she could see inside the observation lounge window at the top of the ship.

"GO for Emergency Thruster burn, NOW!"

The tiny thrusters attached to her head pivoted to the correct angle, and the viewscreen inside her helmet showed the new trajectory. It ended inside the open bay doors.

The course correction was swift, as the thrusters made their start with a jolt. In three, two, one, she was traveling at breakneck speed, headed directly for the open cargo bay doors. As usual, there was another problem. The angle she was now traveling wouldn't allow for full sunlight on her sail. And as soon as she turned, she started to lose speed. Her asteroid competitor started to gain an edge in distance and speed ahead of her.

"Come on, come on, COME ON!" She roared to no one in particular, but it was too late. The asteroid now had the advantage. Its speed increased, while she had only a corner of the sail to catch the light of the sun. It was like watching a slow defeat.

As she approached the giant open rectangle, two thoughts kept running around her mind. First, how was she going to stop... and second, *HOW* was she going to stop? Her speed was intense, thousands of kilometers per hour. She didn't have anything to slow her down. She prayed that somehow this wouldn't end with her being squashed like a bug on a windshield.

Oni turned and watched the asteroid slam into the bigger asteroid it called home. She couldn't tell from her angle if there was an opening or not. Perhaps it crashed, like she was about to.

The closer she traveled to the rectangular opening in the ship, the more she could see why it was glowing white. The opening was covered in a white crisscross mesh, like a chain link fence, or a fishing net. As soon as she had the thought, she knew: *a net.*

Her speed was incredible, and she was just shy of hitting the top left corner of the ship as she dove in, headfirst. The glowing white net scooped her up and surrounded her completely. As soon as she crossed the force-field barrier into the cargo bay, gravity hit. She flailed in the net for a moment, unused to the sudden gravity, and still blazing like a white-hot comet! Oni zoomed across the half-mile bay till she finally hit the ground hard, bouncing and rolling along the floor. But the net did its job. Somehow it had stopped her.

When she glanced up, she saw the entire team and Liew running toward her.

"DON'T TOUCH HER!" thundered Liew. "Stand back, everyone, please." Near where Oni had landed was a control panel. Liew sprinted over to it and pressed a button.

Margit raced to his side. "What is that thing?"

"An inertia net. It dispersed all her kinetic energy."

The white glowing net around Oni, slowly disappeared, link by link. She watched the net disperse, catching her bearings. When the last link fully dissipated, she waved at the team and Liew. With a little difficulty, she tried to stand on her feet but ended up on her butt. Liew charged over and removed her helmet.

"Congratulations, Ms. Di Mateo. You completed your heat!"

The team erupted in applause around her. Oni looked like she had been through the ringer. Her spacesuit was darkened in certain spots—there was dirt, dust, and remarkably, frozen crystals of water in crevasses along her elbows and feet. It still felt warm to the touch. She lifted her hands to show the tattered golden sail, like a flag that had seen one too many winters.

"The solar sail didn't make it, I'm afraid." Oni showed Liew. "I'm not sure if it was the last thruster burn or that net." Oni motioned to the ribbons that were left. Yosi and Ari gently touched the remnants of the sail. They too were still warm to the touch.

"Wow!" said Ari tenderly handling the foil-like sail. "This is fantastic."

"Are you OK, physically?" asked Liew, looking highly concerned at his pentathlete.

"I'm a little sunburned," answered Oni, laughing, with a smile on her face. And it was true. Her face was red, be it from exertion, worry, or the Olympic Flame sun.

"Yes, you are officially our Star Diver now, solar sailor!" Liew chortled. "Still, I want you in the Recovery Chair immediately to check for anything we can't visibly see."

"All you will find is a broken heart," she answered reluctantly. "I didn't win, did I? *It* made it back to its ship first."

"Yes, Oni. You are correct, but by only a few seconds. It was a very close race."

"What does it look like, Liew? Is it rock all over?"

Liew helped as Oni took the gloves off her space suit. "No, like you, it needed a special exterior to adapt to space. That's why you two were put together for this heat."

"Never thought of an alien using an asteroid as a spacesuit."

"Their home world is very close to a large asteroid belt, much like your solar system has between Mars and Jupiter. They used what resources they had around them to adapt."

The team started walking out of the bay. One glove given to Yosi, the other was taken by Ari, both beyond enamored with the spacesuit and their new hero Onorina.

"Everyone back upstairs," declared Liew.

"Please tell me we can use the elevators this time," wondered Manny, obviously still traumatized by the long trek down twenty-eight floors.

"Yes, Mr. Suarez."

Stoke ran up next to Liew as they crossed the enormous cargo bay. "Answer me this, Liew. I thought you said the only technology on this ship was stuff humans had used or imagined before. I'm a *huge* sci-fi fan and I don't think I've ever heard of an inertia net before."

"It's from a science fiction book from way back in 2020s. So technically, the inertia net was imagined by a human being before."

"Never heard of it. What's the book about?"

"Olympians, much like yourselves."

"Really? Sounds cool. I never read it."

"You don't have to, Mr. Townsend." Liew said with a smile on his face, as all of Team Earth walked out of the cargo bay. "You don't have to."

Chapter 9

Human Time

Ramon waited in the entranceway, counting heads one by one as they went by. "Ten, Eleven, Twelve..." He confirmed out loud, as a blond head, quite a bit shorter than his, looked up. "Thirteen. You're lucky thirteen, Margit."

"Always, Ramon," replied Margit, dressed head to toe in snow gear. "Stoke's already in there."

"OK, then—fourteen, fifteen," as husband and wife pair, the Hallperans, walked by, holding hands.

"Sorry, Mate," screamed a very wet Josie from far down the narrow hall as her twin sister trailed behind. "We only just now realized the time," she finished apologetically.

"You're, fine. You're, fine. there's always time. No strict deadline. All's good." Ramon smiled and waved them through the doors.

"Yeah, with two extra hours, it's like, these days NEVER end!" added Jodie who was last through the doors.

"OK. Oni's in Recovery, so that leaves me," Ramon said to himself. "Seventeen, lucky seventeen; Team Earth all accounted for," he said to no one in particular. He quickly about-faced and walked through the large doorway. Within two steps of passing the threshold, his feet crunched on hard snow.

"*HOLY* crikey!" screamed Josie oh-so-not-subtly, "What the heck is *THIS PLACE*," she marveled as her flip-flops slipped on the snow and a large snowflake passed by her face.

"I thought this was going to be an indoor snow run!" finished Jodie. "Where the heck *are* we?"

"Welcome to the Snow Room," said Margit to the whole group of athletes huddled together in a sort of semicircle near the opening of the door.

"ROOM!" exclaimed Jaysen, his eyes popping. "How is this a room?"

He was right. There weren't the four closed-in walls, a floor, and a ceiling that would normally delineate a "room." Again, Liew got his words mixed-up, like the cafeteria. The team was standing on the side of the mountain, rocks, and snow below their feet, next to a steep vertical slope. There was an endless blue sky above, a few clouds, with slight flurries floating to the ground.

"*This* is a mountain," finished Jaysen, picking up some snow and forming a hard snowball.

"Liew's got to work on his words!" hollered Jen, looking around in astonishment. "WOW!"

"Hey, that's my word, lady," answered Jaysen, winking. "Time to find one of your own. Try… Ride."

"Ha, ha…" responded Amy half-rolling her eyes, "Taken." Amy pointed to her own light blue T-shirt adorned with a wave and the words, 'Let's Ride.'

"How far down do you think it goes?" asked Jen, staring down the long ski run that ran the length of the mountain.

"A little over a thousand meters," answered Margit. "This is halfway up on one of my favorite runs in Norway, Olympiabakken. It was used for the 1994 Olympic Games downhill event."

"*Wait?* Are we back on Earth?" speculated Pappie, taking in the scenery uneasily. He was careful not to step on the edge of the ski run with his thin spiked biking shoes.

"I don't think so," answered Margit. "This particular run is usually very crowded and has hundreds of people skiing or snowboarding on it daily. It's only us here."

Stoke quickly snowboarded by the group howling and waving. "What's up?" he crowed, and turned his board, creating a little wave of snow that hit the crowded athletes. "Back in a sec," he shouted then continued down the mountain.

Everyone was silent as they watched him snowboard down the run toward the bottom of the mountain.

"How does it go on and on?" asked Sito, the quiet giant from Japan, who rarely ever spoke in group settings.

"I haven't figured out the physics of our 'Snow Room' yet," answered Margit.

"Is it a hologram?" asked Jen.

"No, watch. Stoke will make it all the way down the mountain. It's real and there is actual distance. I've already done this run twice today."

"I don't *think* a hologram could do that," conjectured Mark while turning to his wife Justine, who was nodding in agreement.

"I'm beginning to suspect it's para-dimensional," replied Margit.

Stoke looked like a tiny speck of color in the white snow much further down the run. He was zigzagging down the slope, occasionally jumping and grabbing his board. He was too far away to hear the hooting and hollering.

"I think that is beyond the end of the ship," stated Dmitri, whose deep baritone voice made the group jump because he rarely ever used it. "I don't know about para-dimensional," he said, very impressed. For this quiet Russian athlete to be impressed, it took a lot.

"Huddle up, everyone," said Ramon. He motioned to the group to get closer, not only for the intended meeting, but also for warmth.

"We can debate physics para-dimensionality later. We have pressing business."

"Yeah, it's super freezing in here," muttered Amy, who was also very inappropriately dressed for the side of a snowy mountain, wearing only shorts and a tank top.

Margit took off her top layer and handed it to Amy. Margit still had at least two other down jackets underneath.

"Thanks, Margit." Amy smiled at her fellow teammate.

"I wanted *all* of us..." started Ramon but was quickly interrupted.

"Oni's not here," stated Jen, "or Stoke."

"All of us, sans Oni. Stoke is still technically in the room so it counts. We need a group meeting without the Ambassador, in case any of you had concerns or complaints, or anything we wanted to address as a team from Earth."

"Like a Human Meeting!" interjected Josie smiling.

"Yes," answered Ramon.

"Team Earth, Human Meeting number one, in session," Jodie piled onto her sister's comments. "I'll take minutes. And go..."

"Now, does anyone have any questions or concerns so far?" Ramon looked around the group.

As was often the tendency among a crowd, everyone was hesitant to be first, even Pappie. Ramon got the ball rolling, "I was wondering, Amy, since you have already gone, could you share with us what Liew told you? About your event or anything else about your experience in the competition."

"Liew did say something very interesting, after the fact. He said that each of these events were going to challenge us intellectually, physically, emotionally, and spiritually. And to be prepared for all four parts, because honestly, I wasn't. I had to intellectually problem solve one of the gates, I was emotionally pushed to the limit by swimming into the cave, and was physically spent at the end, racing against Aule," she responded.

"Who's that?" asked Ari.

"The blue whale creature. I literally had nothing left to give at the end of my event."

"And spiritually?" asked Jen, who wasn't sure how the spiritual aspect played into her event.

"I'm not ready to talk about that yet, Jen."

"Fair enough," nodded Jen.

"And let me say, for the record. Everyone. I am sorry I took second place," Amy said contritely to the team.

"No apology necessary," said Ramon very forcefully. "You put in a good show for Humanity."

"What else," asked Eric, "did Liew mention?"

"He told me that the President of the Universe Olympic Committee already told us these things already, but I wasn't paying full attention."

"Neither was I," said Pappie, turning to Ramon. "We were too busy assessing our bet. And noting how remarkable the turtle was. Took me off my game."

"As it did most of us," retorted Ramon. "So, each of us needs to be ready for all four components of our individual events."

They nodded in compliance.

"Yes," answered Amy, "and… not to put a wrinkle in this, guys, but he told me to keep training. I've got to be honest I have a feeling; I'm not done yet."

"Really?" pondered Jaysen. "Athletes may be in more than one event! Wow. Good to know."

"That's just my feeling. I'm still training like I haven't raced yet. And I hope I get the opportunity too. I'm kind of disappointed with my first outing, if you know what I mean."

And everyone did. Nodding in accordance. This was a circle of champions. No one took losing lightly.

"Do we know who's going next?" asked Jaysen revved up, throwing his snowball like he was throwing a shot put. "That info would help."

"Nope," said Ramon, "And I suspect there might be a reason for that."

Oni suddenly ran into the room. "*Madonna Mia*," she yelled as she slid on the ice, wobbling. Ramon, who was closest to the door, caught her mid fall.

"*Grazie*," she said, regaining her footing. "I'm sorry, I just finished in the Recovery Room, and I just found your note stuck on my cubby," she said looking at Ramon. Oni reached down and took a handful of snow. "What I would have given for a handful of this in my suit when I was passing the Olympic Flame sun," she rubbed a handful over her sunburnt face.

Everyone laughed.

"My face is still hot," she laughed.

"You're cleared from Recovery?" asked Jen, concerned. "Why are you still sunburned?"

"*Si*, I was cleared, but I asked Liew to leave a little tan as a reminder of what I went through. I earned a little sun." Oni picked up more snow. "Liew wouldn't have let me out if I wasn't fully recovered, I got his speech." She perused all the members of the team. "What are we doing?"

"Meeting," answered Ramon.

"*Si*, for what?"

"To answer or ask any questions."

"*Si*." The group stared at Oni, in hopeful expectation. "I don't have any, right now, *grazie*." She smiled at the group. "I'm *finito*."

"Well, you may not be," responded Amy. "We might be up again."

"Oh?" nodded Oni. "As Team Earth's alternate, I will always be ready to help. And let me apologize for not winning my heat. It leaves an ache in my heart." Her hands covered her heart. "I was hoping to do better for Humanity. I hope you all don't feel my event was wasted on the alternate."

"Truthfully," answered Jen. "I wouldn't have gone out in space… hmmm… nnnnn. *NO WAY*, Jose. Would never have happened! Event over!"

"Obviously, that is why you were picked, Onorina," smiled Margit in acknowledgement.

"No other human would have competed in space," offered Ramon, "or in a spacesuit, for that matter."

"You were amazing!" excitedly squealed Ari. "It was the coolest thing I have ever seen." Ari cozied up to Oni gleaming with slight hero worship on her face.

"You aren't upset I didn't win?" wondered Oni.

The whole group answered in unison, "No."

"*Grazie,*" answered Oni with true gratefulness in her heart. "Liew did mention to me that he wasn't allowed to divulge too much about each contest. Part of the rules. Humanity had to be tested for adaptation."

"Yeah, I was starting to wonder. Liew hasn't pulled each of us aside to prepare us for our individual events." Ramon was nodding and talking more to himself then to the others. "All the more reason I'm glad we're meeting. This is important to know. Adaptation."

"Whose rules, Oni?" asked Pappie.

"The Universe Olympic Committee, I think. He petitioned them to let me compete in a spacesuit in space."

"Wonder what else he's petitioning for?" announced Pappie with a slight hint of worry, "We must all be prepared."

"We'll be ready for whatever comes Humanity's way." Ramon winked at his friend.

Stoke finally hopped off the T-bar that was slowly creeping up the other side of the mountain.

"Dude, what did I miss?" asked Stoke. "That thing takes foreva," he motioned to the T-bar.

"Perhaps you should have stopped your run and taken part in the meeting instead of wanting a quick summary at the end, when you were ready, Stoke," said Jen vehemently.

As the whole group was standing together chatting, there was a general beeping sound, like an old-school beeper. Everyone began looking around, searching for the origin of the sound.

"Where is that coming from?" wondered Margit, looking around at herself and the closest athletes.

"Stoke, dude, it's coming from you, buddy," said Jaysen matter-of-factly.

"Me?" he said, lifting his hands up and down, looking around endlessly.

"Check your patch," stated Jen.

Stoke pushed back his puffy jacket. On the hoodie underneath, sticking to his arm, the clear patch was emanating the beeping sound. The display was divided into two options: Green said Talk, and red said Decline. Stoke stood there amazed at the flashing green and red lights on his translucent patch. The beeping sound persisted.

"ANSWER IT!" yelled Jen.

Stoke pressed the green side. "Yeeeah."

The voice emanating from the patch was familiar. "Mr. Townsend."

"It's Liew!" announced Stoke to the others, pointing to his patch.

"Who else is it going to be?" answered Pappie, snickering to Ramon, who laughed back.

"I don't mean to bother you in the middle of your workout," continued Liew, "but I need to inform you that in a little over an hour we will be heading out for your snowboarding event."

"FINALLY!" breathlessly answered Stoke. "I've been waiting forrrevvveraaa."

"Come on man, you're only the *third* person to go," snapped Jaysen, not so amused.

"Could you please meet me in over an hour, at the small shuttle entrance? You know where that is?"

"Yeah, easy-peasy, Liew, my man," happily finished Stoke.

"Thank you. I started a countdown on your patch as a reminder."

"Cool…" said Stoke watching as a small digital clock appeared on his patch and began a sixty-five-minute countdown. "I'll have just enough time."

"Time for what?" questioned Jen, but she got no answer from Stoke.

As Stoke reached down, about to press "End," he suddenly yelled. "Wait, Liew… Has this patch thingy been listening in on everything we are doing?"

"No, Mr. Townsend, that would be an invasion of your privacy, and against the contract you signed. It works like a mobile phone. You have to accept the "call" before I can hear you."

"Oh, phew…" said Stoke looking around at the group who were still listening. At this point it was more like a conference call, than anything else. "Can I call you? *Or* can I call another member of the team from this thing?"

Liew paused for a moment. "Yes, you can," he answered, with an inch of hesitation in his voice, "but I encourage you to do so only if the call is of the highest priority, like this one."

"High priority got it. Awesome!"

"See you in a little over an hour. Please, do not be late, Mr. Townsend." Liew hung up the call, and the patch went back to its normal translucence, but for Stoke's playlist of music.

Without a moment's hesitation, Stoke immediately pressed the patch and said, "Call, Amy."

A beeping sound emanated from across the gathered circle, on Amy's bare arm. She looked down at the flashing lights of her patch. It was stuck to goose bumps, as she shivered in her summer outfit amid the snowstorm.

"Aren't you going to answer it?" asked Stoke.

Amy just stood still waiting for a long moment. "Stoke, I am five feet away from you."

"Still calling…" answered Stoke, ignoring her.

"Stoke, please ask yourself," interjected Jen, "is *THIS* a high priority call?"

"Yup," came the quick retort from Stoke. "Checking my equipment."

After another long pause, and a deep eye roll, Amy finally touched the green "Talk" button.

"See, now we can talk, anytime," declared Stoke with a wide grin on his face, his voice echoed across the circle in stereo.

Amy simply pressed the red END button without a word.

"All right, Stoke, you better get ready. Liew said you have about an hour," hinted Ramon, pointing toward the Snow Room exit. "Time to go."

"Yeah, got to jam." Stoke quickly snapped his boots off the snowboard, "Get it… JAM!" He winked then smiled, but no one flinched at his stupid, not-so-witty quip of his name. He zoomed toward the Snow Room door. "Peace." He said as he held up the universal two finger 'Peace' hand sign.

"Lord help me, that boy!" said Jen when Stoke left the room.

"Little humans," answered Ramon trying to hide his amusement.

"I vote to adjourn the first All-Human Meeting of Team Earth. I'm freezing," proclaimed Ari, who was in even less appropriate winter clothes than Amy. She had on a wet bikini top and wetsuit rolled down to her waist. "On grounds of the weather."

"Agreed," said most members of the group, including the twins in unison, who were holding onto each other to keep warm. Yosi was in a leotard, Amy in shorts, Manny in a one-piece swimsuit, Pappie in tight cycling shorts, and Sito in shorts and shirt worn for sport climbing. They were all dressed for summer sports.

"Yeah, next time let's meet in our pool room, or someplace warm. This is ridiculous," balked Josie.

"My toes are blue!" shouted Jodie.

"That's your toenail polish!" retorted Josie.

"No, around the nail polish!" finished Jodie, "It's blue!" The girls promptly headed for the Snow Room door.

"So are mine," stated Amy, wiggling her cold toes and feet in her flip-flops. She walked out directly behind the twins.

"Human meeting adjourned," finished Ramon, though half the humans were already gone. Ramon himself was in the tight one-piece worn by most bobsledders. But he was used to being cold. Most of these other Olympians lived and competed in warm weather only. He promised himself, the next time he would do a better job picking a location for their Human Meeting.

*   *   *

Stoke was in his bathroom next to the sink when he heard a familiar voice emanating from his bedroom. "Dude…." said the voice, slowly dragging out the word as though it were a paragraph. It wasn't another member of Team Earth at the door, or Liew from his patch. Stoke knew the voice, but he was a little confused as to why it was coming from his bedroom.

"Dude…" stated the voice again, only this time the word was held on long enough to be a sentence.

Stoke popped his head out of the bathroom door, wearing a shower cap. Stoke half expected the person to be sitting on the edge of his bed. Instead, his entire wall was filled with the image of one of the most famous snowboarders that had ever existed. He had aged in the previous decades—his hair wasn't the flaming color of his youth but was lighter with silver streaks along the temples. There was still a boyish mischievous sparkle in his eyes, even though the wrinkles around them claimed a few more years. His smile was as wide as the day he won gold in his third Olympic Games, way back in the day. He emanated joy, pride, and calm as he looked straight at his young prodigy, the future of their sport.

"Dude!" Stoke yelled in a quick sharp voice full of wonder. He felt joy, just seeing the familiar face on the screen taking up one side of his whole bedroom. Translation: (What are YOU doing here?)

"Duuuuuude," retorted the man on the wall, holding onto the U sound for an unuuuusually long time. Translation: (What are you up to, my brah? What up?)

"D....u....d....e" (The stuff I've seen here is cra-cra exciting, man. You wouldn't believe it.)

"But, Dude?" continued Stoke quizzically. (Why are you here now?)

"D-u-d-e." stated the man, understating the seriousness of the tone. (I'm here for a reason. This is important stuff.)

"D! U! D! E!" answered Stoke, pleadingly. (I'm one of the first humans to be on a spaceship. Not any old spaceship but all of them combined. It's super righteous, man.)

"Dudeee," countered the man. (I know... but you need to listen.)

"Dudddddddde." (And there is this whole planet just for snow events. A WHOLE SNOWY PLANET!)

"DUDE!" sharply finished the man. (Stoke, it's time to hush up. I have to talk, serious time.)

A single word often has a lot of meanings.

Stoke pushed aside the pile of stuff on the messy bed and sat down at attention.

"Stoke, my man," started the man on the wall. "It's time."

The young snowboarder nodded his head in acknowledgment.

"We have worked together and hung together for a long time. So, I'm not here to lecture you on all the things you can't do."

Stoke remained silent.

"I'm going to tell you all the things you *can* do."

"Word!" answered Stoke.

"First, you can do anything you put your mind to. Finish."

Stoke nodded in silent agreement.

"All you need to do is focus on the task ahead. Imagine yourself putting in the most righteous run in all of the history of Humanity."

"Second," continued the man. "This is *not* the time to try anything new. Go with what you know!"

Stoke nodded. He knew exactly what the man was talking about. In the 2034 Winter Olympic Games, he had almost lost the gold medal because he tried his new trick on his second of three runs, the half-baked chicken-salami-Italian sub with a twist (he made up the name, piling on previous names to his new one). It nearly ended his Olympics. The lip of his snowboard caught the side of the pipe and he flipped sideways, crashing hard to the bottom, breaking his nose, and bruising a rib. Luckily, they patched him up and he stuck to his well-trained run and won the gold in the halfpipe event. Afterwards, it took him almost three months to fully heal.

"No chicken-salami-Italian subs with a twist," Stoke replied to the man.

"Third,"

"Oh, come on man… *THREE!*" Stoke griped to the wall.

"I know you hate three's but there's no choice. You need to listen to Ambassador Liew. I feel he's a sincere, righteous soul and has your best interest at heart." The man for the first time took on a stern and adult posture and voice. "Whatever he says, you do. Got it?" The man pointed directly at Stoke, his finger looming large in the viewscreen.

"Fine… fine…" answered Stoke half-heartedly.

"I know deep in my heart you can do this. I have never seen a snowboarder who is more gifted than you. You have all the instructional wisdom I can offer. You have an instinctual reaction with the board. I know whatever the run, however the snow, you can adapt and 'Be One with the Board.'" The man bowed his head, hands in praying position.

"I am so proud of you, Dude, my heart is swelling with love, gratitude, and good wishes from Earth, and for this chance you have been given. It is the game of a lifetime."

Stoke smiled.

"On the powder, be chill like fungi!" urged the man on the wall.

"Go out there and kill it. If it's pipe, slopestyle, or whatever that mountain may be, you get on that board and own it. It's your snow."

"Thanks Coach!" responded Stoke.

"And…" Stoke's coach stared at someone off camera for a second. "Your mom says hi." He leaned into the camera. "She thinks you're in the Alps BTW."

Stoke's patch beeped—the hour was almost up. "OK! I've got to go finish my rockin' hair," he waved bye to his coach and ran back into the bathroom.

After waiting at the designated spot, Jen and Ramon were standing patiently next to Liew. Stoke was running down the hallway, his patch beeping loudly like an old school alarm clock. You could hear him coming a mile away. "I'm running," he bellowed.

"Dear Lord! What did you do to your hair?" called Jen as he ran up.

"Getting ready for my 'dominance.'"

Jen quickly turned to Liew, "I thought you said there was nothing bad stashed in his room?"

"And there isn't, Mrs. Washington Lee. Hair dye doesn't count," answered Liew.

"I think it looks good!" said Ramon with a slight chuckle. "We can easily spot you in the snow now."

Stoke's hair was still wet but it was now dyed, bright red along the hairline, white a little further up, and bold blue at the tips.

"It's coolio, Jen," said Stoke combing, his fingers through his long shoulder length hair. "It's the American flag colors."

"I guessed that." She answered snidely, "I'm American, too, Stoke. Would you like me or Ramon to come with you to the start of your event?"

"Nah, I'm good!" He answered more referring to his hair than the actual question at hand. He stared at the tips of the dye job. "I think my hair has some split ends."

"Yup," she said, shaking her head. "I leave you alone for one hour."

"He will be fine, Jen," retorted Ramon, who was still trying but barely suppressing his hysterical laughter.

"If he is OK with it," Jen shrugged, having had it with his shenanigans. "We just wanted to give him, and all the younger ones, the option of human representation at the beginning of their events."

"Very thoughtful of you Mrs. Washington Lee. I will remind the other contestants of that option when it is their turn."

"You'll be at the finish line, right?" asked Stoke.

Ramon turned to Liew, waiting for the answer.

"I think it is an established trend at this point that the whole team, or whomever wants to join, has the option of cheering you on at the finish line of your event," answered the Ambassador.

Jen looked down at her attire. "Then perhaps I should dress a little more warmly, assuming this one isn't in space again."

"No, it's not," smiled Liew, but not really giving any other definitive answer. There was always a remote possibility they could end up on the first rocky planet for all they knew. Anything seemed to be possible at the Universe Olympic Games.

Liew turned to Ramon, who still had the largest grin on his face. "May I look to you to remind the other athletes of that fact, Ramon? We wouldn't want Josie, and Jodie to dress inappropriately for the cold weather, and get blue toes again."

"Yah, OK." Ramon was momentarily confused as to how Liew knew that fact. It was supposed to be a "private" Human Meeting. He wasn't on the mountaintop or anywhere near the workout arena. Maybe he spied on them? But that didn't seem to follow with the code of ethics Liew had for himself or the rest of the team. The contract didn't specify what the limitations were on privacy for the people of planet Earth. He reminded himself to ask Liew how he knew that random fact at a later time.

"Are you ready, Mr. Townsend?" Liew looked down at the top of Stoke's tri-colored head.

"Yup, let's roll! It's Snow Time."

Chapter 10

Snow Time

The small shuttle landed on the top of a large mountain somewhere on the snow planet. It wasn't exactly the tippy-top, but close enough—the zenith was above them. They stood on a plateau just beneath the peak. It had enough room for the small shuttle, Liew, and Stoke.

"OK, Liew, talk to me," said Stoke to the only other person on the mountain, quickly putting on his snow gear and jamming his snowboard upright in the snow.

"Mr. Townsend, for your event, you have to make it down the mountain."

"Easy enough," said Stoke, who had traversed far more dangerous and edgy terrain than the one below him. His scariest, to date, was on a higher peak in the Himalayas. That time, he had to start by jumping out of a helicopter. The snow was a bit too powdery, and he caused a mini-avalanche as he raced down the side of the mountain. But it was all worth it—the visuals made for the perfect viral endorsement for some energy drink sponsor or some such nonsense. This mountainside looked like beginner blue-green difficulty, by comparison.

"Here are your goggles."

Stoke grabbed them from Liew's hand and put them on.

"You will notice a new digital display we put on the Plexiglas."

"I don't see it," said Stoke shaking his head all around.

"Look for the large green circle markers in the distance."

Stoke stared down the mountain. A bright pair of green circles was directly ahead of him, almost like what mogul skiers used in their course.

"Got it."

"You have to go through each of those markers until you reach the finish line at the bottom of the course, or you will be disqualified from your event."

"Easy-peasy, Liew."

"No matter where they are."

"No problem, bro. Looks easy enough." Stoke perused the slope and snow that seemed a decent descent angle and snow gradient. There weren't too many rocks or obstacles down the course, and the green markers were only fifty feet below. Honestly, it looked like an easier course than what he and Margit were using in the Snow Room this morning.

"Mr. Townsend let me caution you slightly. This is not a 'kiddie' course."

"So weirdo—I was just thinking that!"

"Let me remind you, please. No chicken-salami-Italian subs today. You are in uncharted territory here and it is a master-level, so you may want to…"

"Dude, *STOP*. I got this!" stated Stoke sharply, cutting Liew off. He put in his ear buds and activated his 'Jelly Jam' playlist on the patch.

"Very well, Mr. Townsend." Liew remained silent for a minute, and then looked down at the patch on his own sleeve with a countdown clock. "Please prepare yourself."

Stoke adjusted his goggles and strapped his boots into the bindings on his snowboard. Once on his board, he swayed back and forth testing the firm snow. It had a nice feel to it, not too hard, not too soft. He had a good ride ahead of him, one he was going to easily win.

A sequential beeping sound came from above.

Stoke pressed play and the first song started playing in his ear buds. It was classic hard rock all the way.

"Good luck, Mr. Townsend. In three, two, one." The loud elephant honking sound blared from above. "Go."

Stoke without hesitation, took off down the mountain, leaving Liew in a cloud of snow behind.

In a matter of seconds, he zoomed down the mountain and sailed through his first pair of circular green markers. As soon as he passed by them, they flashed.

"Awesome," shouted Stoke not only for himself, but for the entire mountain to hear, and perhaps Liew as well. "This is going to be easy-peasy."

Stoke found it borderline insulting that Liew was trying to baby him before his event. He had Liew, Jen, Ramon, even his coach talking down to him like a stupid kid, and it felt like everyone was babying him. He was on top of the world. Literally, on the top of a mountain on a world that was all snow. Life couldn't be better. What could possibly go wrong? Unlike Amy and Oni, and he meant no offense—they were just girls—but *HE* was about to show Team Earth how to win their first gold.

Up ahead, another fifty feet away, was the next set of green markers.

"Boom!" he shouted as he swiftly glided through the green circle.

He wondered if there was a time trial as well to his event. Liew had only mentioned making it to the bottom, which was easy enough. But if he made it in record time as well, would there be an extra special gold in it for him?

The next gate appeared slightly off the ground in the air a few feet up, with a small ramp leading up to it. Without even thinking, he easily jumped through the flashing gate.

It was a neophyte course. Stoke was jumping through this type of stuff at five years old. He was beginning to wonder if they really needed Earth's gold medalist for this course. They could have brought in a tenth or eleventh place snowboarder for this event and they probably would have still won.

With every gate down the mountain, the green circle was slightly higher off the ground and the ramp before it just a smidge higher to effortlessly make it through with no problem.

To make it fun for himself—he was bored stiff at this point—as the progression of gates continued, Stoke started to add in a few moves with each gate. The first was to grab the edge of his board, as he flew through the green gates, then next he took off switch backside flat spinning, ending each jump with a *STOMP*.

The fifteenth gate was taipan grab double backside rodeo fourteen-forty.

By the sixteenth gate he was doing complete flips with a switchback triple, two flips landing switch.

The seventeenth was particularly high and the ramp leading up to it was what he needed to jump properly through the gate. He crouched down, picked up more speed, doing a backside quad cork 1800 through the mid-air gate. His body cleared the gate sideways. It was tremendous.

"STOKED!" he howled.

The terrain on the mountain suddenly changed. He passed through a few gates strategically placed on the ground to help guide the way through a low cloud and around the mountain. The wide-open course suddenly gave way to cliffs, rocks, and crevasses in the mountain. It was edgy and dicey.

The next gate was on the other side of a tiny crevasse. A slight up-slope preceded it.

Stoke easily glided over the gap, making it through the gate that flashed when he completed it.

The next gate down the mountain was a little further back, with the fissure a little wider. And the ramp climbing up the side of the mountain, was like the side of a Half-Pipe.

Stoke glided up the clear-cut Pipe, jumped over the crevasse, and completed the gate without a second thought. This was an afternoon pre-workout exercise for him. Deep down, there was a little embarrassment for the Universe Olympic Committee that they thought this was going to be worthy of putting in the Universe Olympics, or in any Olympics.

The next obstacle was not only one but two gates—one was located halfway up the Pipe and also one was on the other side of an even wider crevasse.

Things were getting a little tricky but Stoke knew that he was perfectly capable of doing this. This was no more difficult than his usual moves; he even rigged stuff like this for himself at home.

When those gates were completed with a moderate effort, he glanced down the course. What he saw took his breath away.

Up ahead was a full barrel roll: Kind of what you'd imagine in a cartoon with the Road Runner. With three gates in total, it was a living embodiment of the corkscrew. He hated threes. The first gate was halfway up the side of the mountain, the next was underneath the upside of the barrel, and the final gate was on the other side of the widest crevasse yet. The giant ravine was too wide for him to jump over without completing the corkscrew and he had to clear all the gates, or he'd be disqualified. The green circle dangling in mid-air on the underside of the corkscrew was his problem. The only way across was up and through ALL the gates.

Stoke crouched down, trying to gain a little more speed, almost like a surfer taking on a wave in front of him.

"You can hang ten, dude." Stoke said reassuringly to himself.

Before he could finish the words, his greatest challenge was under foot. In a squatting position, he sailed up the barrel ramp running up the side of the mountain. He dipped his shoulder with the wall. He continued naturally turning upside down, clearing the gate at the crest of the barrel. Stoke barely had enough momentum and caught a little too much air as he passed the deep crevasse. His eyes momentarily caught sight of the endless dark abyss below him. His instinct was to close his eyes, but he couldn't. He needed to complete the gate on the other side.

It was the *ultimate*, as he caught the other side of the barrel and barely whooshed through the last gate.

"Whew!" Stoke yelled, but he had little time to celebrate. Another barrel roll was only a few hundred feet ahead of him. This one was even larger and if his eyes weren't deceiving him, instead of white snow beyond it, it looked like there was another barrel roll there, as well.

His stomach turned for a moment. There was no trick in his book to make it up and around safely to the other side while hitting the green gates. It was going to have to be old-fashioned centrifugal force that helped him clear the next two rolls. And if he was being honest, he wasn't sure if he could do it; he was barely one hundred and forty pounds, wet.

Stoke bent his knees as far down as they could go to speed like a bullet. He gained momentum, praying there would be enough energy to make it successfully through two-barrel rolls.

"Here we go," he said with an edge to his voice.

The first barrel was the largest one yet, at least three stories tall. Stoke made it up and around over the deep crevasse, passing through the gates, eyeing the hollow chasm below to the opposite side of the barrel. It was a little like his favorite roller coaster, only he was the coaster.

The second barrel was slightly smaller than the first. It was tightly coiled together like a slinky. He hardly picked up any speed between the corkscrews and caught a bit too much air around the top.

He missed a portion of the back side, and barely passed through the last green gate at the bottom of the second roll.

"Yeah!" hollered Stoke.

Making it through was glorious. He had done the impossible. No snowboarder had ever gone up and around two-barrel rolls before. He wondered what new name he should give what he just accomplished. 'Double brew' was lingering in his mind.

After gliding over a few hundred feet of snow ahead of him, he couldn't believe what he saw around an outcropping of rock. Again, it was endless barrel rolls. Stoke guessed there were at least three. They just kept going on and on, creating an optical illusion. It was the ultimate corkscrew.

"I *hate* three's," Stoke screamed. Bad things always came to him in threes, and this was the worst.

Like every kid, he imagined taking a swing on a swing set and doing a full circle around the bar. Stoke had tried it once as a kid. He didn't have enough weight and speed to make it all the way around. He fell on the bar and broke a rib. But there would be no hitting the bar this time. If he didn't have enough momentum behind him, he would simply fall down into a deep crevasse, never to be found again.

He readied himself for what seemed an impossible feat: three-barrel rolls in a row. It was beyond human capability. Stoke took in a deep breath, tried to gain even more speed down the mountain because up ahead was the ultimate corkscrew. He just hoped he wouldn't get screwed. The mountain was crazy. The long "O" in front of him, endless crevasses, and twists mirrored his feelings inside.

The first barrel roll was enormous—much bigger than the previous two. It was the mouth of the monster. Stoke zipped through the first gate, up and around to the second, skimming along the apex. He had yet to formally take physics in school, but he soon innately realized the downward rotation helped him gain enough speed to quickly go up and through the smaller second barrel roll. Hitting his gates, he made it to the final dreaded third roll.

He lost a lot of momentum in the second roll, so he crouched down in the short interval between the second and the third, praying it was enough to help him gain velocity without falling into the precipice.

The third barrel was the smallest of the three, thank God. As he scaled up and around, he just barely hit the gate at the top, lost all momentum, stopped for a split second and fell…

…down.

In retrospect, Stoke would tell reporters how he fell down the back side of the barrel, like when he was a kid, but this time, he hadn't hit the bar on the top of the swing set. He knew his only option was to extend his body and board—hopefully some part of it would make it through the final gate at the bottom of the third barrel.

Officially, Stoke's snowboard and ankle fell through the last gate as he came crashing down. It took all his dexterity, like a cat, to swing his full body around to land. His snowboard stomped on the ground. His shirt flew out of his pants, blinding him for a moment; the fabric had caught the lip of the crevasse that divided the barrel.

Once Stoke stopped on the ground, he took a quick moment, regained his stance, and continued on. Just as suddenly as the corkscrews began, the spirals ended. A bright open mountainside lay out ahead of him.

Stoke cheered, "That turnt!"

It was either gravity, luck, or a combination of both, that got him through the barrel stage of his event. Stoke had a passing moment of fear for what was next—he didn't have four-barrel rolls in him, and neither did his stomach.

The Olympic Flame sun shined above, the snow was bright and soft, and the incline of the mountain changed. It wasn't too steep or overly rocky. A green gate beckoned further down the course, seemingly clear of crazy obstacles.

Stoke surveyed the terrain, but picked up speed, in case there was another, unforeseen challenge ahead.

Hunching down in his aerodynamic position, Stoke felt with each passing minute that perhaps the worst was behind him.

The gates zigzagged to the left and right down the mountain, but nothing was out of the ordinary, which worried him even more at this point. Nothing meant something.

Stoke switched around to glance back up the mountain. It was colossal. The top part, where he started, was barely visible, still in the clouds. Only by being far down below, almost at the bottom, did it become apparent to him how large the mountain was in relation to others. It truly could have been one of the highest elevations he ever boarded.

When he turned back around, something caught his eye to the right. He quickly swerved through the next gate and glanced down the course, to see how far he had until the next gate. Far off to his right, incoming at a rapid pace a large snowball was hurtling down. He slightly veered over to get a better look. The snowball, oddly enough, got closer as well. Given the background, it was hard to tell its exact dimensions, but as it got closer, he realized it was big—at least six feet long and five feet high. And it wasn't a perfectly round snowball either. It was oblong, like a bullet.

Stoke's curiosity got the better of him, he got a little closer, still eyeing his next gate, when the white snowball suddenly changed. It opened a large black eye.

"Whoa!" he yelled and jumped a little as the snowball pulled out from a tucked position. Like a seal, its wings or fins had been digging into the snow, mushing itself along. The snowball turned its full head to reveal a bright orange and black beak, and legs appeared from the back of the ball. So, it wasn't a snowball after all. It was a furry creature.

"WHOOOOOOOOOA!" laughed Stoke, even more thrilled. He realized he was racing what looked like a giant six-foot penguin that was on its belly. Almost like a person would use poles skiing, his competitor was using its short wings and feet to steer.

"DUUUUUUUDE!" Stoke screamed. He finally met his competitor. This thing was fast too. With a push of its fins in the snow, he gained an inch on Stoke.

The black eye never took its stare off Stoke. He wasn't sure what to do, and the only thing that came to his mind was simple. Stoke held up his hand waving.

"Peace!"

A clattering sound came from its beak in response, then it quickly tucked its head back in position. Creating the bullet shape again, and using its feet to steer away from Stoke, the huge creature raced ahead.

The proverbial foot race had begun.

After giving his competitor a friendly wave and quickly swerving left to pass through his latest gate, Stoke knew what he had to do. He hunched down close to the ground, making himself into a ball as well. Using all the skills he could think of, he gained on the snowball.

They went up and over a mogul, never out of each other's sight. Jumping up and over around the mounds of snow, occasionally passing through the mandatory gates. The snowball followed in perfect unison. One after the other, it was a true race. Each taking a slight advance with a move or cut down the mountain. Back and forth, up and over, a jump here, a swerve there, they were equally matched.

Neck and neck, they battled down the mountain. Their speed was tremendous. Stoke's legs began shaking. He glanced down below and saw the final gates leading to the bottom of the mountain. He could have taken the easy turn left. But Stoke saw an excellent two-fer opportunity.

There was a ledge out ahead. He could go over it, gaining in time and distance versus swerving to the left around the rock. Stoke also wanted to show that snowball what humans could do, and up ahead was his opportunity. The gate, far below the mountain, was to the left of a slight outcropping of rock. If Stoke played his cards right, he could do his righteous chicken-salami-Italian sub move. The snowball would be *uber* impressed since it only seemed to use its belly as a board. Stoke doubted if his snowball buddy could jump or flip in the air like humans—you needed a board for that. And then the snowball would want to tell his other snowy friends about how cool that Earthling was while winning the gold medal. So not only was Stoke going to win the race, but he would also put on a show.

The opportunity was upon him. Stoke swerved to the right, went up the slight bump and then over-executed the most perfect chicken-salami-Italian sub in the history of history. And to add a little magic to it, he Taipan-grabbed the edge of his board between the bindings. On Earth, they would have given him a perfect ten for such advanced board work. He landed on the softest powder, so the landing was extra cushioned.

Stoke quickly made his way out of the landing in deep, loose snow, then headed down to the left and through the next gate. At this point he lost sight of the snowball. The mountain had divided, and he was lucky to get the move in when he did, but he wasn't sure if Mr. Snowball caught sight of his perfection.

As he zoomed through his next gate, he turned around because he heard something. The spot where he had landed from the magnificent chicken-salami-Italian sub wasn't there anymore. The snow, and everything with it, had started piling up and moving down the mountain.

He reminded himself that this often happened. That time he was dropped by the helicopter, it started a mini-slide, but he usually was well past the accumulation of snow and out of the way, or a bit of rock stopped the flow.

The next gate was upon Stoke before he realized it. At these high speeds, he was more alpine skiing than snowboarding at this point.

When he glanced back again, he was surprised at what he saw. Not only was the snow accumulation growing, it was gaining speed. What was once a bunch of fluff now was becoming a wave. It worried Stoke an inch. He peered down the mountain at the mile-long path of gates in front of him. The glowing green circles extended far below him, there was nothing that would stop the flow of snow from engulfing him. His gut, with his knowledge of snow, knew what to do: He needed to deviate far off to the left, out of the way. Unfortunately, the only way to win the contest was directly below him.

As Stoke raced at full speed down, he finally spotted the finish line. It was far in the distance. The last green glowing gate was followed by a glowing red line, after a straight-away. Behind the finish line were what looked like tiny black rocks.

Stoke turned back to glimpse the wave of snow. It was bigger and catching up with him as he sailed through the next green gate. The gates now were in a zigzag pattern down the mountain, which was very, very bad. Every time he turned, he'd lose speed, and the… avalanche, there he said it, was catching up to him. Stoke needed every second, every inch, every advantage, to stay in front of the wave of snow. Liew had said he couldn't skip a gate, or he'd be disqualified, but there were bigger problems at hand; disqualification was the least of his worries.

Stoke turned sharply to his right to swiftly clear his next gate, and the snow wave was much closer than he thought. And he knew it too. The noise of the snow wave was gaining on him—it was a roar that couldn't be ignored.

Side to side, he swooshed through the green gates. Foot-by-foot, the avalanche caught up to him and accumulated more snow. Stoke's heart sank. He regretted hot-dogging off that cliff outcropping. It was catching up to him.

Back and forth he went, left, then right, through the mile of gates. Stoke was so worried about what was behind him, that he never took the time to study what was in front of him. The long red banner finish line looked just like what it would be at home. He was zipping toward the long red banner as fast as was humanly possible.

He quickly peeked behind at the avalanche. It was all but upon him. As the roaring mass rolled, it gained more and more snow. It had become a tsunami of snow behind him, and it wasn't just made of the fine fluffy snow anymore. It had accumulated hard snow chunks, bits of boulders, and rocks. It was now a ten-foot-tall wall of cement coming for him.

At that moment, he decided to stop going through the gates, disqualification be damned. Ironically, he realized the next green gate was actually directly ahead. In fact, the rest of the gates were in a perfectly straight line to the finish.

Stoke crouched down in a ball, trying to gain speed, using aerodynamics in his favor. He gained some speed, but not enough to escape the avalanche. It was right behind him and towered a story over him. He could no longer hear his inspiration music playlist anymore—the only sound in his ears was that of crushing snow at high velocity.

He glanced back, and the snow wave was only twenty feet or so in his wake. His heart sank with the understanding, the acknowledgement, that he wasn't winning this physics game or any game.

Stoke was practically in a ball when he finally assessed how far away the finish banner was in front of him. As he reached the bottom of the mountain, he recognized what was immediately behind the finish line—it wasn't rocks, it was something else.

"Oh, DUUDE NO!" yelled Stoke, but to no avail. The avalanche muted all other sounds.

He grasped that what he had assumed was a group of dark rocks from high above, was actually something worse. Right behind the finish line—just a mere few feet behind, in fact—all of Team Earth huddled together wearing dark jackets. He had totally forgotten about the request he made—to have the entire team congratulate him. Standing in the middle of the group, he could make out Amy and the twins.

He was heading straight toward them, which also meant the avalanche was too. A sob reached his heart and made its way up to his mouth.

"DUDE!" he yelled in a panic, "Get out of the way!" He motioned slightly for them to get out of the way. The gesture was lost amid the snow and rubble passing his head. Stoke knew, as bits of the avalanche passed around him, that not only did he kill himself, but he was also about to kill all of Team Earth and their Ambassador. He wasn't bringing them their first win of the Universe Olympics; he was bringing them the grim reaper.

He hit the last flat straight-away right before the finish line. He knew it was the death knell. He wasn't gaining enough speed; he was losing it. The avalanche continued its march and it finally caught up with him.

A cry, unlike anything he had ever heard before, came out of his mouth and took over his soul as the wall of white overtook his whole body.

*   *   *

A bright light slowly came into view. It was an orange-yellow sun setting along a lovely white beach. The waves of a blue-green sea crashed against the sand. The light refracted from the sunlight made a momentary rainbow in the spray of a splashing wave.

Stoke, lash by lash, slowly opened his eyes. He knew he had died and gone to heaven, which looked a lot like the Hawaiian coast. It was a bit of a surprise because it wasn't the first place he thought of when he imagined what heaven would look like. The first place probably would have been the mountains of Colorado.

"Mr. Townsend."

Stoke heard his name spoken. He wasn't sure if it was God or perhaps a spirit that had helped guide him to the Other Side.

"Mr. Townsend," the voice said sternly and a little louder.

The waves crashed again. He could see a sandpiper running up and down the sand, coming and going to avoid the wave. Stoke wasn't sure if every person started their journey to the Other Side along Hawaii's Big Island, but it did provide him with the sense of peace that he had always imagined heaven would bring.

"STOKE!" A female voice yelled. It wasn't a voice he would have associated with heaven. In fact, it reminded him of that other place he was afraid he'd go after death. Maybe he was denied entry into heaven? Was this Purgatory? Or the other place…?

"Mr. Townsend. Please, gently turn your head forward."

"Where am I?" When Stoke spoke, he realized his mouth and nose were muzzled. "If this is heaven, why am I hearing Jen? Am I in the other place?"

"Dear Lord, child."

Stoke opened his eyes wider, focusing further than just his lashes, slowly turning his head.

Standing directly in front of him was Ambassador Liew. Behind Liew, the entire team from Earth hovered anxiously.

"Did I kill you all? Are you here too? Did we die?"

"No, Mr. Townsend."

Stoke heard his muffled voice and reached up to remove a clear mask that was covering his mouth and nose.

"Leave that on, Mr. Townsend. It's helping you breathe."

"Where am I?" asked Stoke again, still struggling with the fact that he was seeing the entire Team, wearing snow jackets and pants, standing in front of a beautiful beach.

"This is the Recovery Room."

"Dude, Liew, you have to work on your words." Stoke mumbled, and then tried to sit up but couldn't. "This is H-E-A-V-E-N."

"No, Stoke," said Jen firmly. "You lay back down!"

"Mr. Townsend, please lay down. We aren't done with the initial analysis."

Stoke leaned back onto the bed.

"You aren't dead," continued Liew while also touching features on the 3-D hologram scan of his body on the wall panel. "You are on Team Earth's spaceship participating at the Universe Olympics."

"Oh yeah…"

"You have not completed your full recovery, and you need to remain still and within the light around the Recovery Chair."

"Yeah, you're nowhere near it fixed, Buster," retorted Jen. "All you did was regain consciousness. You're in here for a while."

Stoke momentarily welled up with anger at her barking orders, but then another thought washed over him. He suddenly remembered his last moments, racing the snow avalanche and the team directly in its path.

"Jen, I thought I killed you."

"Lord, no," chuckled Jen. "You are stuck with me for a while. At least until the end of the games, Buster."

"Liew, how did you all survive the avalanche on Claw-Bear? I named the snow planet, FYI."

"Well, Mr. Townsend, that's a long story. First, let's allow the whole team to return to their rooms to change out of their snowsuits. They all wanted to make sure you woke up." Liew motioned to the soggy crowd. Snow melted off their puffy clothing in the heat of the room. "My guess is they didn't believe me."

"Oh, we did, Ambassador," finished Ramon. "Let's call it a little human thing. Making sure each of us *survives* the games."

"Mr. Townsend will make a full recovery, in time, I promise. No human being will die under my watch, Mr. Stead," answered Liew diplomatically. "Now, please. Everyone return to your daily practices and routines. I will remain here for a while and meet you all at dinner in about an hour. Mr. Townsend will be here overnight."

"Really?" asked Stoke.

"At the very least kiddo," answered Ramon. "It was *BAD*."

Most of the team started to exit the Recovery Room, not saying much.

"You coming?" wondered Ramon, leaning in.

"Nope," replied Jen, taking off her puffy black jacket. "Little humans."

Ramon nodded his head, patted her shoulder, then left the room with the rest of the team. Amy gave a quick wave and smile to Stoke as she exited.

Jen wrapped her jacket around her waist and pulled up one of the two chairs. Liew returned his full attention to the wall and 3-D holographic scan of Stoke's body. Most of it was in red and flashing, especially the chest area. He was touching a blue area on the wall and dragging it over to Stoke's lungs.

"How's he doing?" asked Jen.

"Alive—and breathing," replied Liew with just an inch of relief in his voice.

"I wasn't breathing?" asked Stoke.

"No, Buster you weren't," answered Jen. "You inhaled too much snow."

"Why do you keep calling him Buster?" pondered Liew, never taking his eyes off Stoke's recovery.

"Yeah? What happened?" queried Stoke pleadingly. He tried to sit up a little in bed, but the head of the chair rose up, following his gesture.

Jen glanced over at Liew for permission. "Yes, tell him, but try not to agitate him too much, Mrs. Washington Lee. He still has a lot of healing ahead of him."

"And breathing," interrupted Stoke.

"...to do," finished Liew.

Stoke quickly returned his attention back to Jen. "We could watch it all. We were waiting at the bottom of the run. You just finished your eighteen-hundred-degree double half tip, roast Italian sandwich stir-fry, bobble till you topple, signature 'show off' move."

"*NOT* what it's called," added Stoke half rolling his eyes, half laughing.

"From that cliff, and we saw it begin..."

*   *   *

High up and halfway down the mountain, the team could see flicks of red, white and blue flash by in a blur as Stoke swerved in and out of rocky points.

"There he is!" shouted Amy, pointing up.

The group had gathered together in a cluster behind the finish line. It was difficult to see with the Olympic Flame sun reflecting off the snow-covered mountain. The sun was shining, creating a giant reflecting mirror on the snow. It was bright.

Only the skiers on the team had remembered to bring sunglasses.

"I can see him," shouted Eric, who was fortunate enough to be wearing a pair, but unfortunate enough to be nearsighted. "He's moving fast. Looks like something is moving next to him. A giant white fluffy snowball."

"That's his competition," explained Liew.

At that, the whole team stared up the mountain, trying to get a glimpse of what the other sentient life form looked like. But Stoke and the white fluffy ball had already disappeared behind an outcropping of rock.

Unexpectedly, Stoke burst over the edge of the cliff, upside down, and backwards. He was turning, twisting, rotating, and flipping all at the same time, while holding onto his snowboard through the air. The spectacle was impressive. They were witnessing one of the greatest moves known to 'snowboardom,'—the trick that almost cost Stoke the gold medal a few years ago at the Winter Olympics in China. This time, Stoke landed it perfectly in a soft patch of snow, well below the cliff. No one noticed the beginnings of loose snow that began to shift behind him.

Stoke continued his descent down the clear slope at a steep decline. All eyes were on him as he zipped back and forth through something that was invisible to the naked eye.

It took the team a while to recognize the gathering snow as it rushed down behind Stoke. Oddly enough, it was the surfer who spotted it first. She had an eye for waves.

"Oh my God!" yelled Ari. "The snow is starting to build… like a wave." She was forever looking to the horizon, calculating the movement of the water. A skilled eye could spot a good set of waves miles away.

"Or an avalanche," yelled Pappie.

"Oh no!" said Amy as she quickly turned around, "Liew, can you do anything?"

"Not yet, Ms. Ride. Not yet." Liew stared like a keen-eyed cat at Stoke, who was making his way in a zigzag formation down the final slope. Liew's stare was deep and sharp. With every zig Stoke made, the avalanche gained ground on one of their youngest. Liew feverishly began touching the patch on his shirt.

They stood horrified, as the snow went from a puffy white color to a darker brownish hue. As the force of the avalanche pulled up more and more snow, the deeper and darker the wave became, as the colors mixed in with dirt. It had gained momentum and its rolling thunder was audible to the team.

"Ambassador!" said Ramon worriedly.

Within seconds, the avalanche caught up to Stoke and engulfed him.

"LIEW!" screamed Jen. "HELP, STOKE!"

The wall didn't stop upon consuming the young snowboarder. The next victims would be the team, trapped directly in its path.

"Get back!" roared Liew. "Behind me." Liew quickly rolled out a long white mat in front of him. Every human scurried to clustered together tightly behind the Ambassador. The older men and women pushed the younger athletes toward the center of the circle, while they guarded the circumference of the group. The two largest men, Ramon and Dmitri, flanked Liew on his left and right side, and Yosi, the smallest and youngest, took dead center in the circle.

The roaring wall of ice and snow dashed toward them. All the girls, and a few of the guys, howled at the top of their lungs as it hit, their screams drowned out by the fury of the avalanche.

Stoke's finish line now served as a stopgap for the avalanche, creating an invisible bubble barrier around the team. The heavy wall of snow went up and around and past the team who instinctively had their heads down awaiting full impact.

Liew remained at a constant vigil, standing tall and watching the wall of snow for signs. He looked down at the panel on his arm and stepped forward, waiting.

The invisible wall literally spit out Stoke's broken body onto the ground. Plopping him down in the exact same position Liew had placed the long white mat.

In the madness of the snowstorm encircling the team, Liew gently flattened out Stoke's body and pressed a button on his arm panel. Stoke's body jumped from some type of electricity. Liew touched the panel again. Stoke's body jumped for a second time. Ramon and Jen watched as Liew for the third time tried to shock Stoke's heart to start beating again.

And just as quickly as it went by, the wall of snow abruptly stopped. The avalanche had passed. The sun began creeping through the flurries from the rushing snow.

Ramon stepped forward toward Liew and Stoke.

"Don't touch him!" snapped Liew, who crouched down, touching the sides of the mat. White light buttons appeared out of nowhere.

"Is he alive?" questioned Jen watching Liew at work. She half turned to the younger ones in the group, ready to force them not to look.

When the thunderous sound of the avalanche ceased, the team was huffing, puffing, and coughing from the remnant snow. They noticed they were no longer on the surface of the mountain, but eight feet below a new floor of snow. One by one, the stunned athletes realized that the protective bubble seemed to be gone. They watched Stoke's limp body on the ground and Liew hovering over him.

*   *   *

"*WOW!*" said Stoke happily, alive in the Recovery Room bed. "I don't remember any of that. Sounds like it was a close shave."

"Too close, Buster. Tooooo close," concluded Jen, eyes tearing up.

"Was it my jump that started the avalanche?"

"Yup," answered Jen. "Ari, saw it."

"You should have stayed on the designed course, Mr. Townsend," said Liew.

"What do you mean?" asked Jen, confused.

"Oh, I had circular gates to go through. I saw one far below and I kind of decided to take the alternate route, over the cliff to get down to it."

"To hot dog... child, I'd kill you, if you hadn't already basically died. Your body paid such a heavy price," answered Jen.

"Here I was thinking Amy and Oni didn't cut it, not winning."

"They fared much better than you," she sharply answered.

"Yeah, they did. Was I disqualified, Liew?" wondered Stoke.

"No, Mr. Townsend you didn't. You cleared every last gate, and surprisingly, you crossed the finish line."

"More like pushed over it..." scorned Jen.

"But unfortunately, you didn't win the heat," responded Liew.

"But you won *LIFE*, Stoke," countered Jen, raising an eyebrow. "You won life."

"Yeah, I'm not surprised that fuzzy white dude…"

"The Tonkken," interjected Liew.

"He was super-slick fast on his belly. Liew, he winked at me."

"Did *SHE*? Must have liked the new red, white, and blue hair," mused Liew. "But I must ask you to stop speaking, it's hindering your lung recovery."

"Jen…"

"I ain't going nowhere, Buster."

"Good." Stoke mouthed the words then smiled. He laid back staring at the Hawaiian shoreline, a.k.a. heaven. "You can stay in my heaven," he whispered as he dozed off to sleep.

Chapter 11

The Real Jungle

Margit knew exactly where to go. Curiosity had always gotten the best of her. While everyone was in their evening training sessions, she had let Ramon have the Snow Room to himself—not like he cared if she was there anyway—and she followed Liew after dinner. She knew the roundabout area where his room was located; but perhaps on giving it another thought, it wasn't his room. It could have been his bathroom, for all she knew. But it was the first place she could think of, because she wanted to try and speak with him alone.

She had followed Liew the night before last, down this hallway. The path was long and empty. It was a little creepy. She glanced back a few times, trying to orient herself to the last turn she made. The walls had no markings or discernable way for her to make a mental note on where and how long she was walking. She touched her patch and marked the time. She could at least calculate how long she had been walking, using her stride, and coming up with a rough estimate. It reminded her how big this ship was, and that they had only begun to scratch the surface on what lay within it. After a few minutes—and one hundred yards by her calculation—she found a pair of doors. They were the only set along the long hallway.

Margit knocked.

There wasn't an immediate answer.

She knocked again, louder, wondering if there was a possibility that he was still in the Recovery Room with Stoke, or back in the workout arena. This ship was so vast, the possibilities were endless. She thought for a moment and pulled back her shirt to reveal the clear patch on her skin. She touched it, about to call Liew, when the doors slid open.

"Ms. Housman," said Liew speaking in Norwegian.

Margit jumped. "Ambassador!"

"Hello, what can I do for you?"

"Sir, I'd like to speak with you for a moment." The sound of a very loud howler monkey came from inside the room. "Please…" She trailed off peeking around the side of Liew to catch sight of what she heard.

"What have you got in there?" she asked, full of both wonder and trepidation.

"You may come in, Ms. Housman, but only for a few minutes," said Liew as he stepped aside.

As soon as Margit crossed the threshold, she felt a difference in the room. She looked around at the wide space in wonder. It was nothing like what she expected. Part of her expected it to be the bridge of the spaceship, full of electronics and gadgetry. What lay in front of her was a perfectly designed living room. It was the most calming, serene, beautiful setting she had ever seen.

"Wow," she said, breathlessly.

Everything was made of wood. The high ceilings, floors, walls, and furniture were all made of a light brown wood. On the right was a long couch, with light green cushions, but it was big enough to accommodate for Liew's seven-and-a-half-foot height. A wood table, carved with an ornate geometric design, was surrounded by chairs of the same make. All this furniture was built into the wooden walls and floors, perfectly set below giant palatial windows.

"Would you like to sit down, Margit?" asked Liew, disrupting her slow meander through the room. Liew walked past two chairs facing each other, and a wooden table to the most curious sight of all. The room had only three walls—the fourth was missing. Instead of a wall, it opened to a large wooden balcony. There were no doors; he just crossed the room into the outside.

Margit passed what might have been a kitchen to her left. It was difficult to tell, but everything was out of the same wood, all carved out—the floor, walls, and ceiling. She walked out to the balcony and her breath was taken away.

"Oh my God! Liew!"

She scanned the outside. The balcony wasn't just a balcony. It was built into a large branch. The largest branch she had ever seen in her life. And the view was unfathomable to her.

They were sitting in the middle of the biggest forest she had ever seen. Unlike the trees of Earth, which were lucky to reach eighty feet, these trees were a thousand stories tall. The leaves on the branches were the size of city buses. As she looked down over the carved balcony, she realized they were halfway up the tree. At the roots, were a river and a small 100-meter waterfall that flowed off into the distance through the never-ending forest. A cockatoo-like bird sound could be heard far off. It returned Margit to the present.

She turned and smiled at Liew, "Just like the cafeteria."

Liew took a seat in one of the wood chairs in a sunbeam.

"This is Beiahisa, isn't it?"

Liew smiled, "Yes, this is my home planet." He leisurely sat back, taking a moment to stare at the view with her.

"And it's a... *jungle*," marveled Margit in a suspicious tone. "A real jungle."

"Of sorts, yes. Ms. Housman."

Margit sat down on the end of the overly large chair across from Liew. "I knew the jungle cafeteria was too bizarre. You purposely made the jungle to remind yourself of your home, didn't you?"

"Actually, no, Margit. My first intention, as I stated, was that the green foliage would bring a calming feeling to the team, but my secondary rationale was more personal."

Margit nodded, awaiting his selfish affirmation. "Which is…"

"I hope, one day, all of you will be able to travel to my home world and visit me. See my actual home." He motioned to his surroundings, which could only be called an apartment. "And meet my family and friends. It was my small way of helping humans adapt to a new planetary environment. Mine. And when you arrive, my home will feel a little like your home here on the ship. Hopefully, there won't be any discomfort or alienation."

Margit felt a slight pang of guilt in her heart at having projected such a negative intention on Liew. She was always very suspicious of people; she had to remember he wasn't a person, a human. All he was trying to do was help Humanity slowly get ready for the larger universe out there. It made her wonder what else Liew had done, in an attempt to get humans to adapt. The permutations multiplied in her brain.

As if reading her mind, "You see, Margit, any newly aware civilization will have to adapt very slowly to the idea of another one. It isn't something that comes naturally. It takes time. All the steps that we, the Universe Olympic Committee and I, have taken, are made for yourselves, and eventually for all the people of Earth, to begin that process. This is *your* first step." He smiled at Margit, motioning to the waterfall below.

"I thought we weren't able to go see alien civilizations on other ships... this is..." she said pointing outward.

"On your ship. The rules state specifically, Earthlings can't travel to any *OTHER* ship, for the first round. We are home."

"Interesting loophole, Liew." Staring up, the sunlight caught her eye. Another set of long branches protruded from high above. It all seemed to be made for giants. While Liew was a tall being, he wasn't 'Jack in the Beanstalk' tall.

"Back on point. What would you like to speak to me about, Ms. Housman?"

"Oh! I almost forgot. I wanted to let you know that we had a Team Earth meeting this morning to discuss the games."

"Wonderful! I was wondering when the team was going to do that."

"You don't mind you weren't there?"

"Of course not! You will have singular human issues I can't solve, but your teammates can. While I studied Humanity extensively, there are problems that only another human being can answer."

Margit nodded in affirmation. "That's probably true."

"Also, you're a team for a reason. I hope you have more meetings. You'll find it will aid the process of digesting what it is that you are going through—how to comprehend the immensity of it. Because this experience, the Universe Olympics itself will take a psychological toll that only the comfort of other humans can uplift. The team dynamic and shared experience will help you process and adapt to this new reality."

"Very true, Liew."

"Please let me know if there are concerns, or anything that I can do to aid the team and make these games a more unifying experience for you."

"So far, it seems, everyone is doing all right. No major bumps. Mostly the little ones talking about their experiences."

"Yes, as they should. Humans learn, adapt, and evolve through communication. You're a very social species. It's why I like you so much. Others are solitary until mating season, but humans learn through combined culture. You will talk about this experience together for many years to come."

And Liew was correct: Every question that Team Earth athletes were asked upon first introduction, every event they attended, and every speech they gave for the rest of their lives, as well as their lasting legacies and final epitaph, was about attending the Universe Olympics.

Margit looked again at the nearest tree. Before it seemed to be a replica of a large jungle tree. But now, she saw a glimmer of light shining among the branches, as the sun reflected off something. She squinted her eyes. "Ambassador, is that another...?" She could barely finish her question.

Her eyes focused intensely for the first time on the large tree across the way. She could see inside. There were wood furnishings much like Liew's, and a large sitting area which also opened to a balcony atop a large extended branch.

"Yes, they are what you call 'apartments', carved into the tree."

She stopped and looked at another tree, then another; there were hundreds of windows. She stood up to get the full view, looking up and down the enormous trees. "Wait, Liew! This isn't a jungle—this is a *metropolis*."

The full impact of the thought made her dizzy. They were sitting in the largest jungle, with the biggest trees she had ever seen; but instead of it being a rainforest, they were in a city. Not one made of silver metal skyscrapers, but a city made up of trees. It was an awe-inspiring sight, and her head was spinning. She lost her footing for a moment and braced herself on the patio table just as Liew caught her.

"It's time to go Margit. You've been in here too long."

"I feel very dizzy," she said as Liew started to guide her back through the patio, toward the door she came in.

"As you should. The oxygen levels in our atmosphere are more than three times that of Earth."

"It's the trees!" she roared, pointing up, feeling a little punch drunk. As she walked, she became even more lightheaded, and her body began to uncontrollably twitch.

Practically carrying Margit as they walked through his living room, Liew specified, "Actually, oxygen is one of our main exports."

"THAT… is…. *amazing*," finished Margit as Liew finally crossed the threshold into the ship's hallway. Her body was now convulsing. She could immediately tell the difference and began taking in deep carbon dioxide filled breaths. She could no longer stand on her own.

"And… that earned you a quick visit in the Recovery Room for oxygen poisoning, next to Stoke."

Margit, still a little punch drunk, protested, "But I'm fine!" She stopped, pulling her arm out of Liew's.

She suddenly, violently dried heaved as the nausea kicked in. Hunching over and pausing she gave in, "Fine. I'll go. I hate being sick to my stomach."

"Thank you." He gently took back her arm and guided her down the hall.

*   *   *

"Dude! A chair just appeared out of nowhere!" said Stoke, who was now wide-awake. Stoke stared as Liew gently placed Margit in a second Recovery Chair a few feet away from him. "And the room is slightly bigger. Where's heavenly Hawaii and Jen?"

"Getting a late dinner, Mr. Townsend."

The walls of the room were black again.

"The viewscreens turned off when the room expanded," answered Liew. Directly next to the 3-D holographic view of Stoke was another human being. The longer room accounted for the extra space needed on the wall. It was most obviously a woman's frame.

"Can you perhaps put up a screen in between us, Liew?" asked Margit in Norwegian.

An opaque screen appeared from the floor and stopped in between the chairs.

"Really?" said Stoke with insult in his voice, raising his hands so they could be seen over the barrier. "We're snow buddies."

Margit sighed audibly, "As long as you let me recover in peace, Stoke."

"I promise. *I promise*, Margit."

The barrier just as slowly returned inside the floor.

"I'll be nice, and chill like fungi, my friend. I need company; I'm super bummed right now."

A light appeared over Margit's Recovery Chair and her stomach instantly felt better. She no longer wanted to vomit. She turned her head back toward Stoke, able to focus some attention on her "snow buddy."

"Because you lost? Or something else?"

"Yeah, totally bummed, like in my heart. It's the first time since I was like ten years old."

"So last year…" Margit couldn't help herself, and she was now able to breathe and tease.

"Ha, *HA*! Really, I'm too old for this," retorted Stoke.

"Too old to lose? Stoke, you aren't. Losing is a part of life, at every age. You've been lucky you haven't lost in, what, six."

"Seven."

"Years."

"It's almost half of my life."

"Truthfully, I'm going to say this… I'm glad you lost, Stoke."

"Really?"

"It's unrealistic. Loss in every form is an important part of being human and growing up. Adolescence is bright splendid happiness. But this is your first step into adulthood. And you are fortunate to have finally learned this lesson now, Stoke, with caring friends and teammates around who are taking care of you."

"It's a bummer."

"Yes, but what is important about this lesson, isn't just how you cope with the loss. But how you move past it. Persevere through it. When we lose, especially in sport, we have to get up and try again."

"Still sucks though."

"Not going to lie, this first loss, this disappointment will be one of the hardest. Yes. You lost today."

"*Big* loss, *big* time, on the *biggest* day, ever!"

"Take that heartbreak and use it, Stoke," continued Margit. "There will be another chance. Learn from your mistakes today, so next time you can be a *better* snowboarder, and a *better, stronger* person as well."

"I know. I shouldn't have hot-dogged and shown off down the mountain." Stoke had a heap of regret in his voice. "Just glad no one got hurt in my avalanche."

"Liew made sure of that. You only hurt yourself today, inside, and out."

"But not for long, at that!" Liew, who had remained silent up to this point, announced from the wall panel. Both athletes had forgotten he was there, working diligently. He examined the 3-D hologram scan of Margit's body. "You're looking better, Ms. Housman. Your blood oxygenation is reaching normal human levels again. Brain and stomach are nominal, but you still require a little rest before you can leave."

"Thank you, Ambassador."

"Thank *you*, Margit," finished Stoke smiling at his friend. "Taking heart. Persevering with my snow buddy." He held up his hand and made the universal peace sign with two fingers. The new Snow Buddies sat in the perfect quiet of companionship.

Chapter 12

J.W.L.

Jenefer Washington Lee's usual routine was to get in an early morning run before 5:00 a.m. But she hadn't slept at all last night; she had gone in to check on a snoring Stoke a few times. Finally, at around 4:00 a.m. Universe Olympic time, she gave up the ghost and decided to go for her early morning run, extra early.

When she walked in, no one was in the workout arena with her. She placed her bag in her personal cubby and walked over to the running squares in the middle of the floor. The whole room was dark, except for a few basic emergency lights here and there. It was perfectly quiet and empty. A few overhead lights turned on just ahead of her steps. She preferred to be alone. And after everything the team had been through in the past day, she needed the time alone to think.

Her mind was racing with thoughts as she began her routine. She kept replaying Stoke's avalanche over and over again in her mind. It was on repeat—the screams, the snow, him being engulfed by the wave. She had to admit that she was worried sick for the little ones and the position they had been put in. She was surprised they weren't more traumatized. She was. Maybe it didn't bother them as much, but she didn't have the stomach for all this.

Jen strode on, faster and faster, but the square met her increased pace. The arena remained dark and quiet.

Her meditative state was broken by a sound.

"Mrs. Washington Lee."

"Aww…" Jenefer jumped over to the adjacent square.

"Oh my God, Liew." Jen hunched over to catch her breath.

"Good morning, I saw you were up and wanted to inform you that your event would be the first today after breakfast."

Jen walked a slower pace on the square to cool down. "Thanks, Liew. You're up early too?"

"I was just checking on Mr. Townsend."

"Yeah, me too, at 2:00 a.m. He doin' better?"

"Yes, and he will be fully recovered by breakfast."

"That's amazing. How does that chair do it?"

"When the games are finished, Mrs. Washington Lee, I am allowed to tell you, and all of Humanity. But only then."

Jen continued her cool down walk. "We only get the tech if we pass the test, don't we?"

"That is correct."

"Hey, I'm just glad it worked. I'll take it. Thank you for saving Stoke, Ambassador. I wouldn't have handled his death well."

"Neither would I, Mrs. Washington Lee. Please understand, no one will die on my watch—that is why *I* am your Ambassador. These are *sport* games, not life and death games. Please remember that."

"Does every new civilization keep coming close to death, like us?"

"No, Humanity is a special case, and why I was specifically chosen. Did you know I was a doctor on my home world?"

"Were you?"

"Yes, before I was chosen to be your Ambassador, I spent my entire life saving others."

"Wow."

"In the twenty years I studied Humanity, before you entered the Universe Olympics, I extensively spent time learning your anatomy, down to individual cell formation and mitochondrial recovery. Many of the medical devices we use in the Recovery Room were designed and created by me for humans."

"The mat too?"

"Yes, the mat too. It's a portable Recovery Chair. We had to heal Stoke's broken back before I could move him."

"I'm impressed, Liew."

"Don't be. I am one of many who are watching over and caring for every member of Team Earth, and Humanity."

"That takes away an inch of the stress here. I'm absolutely terrified for the little ones."

"Don't be. Every precaution has been taken to ensure their safety. Stoke was a unique case."

"Boy is he."

"Until he made the free-will choice to make that jump, all I could do was be prepared for it. There was a small chance he would have decided not to do the trick.

"Oh, he chose, all right," she responded.

"Doubtful he will ever choose it again."

"Good. My ulcers can't take it."

"But please, ease your worries and prepare yourself for your event today."

*   *   *

Jen marched through the door of her bedroom. Every time she stepped in, she was momentarily caught off guard, half expecting to hear familiar voices and see faces. Her large king bed was already made, and in the middle of the pillows was one that didn't match the other brown accent pillows. She gently picked it up and shook the pillow with the smiley face and petals. It had bells in it and sounded like a fairy flying away.

Jen glanced to the wall; her eyes were met by a familiar face that took up the whole space.

"Hi babe," the man said. He was hunched over, hands clasped together.

At this point, nothing seemed to ruffled Jen's exterior feathers, but inside she was in knots. She took the sudden appearance of the man with ease.

"Hi," she returned back, undeterred.

"How you doin' today?"

"Been better…" Jen trailed off, looking down and shaking the jingly pillow again.

The African American man on the wall didn't respond to her. He just kept talking. "We were told to make a few vids, so this one is for your official competition day."

"Yeah… it's today," replied Jen with no oomph in her voice.

"And I wanted to take a moment and remind you to warm-up a little extra today. That quad muscle has been a sticky issue."

"OK," answered Jen, lost in thought.

"Take in a few extra carbs and a dairy protein shake to settle your stomach."

"It's a double ulcer now, thanks to Stoke."

The man leaned in closer to the camera. "I feel so blessed Jenefer Washington, to be both your coach and your husband. I thank the Lord every day that we met."

"And I do too, Mr. Lee."

Jackson Lee reached off camera. "I know it's only supposed to be coaches making videos but…" He stepped out of view and came back with the cutest small baby you have ever seen.

"Ah, there he is…" Jen teared up, her full attention now back to the wall. "Hi baby."

The man bobbed the baby up and down on his knee. He looked maybe six months old. "I was thinking perhaps you needed a little extra hello to motivate you for your event today."

Jen got closer to the wall.

"We just wanted to wish you luck. Know you're my heart and life. We know you can do it. I say a prayer for you and the team every morning that the Lord watch out for you and keep your feet on fire."

Jen laughed and wiped away the tears. "I'm fired up."

"Eotan and I know you are the fly-est, fastest, fieriest woman on the planet. We miss you and love you."

"I love my babies."

"You keep that spark in your step and beat the pants off whomever you chase."

"Oh, I will Jackson, I will."

Eotan smiled and Jackson caught sight. "See, he knows we are talkin' to you. He smiled for mama."

Jen practically touched the wall and baby.

"I love you," Jackson finished, "and go get them. *Fire* them up." The baby shook the same pillow that Jen was holding a few moments earlier and cried out with laughter.

"I'm on fire now!"

*   *   *

Both Jen and Liew took the small shuttle down to the main green planet. It was the one of the four that looked most like Earth, albeit a lot smaller in circumference. It did have ice caps at both poles, and it was covered in green with the occasional blue stream, river, or semi-large body of water. But nowhere near the size of the singular ocean planet Triton.

She thought for a moment. It seemed to be an emerging tradition that whoever set foot first on one of the competition planets, got the honor of naming the place. Triton was a wonderful name for the ocean planet; thank God that Amy had studied a bit of Astronomy and Greek myths in school. It seemed an appropriate name. Jen could barely wrap her head around Stoke's name for the snow planet, Claw-bear.

Looking down at the lush savannah as Liew and she were approaching from above, the naming possibilities were endless. It was so green and vibrant, with the high grasses and spotty trees here and there. The landing on a solitary continent of savannah was effortless.

The shuttle door opened, and Jen began her stretches and warming up her legs.

"OK, Liew. What can you tell me here?"

"Yes, Mrs. Washington Lee. This won't be as long a race as the other events, but that only seems appropriate, given your record is in the 100-meter sprint. But it will be a little longer than you're used to."

"Expected. Actually, I've been expecting the unexpected. I wasn't sure if we were going to land on the ice planet again, or the rocky first planet. I'm kind of surprised we're on the correct planet. I was preparing for everything, anything, even space. Oni warned me at breakfast."

"That's wonderful, Jen. You are open to adapt to any situation, and therefore you are now a perfect contestant for the Universe Olympics. That's what this whole endeavor is about. But for you it will be a little simpler," he added pointing in the distance.

"You see the top of that large tree? It looks like a parasol in the distance?"

Jen looked up from stretching her glute muscles. "Yeah. It's the only tree around." Jen scanned the endless plains that went on for miles and miles.

"*That* is your finish line."

"OK. I can do that. Doesn't seem too far. That's it?"

"Yup, and please get there as fast as humanly possible. This race will be for time."

"NOW I CAN DO THAT!" Jen said, clapping her hands. Her long, splendidly painted nails clicked against each other. Then she began stretching her arms in preparation.

"Are you ready?" asked Liew, looking at his arm and the patch on his clothes.

Jen nodded, surveying the scenery. The Olympic Flame sun was shining. The air temperature was comfortable. Not too hot or cold, just right for a lovely run.

"Patch on?"

Jen held up her arm.

"Good. One minute."

"Can you count it down for me please?" she asked, jumping up and down.

"Of course."

"From twenty." Jen examined the ground where they were standing. The grass wasn't too tall, and the dirt wasn't too hard and firm. She dug her feet into the dirt and created two small divots for her to start.

"In twenty."

Jen wiggled around and slapped her legs getting the blood flowing. "Anything else I need to know, Liew?"

"Fifteen."

Jen crouched down in her starting position.

"Fourteen, thirteen, twelve..."

She lifted each foot up and slammed it into the makeshift foot divot.

"No, nothing else, Mrs. Washington Lee. Be the best human you can be. Focus on the tree, only. I'll be at the bottom."

"Eight, Seven, Six…"

Jen put her head down, ready to shoot off like a gun.

"And ignore the other contestant."

Jen's head popped up.

"Three, two, on your mark…"

She shook off the comment and put her head down again.

"GO!" The same loud honking sound that Amy, Oni, and Stoke had heard blared. Jen jumped from the noise, which came from every direction with no mechanical reason.

She bolted out from the starting position, as fast as any human being was capable of doing. It was perfect. She ran from the slightly shorter grass of the meadow, straight into the long grass of the plains, in five seconds flat.

Her heart racing, her blood pumping, Jen squinted her eyes and only focused on the top of the parasol tree. The large, distant tree looked like it wasn't too far away, maybe a mile, but with such a tiny planet and the curvature of the landscape, she couldn't be too sure about the precise measurement. It really didn't matter. She'd be there soon enough.

As quickly as lightning, Jen zoomed through the now knee-length grass as fast as she could. It would be an understatement to say that she put all her heart into the start of her event. She was hoping to change her luck—that was the only way she viewed it at this point—to give Team Earth and Humanity their first real win.

The terrain didn't look too difficult. The ground wasn't too hard, and it wasn't too soft. But the grass that started at ankle length with each stride got taller and taller. And the ground that seemed a flat straight line, was more in fact hillier.

With each passing hill, up and down, the grass got longer and longer. It was starting to become a hindrance to her stride.

She glanced up at the tree which still seemed to be a considerable distance away.

Jen eased up a bit on the gas, wanting to conserve some energy for the last stretch of the race, whatever it was. The parasol tree, which at the start was just the treetop in the distance, became more and more visible and larger on the horizon with each step.

With each footstep, a sinking feeling crept into her heart. What if it was really far away—like miles and miles. She wasn't a marathon runner. Moses was. But he had turned down the opportunity to be in the Games. What if Liew had put her in *HIS* event because he needed someone for the race? She couldn't make twenty-six miles. She could probably run, on a good day, maybe five to ten miles, but not at this pace. The uncertainty of the distance started to really dig in and give her anxiety. She chastised herself for not asking Liew the actual distance to the finish line. What if she was running Mo's Marathon?

Even after running all this distance, it felt like the tree was a million miles away. She could see only the top canopy with all the leaves pointing up. And there was another new obstacle: the grass got longer with each step. At first, it had seemed lovely, fresh, green, and easy to run through. Now the grass had made it up to her hips at this point, and there was a small hillock ahead. Its shadows were long.

As she ran, she realized that she had underestimated—the hillock was large. The grass now crawled up to her shoulders. She began to fret and worry. What if the grass became so tall that she lost sight of the tree in the distance? She'd lose her bearings and miscalculate the shortest distance to the finish line. It was too much for her tummy; a sharp pang hit her ulcer.

Her speed, which had started out in world record time, reduced to as fast as she dared to run. Not knowing the distance, struggling against the grass, Jen's anxiety also weighed her down further. Not to mention the fact that now some of the grasses were hard and slowly tearing at her legs and arms. Jen recognized that she wasn't dressed appropriately. She needed safari gear with long sleeves and pants, not the crop top and bikini shorts of an Olympic runner. But she would not give up because of a wardrobe malfunction. You just had to push on through them.

Jen thrust through the thick grass, constantly glancing up at the tree. It finally had a little bit of trunk to it, from her perspective, but she was nowhere near the finish line. She was maybe halfway there. She acted accordingly and slowed her pace down a bit, breathing hard, digging into each step. The burn had started in her legs from the strain and buildup of lactic acid. If she lengthened her stride and took deeper exhales, perhaps she could stave off the pain to make it to the end of the race.

She ran down a small valley, then hard up a hill (which she hadn't known was there because the height of the grass obscured it.) When she reached the top, she heard a rustling sound. Off in the distance, to her left, the grass was being moved to the side by something, but she didn't know what. Her heart jumped. It was a short distance behind her and was gaining fast. She still had the advantage, but she had to maintain her current speed to win.

Runners, any Olympic athletes aren't only masters of their bodies—their instrument, as it were—they are also masters of science and math. No one really tells them this when they begin training to be an Olympian. But Jen was a master. Actually, so were all the Universe Olympians on Team Earth. Each person had their own specific concentration in a different field: Amy's was hydrodynamics, Oni had multiple masteries (which now included astrodynamics), Stoke's was physics, and Jen's specialty was kinematics, the geometry of motion. It all made for a grand equation in her head. And with a little calculation, velocity equals distance divided by time—she needed time to win this race. So, like every athlete, the only choice was to change one part of the equation. There were always opportunity costs with these choices—

pain, fatigue, energy, injury, or losing a race—but Jen calculated and saw no other option. Her velocity needed to increase, and quickly.

She lost track of the other contestant as she made her way down the hill. The grass was now completely over her head. It was as tall as corn ready for harvest. She had never seen grass this high before. All she could see in the distance was the very top of the parasol tree.

Jen could hear loud rustling, right upon her; she didn't dare look to her left. Liew had specifically said to ignore her competition. She didn't realize how hard that instruction would be. Her competition was right next to her, and she could hear its labored breathing. It was heavy like hers, and whatever it was, it sounded big—bigger than her, like a horse.

At that moment, for whatever reason, a sermon long forgotten popped into her head. When she was a child, she spent hours every Sunday at Chicago Zion Baptist Church. It was a refuge. Most of her youth was spent listening to Pastor James. This lecture was on the nature of fear. There were five types of fear, he said. And right here, right now, was one of the types.

Pastor James used animal analogies, which is why Jen remembered them so well. She loved animals. The first type of fear was of size: a man swimming next to a whale—Don't fear what is bigger than you. The second type of fear was volume: a lion roaring—Don't fear what startles you. The third was the fear of the unseen: the sound of a bat chirping in the dark, hunting at night—Don't fear what is not visible.

She couldn't remember the other two off the top of her head, but this was the bat chirping in the dark. She mustn't fear what she can't see.

Jen redoubled her efforts and picked up her speed, back to world record pace. She ignored what was next to her. She would not allow the fear of what, or who, was next to her, to take her mind off the game. And the game was to reach that tree first.

Out of the blue, the high grass suddenly stopped. A long flat plain lay in front of her at last. The large tree was at the other end, and she could see Liew and the whole team waiting in the distance.

Jen couldn't help herself at this point. She could hear the heavy breathing next to her, the weighty foot stomping on the short grass. She turned to her left to finally see her competitor, and it was her worst nightmare come true.

Many, many years ago, as a kid, Jen had been forced by one of her cousins to watch a movie she was probably too young to see. Even at seven, this film made an everlasting impression on her. It fed her nightmares from that day on. The velociraptor in the original *Jurassic Park* stuck with her—specifically, the scene where it went after the kids in the kitchen. The fear she felt during that scene never left her; as she grew up, and every time she ran, she'd always visualized a dinosaur from that specific movie trying to catch her. She'd even dream about them! She'd be running for her life, like the blonde lady (whose name she couldn't remember now) retreating from the fastest dinosaur. This was something primal for her. Imagining that beast behind her always did the trick in a race. When she sprinted the fastest time ever in the 2036 Summer Olympics, she envisioned (one of the best coaching methods) a full pack of them chasing her. Only this time it wasn't her imagination—it was a reality beside her.

It had the face of a velociraptor but a longer, leaner snout. Its skin was a scaly brownish-green, blending in perfectly with the long grass. The closest eye was a bright orange, and now looking straight at her. When she caught its eye staring at her, it made the most horrible screeching sound she had ever heard—like nails being pulled down a chalkboard. It was excruciating to hear. She almost threw up right then and there while running.

Jen broke eye contact and stared down, only to see its most impressive feature—its legs. The muscles on Jen's legs were nothing compared to these legs. She hated to say it, but all her mind could think was—*dinosaur*. She was racing a friggin' dinosaur. Obviously, they weren't extinct after all, perhaps only on Earth.

Jen had never been so frightened in her entire life. It was like being in a game show called, "Race Your Worst Fear" and she was living it. Every time the dinosaur stepped closer to her, Jen veered off her course. Each time she moved out of its way, she lost the advantage.

She suddenly remembered the fourth type of fear. Pastor James used a tiger as the animal example, but in this case, Jen felt it was apropos to use a dinosaur instead. At the sight of the thing you fear the most, you flee—flight. She was the living embodiment of it right now.

She was now officially running faster than world record time and could feel the sweat running down her body and legs. Her muscles burned, her heart pounded, her stomach turned as she kept glancing at the creature next to her. And it was fast; each of its strides were two of Jen's. For a moment, she felt as though it was taunting her. When she veered back on course, it would take a step closer to her. Jen out of fear altered her direct-line trajectory.

Back and forth she swayed, as she stepped to the side, it would move in closer. It had the upper hand, proverbially, taking a few steps ahead of her, only to slow and mirror Jen's stride, step by step.

Jen closed her eyes for a moment and meditated: Liew had specifically told her NOT to pay attention to her competitor. She knew in her heart that they would never put a species in the Universe Olympics whose design was to eat or maul her. He said these were not life and death events. These games weren't the Coliseum in Rome; the games were something more. This wasn't sport for killing. It was sport at the most elevated evolutionary level: requiring, mind, body, and soul to work in coordination. It required humans to rise above base emotions, especially fear. This dinosaur-thing *wasn't* going to eat her. This *wasn't* a stupid childish horror movie. These creatures were conscious beings competing in the Universe Olympic Games, just like her. She needed to grow up, and evolve. The only way to beat this childhood fear was to squash it. To prove that there was no reason for the fear to exist. For Jen, and for all of Team Earth to win, they would have to rise above fear to win the game, any game. And this was going to be the first event to do that.

She opened her eyes and looked at Liew and Team Earth: Eyes on the Prize.

As she approached, she could hear everyone's screams, but it wasn't the scream of excitement or joy of cheering on a teammate. It sounded more like the screams of horror. And she knew what they were looking at.

They were only a hundred feet away, standing behind a white line on the ground. The shadow of the tree covered the team and the Ambassador. The entire team was again huddled behind him.

Jen widened her stride and ran like no one else on Earth had ever run. She knew there was no one else who could have done what she was doing. She could beat the dinosaur. And with each stride, she was a slight step ahead of it. She must have been doing thirty-nine kilometers per hour, at least.

Then she heard a weird whooshing sound. It was her nature to look and see what caused it. The dinosaur, much like small lizards still alive on Earth, opened what can only be called a frill around its neck, made of skin. The wind was blowing from behind and catching the extra skin, which was spread wide like a sail.

The physics now were on its side. She couldn't catch it; not once it opened its last trick. It was too fast for her.

With each of her steps, the dinosaur was half a step, then one step, and then two steps ahead of the human.

In the last fifty feet, Jen gave it every cell, every muscle, every adaptation known to Humanity, to try and beat her opponent. Her feet were on fire.

But it wasn't enough. The dinosaur, with the help of its neck frill, crossed over the white finish line almost five feet ahead of Jen. When it crossed, the dinosaur made its way straight ahead toward Liew, and the athletes huddled behind him. A few high-pitched screams were heard from the athletes.

The dinosaur suddenly, sharply, turned left directly in front of Liew and ran into the smaller condensed group of trees off in the distance. It was gone into the shadows in seconds.

When Jen crossed the finish line, she had nothing left to give.

The team roared. Once the dinosaur was gone, they all turned to Jen. They jumped up and down screaming, this time in pure joy.

Jen collapsed immediately and said a prayer, thanking the Lord and Pastor James for the lessons.

Liew walked up to her, wrapped her in a silver-like foil sheet, and handed her a water bottle. "Congratulations, Mrs. Washington Lee. And please drink this immediately."

She sprayed the water in her mouth. It tasted sweet.

"I couldn't catch it, Liew. I couldn't, I'm sorry," she said breathlessly, in between drinks.

"Please, no talking. We need to get you back to the Recovery Room. You put in a stupendous performance, the fastest in human history, Mrs..." he stopped himself, "Jen."

She turned her head up and smiled at her Christian name.

"You have the second-best time in this heat!"

"But I didn't win it, to move on," said Jen very weakly.

"Not this event, Jen. But don't lose heart. You were amazing. I didn't realize humans could run so fast."

"Fastest on Earth. But not here."

"Can you stand?"

"With a little help," she answered, lifting her hand up for help, her long nails clicking.

Liew graciously complied and picked her up off the ground.

Everyone was chattering behind them, letting Jen have some room and air—no one ever wanted to be crowded after a race.

"You were unbelievable!" yelled Stoke to Jen. "And *DINOSAURS* are *ALIVE*! Game changer, man. Total, game changer." He was again, inexplicably, wearing the perfect tyrannosaurus T-shirt for the occasion, with a vampire riding it.

"Thank you," Jen had a very hard time walking and limped a little. "I think I'd like a trip to the Recovery Room, now, Liew."

"Of course, Jen. Let's get you all healed up."

She smiled and let him lead her to the big shuttle sitting in the middle of the field.

*   *   *

The scene on the walls wasn't of any naturescape, or beaches, or rolling hills. They were in the middle of a street; cars were driving around the perimeter of the room and a bus accident was in the intersection. There were also people walking along the sidewalk in front of tall buildings, gawking at the crash.

Jen was in the Recovery Bed and talking loudly over the ambient city noise, "Heal it all, Liew!"

"I'm trying, Jen," he said, touching the panel with her 3-D holographic scan.

The twins walked in and were startled at the cityscape. The honking, people yelling, and city noises reverberated.

"Oh my God, where are we?" shouted Jodie, barely audible above the bus honking.

"It isn't the Jungle!" howled Josie.

Liew hollered before Jen had the opportunity, "Chicago. Girls if you'd like to visit, please sit quietly."

"You couldn't hear us anyway," said Jodie, over the chaotic scene.

"I'm not sure how you find this relaxing," shouted Josie, sitting next to Jen by the chair.

"Gives me something to focus on besides myself." She looked over to Liew, "What's the prognosis?"

"You will need to be in here a few hours, that's all." He answered. "You are a remarkable woman, Jen."

"Thank my mama." She smiled.

"Your body weathered the strain of the race remarkably well. Just dehydration, lactose buildup, scrapes from the grass, and a few tears and pulls, here and there. You're fine."

"Mama always said, 'No one can beat the genetics of a black woman. We hard, we tough, and we can keep going through anything rough.' I think she was right."

"Indeed, she was." Liew touched a small section of her 3-D holographic diagnostic near her knee. "Slight meniscus tear."

"Whatever. Just heal it all, please. Maybe you can touch up my sagging boobs, the flab on my stomach, and the extra skin on my face, under my chin."

The girls giggled to each other.

"I want a better-than-new Jen."

"I'll see what I can do, but the official rules specifically state that I have to leave genetic material exactly as it was pre-games. No new improvements allowed. It's in the contract."

Jen turned to the girls and smiled. "Well, it didn't hurt to ask. Speaking of…"

"DINOSAURS ARE ALIIIIIIIIVE!" screamed Stoke as he walked into the Recovery Room.

Stoke had written on his T-shirt. His sloppy handwriting crammed next to the vampire riding T-Rex. "Like my shirt?" The writing was indecipherable.

The girls looked it over. "If a five-year-old wrote that!" giggled Jodie.

"It was tough to find a marker in my room that worked." He examined the shirt. The letters were off and a little juvenile. "And it kept getting stuck on the fabric."

"Speaking of…" asked Jen. "Liew, can I ask? Was it just me or was that dinosaur-thing taunting me?"

Liew stopped what he was doing. "Taunting you? What do you mean?"

"I felt like it was purposely stepping closer to me, to intimidate me during the race."

"Really? I would venture that wasn't the case. She would have been disqualified if she touched you or hurt you in any way."

"She never touched me. She just stared at me, mirrored my steps exactly. It was a bit creepy."

"Oh," Liew laughed and turned back to the diagnostic. "She was probably trying to get a good look at you. She's never seen a human being before. It may be her only opportunity to see one up close."

"Liew, I'm telling you. She was taunting me. She howled when I first caught her eye. It was the most horrific sound I ever heard—my nightmare."

Liew touched another panel on the Recovery Room wall across from the diagnostic. A holographic small square appeared showing an above angle view of Jen running next to the dinosaur, like a movie."

The kids jumped up to watch. "Hey!" yelled Stoke.

Liew watched them running and saw the obvious howl of the dinosaur. He paused the playback. "Translation in English." He said to the panel.

He rewound the footage again on the panel and as the dinosaur bayed, words scrolled on the top of the image. "Nice to meet you, human from Earth." Stoke read the words allowed.

Jen jumped from the sound of the dinosaur screech. Liew could see the stress in her muscles.

"Dude, he was just saying hello!"

"She... she was." Liew stopped the playback and returned to the patient. "It's discouraged to consort between teams, but it's not a rule."

"Wait? Do you have footage from each of our events?" asked Stoke.

"Yes, Mr. Townsend."

"Can I watch my avalanche on Claw-Bear? Pllleeeeeaaasssseeeeee!" He slowly whined.

"Absolutely not! The record is for official use only to monitor the event in case of a tiebreaker or an injury. This will also be shown back on Earth when you return home."

"Really?" wondered Josie. "So, our families will get to see what we do here, after all?"

"Yes, Ms. McQuenzy, but only at the end. All of Earth will be able to watch the Universe Olympics."

"Cool!" announced Stoke. "Now, I'll be a legend."

"After everything you've been through, that is *ALL* you care about," snapped Jen. "Letting people watch you bust on a hot-dog move, creating an avalanche on the mountainside, nearly killing yourself, and your entire team?"

Stoke thought about it for a second and his momentary thought of fortune and glory faded. "Oh yeah. I messed up."

"Yes, you did, Buster. Big, time. You really that anxious for the whole world to see that?"

"No, Ma'am." Stoke was bested.

"And *why* Claw-Bear?"

"It's the name of a character from the latest Telidayo VR games. It's big and white and they bite. Hey… that would make a cool T-shirt."

"You do love your T-shirts. What did you write on yours?

"I wrote, 'Dino-mite Jen.' To honor your dino-occasion. You were great today."

She smiled. "Thank you, Stoke."

"Now, you all be quiet," Jen waved for them to shoo. "Go, so I can heal in peace."

The twins and Stoke quietly slinked out of the room. "Not sure about the 'peace' part." Josie said in a not-so-subtle aside, as the ambient noise of a yelling man from a window competed with sirens of an ambulance pulling up to the traffic accident.

The Recovery Room was blessedly free from young humans for a moment. Jen closed her eyes to let the white light around the Recovery Chair work its magic.

After about fifteen minutes, Jen spoke up, her eyes still closed. "Liew, can I ask you one question?"

"Yes, Jen." He was dragging a blue color on the diagnostic, over to her red covered stomach.

"Did you know about my childhood fear of dinosaurs?"

There was silence in the room for a long moment, as the red stomach slowly turned blue.

"Yes, Jen."

"OK, that's what I thought. Thank you for answering my question."

"Of, course." Liew returned to the panel and her diagnostic.

Jen was beginning to understand what this meant. All the big pieces coming into play for every member of the team. These games were so much more than what any of them were expecting. This was next-level play. And for Team Earth to win any event, they were going to have to adapt, communicate, and motivate each other. Starting with her.

*   *   *

Team Earth was assembled around the long wooden table perched in the middle of their jungle cafeteria, eating happily, and conversing with each other. Jen squeezed in beside Ramon at the table.

"Look who's back," stated Ramon jovially, fork in hand. "You all healed up? That was quick."

Jen leaned in, "I really need to talk to you, Ramon."

"What's up?" he said curiously. "You're not eating."

"I'm not hungry at the moment, but when you are done can we speak in private?"

"Sure. Everything all right? Have you been hurt in any way?"

"No, I'm physically fine, but I realized something important."

Liew stood up at the head of the table. "I hope everyone is enjoying their lunch. I wanted to give you all warning that our next event will be the Artistic Swimming Synchro event."

"YES!" The twins yelled in unison.

"But Liew, we need at least an hour to do our hair and full makeup," announced Jodie in a panic.

"It takes the gelatin at least a half hour to set in our hair," finished Josie.

"I understand that girls, that's why you are now getting this warning." Liew touched the patch on his sleeve. "Please meet me at the small shuttle in exactly one hour, fifteen minutes. I started a countdown on your patches."

The girls didn't even finish their bites of food. With a loud bang, they dropped their forks and knives and ran out of the jungle as fast as they could, leaving trays and all behind.

After the girls high-tailed it out of the cafeteria, Liew remained standing. "I also wanted to give each of you fair warning—if you are in any way claustrophobic, this is not the event for you to attend as a spectator." He glanced over to Dmitri.

"*Da, speciba, Ambassador.*" Dmitri nodded in his direction.

"Or you, Oni."

"But Liew, I am not a claustro…"

Liew stared at her, shaking his head no.

"*Si, Ambassador. Grazie.*"

"Did everyone get an avalanche warning too?" Stoke asked snarkily, throwing up his hands in defiance.

"No, Mr. Townsend that was not supposed to happen. Your free will choice brought that situation about."

"Oh, yeah…" Stoke had a quick flash of his team members' faces as the avalanche rushed toward them. It put a pang deep in his heart, one he wouldn't soon forget. "I'm sorry about that choice, guys." He sincerely spoke and made eye contact with every team member. "I would never have done the move, if I knew any person could have been harmed." He finished looking at Amy, with a slight tear in his eye.

"Lesson learned, we hope, Mr. Townsend," finished Liew. "Now, everyone else has one hour and twenty-five minutes until your shuttle leaves. Thank you."

Jen leaned over to Ramon, "That's weird. Why claustrophobic? The girls' program is held in a stadium."

"And Oni swims," declared Ramon, shrugging. "But with these games you never know, do you?"

"Ya, that's just it," Jen looked down at Ramon's tray, which was fortunately empty. "Can I entice you into getting a dessert, while I get my lunch tray?"

"Sure, Crème brulée would hit the spot right now."

"Good." Jen stood up and spoke to Ramon as they walked into the meadow with food stations.

Chapter 13

Synch

Liew waited alone in front of the shuttle bay door. He checked the patch on the sleeve of his tunic, and it was well past the hour mark. He was about to press the call button.

"We're coming!" screamed Jodie from down the hall.

The twins were running, gear in hand, down the empty hallway. They made quite a racket.

"I'm sorry, my hair gelatin wasn't setting right," exclaimed Josie as they approached Liew.

"Hurry please, girls." Liew walked into the shuttle bay, with the girls running behind him.

"And I couldn't find the right glitter eye shadow," answered Jodie, adding to their litany of excuses.

"It's fine, please, we must hurry." Liew stood at the doorway of the smallest shuttle in the main shuttle bay.

The twins hustled inside, threw down their gear, and finished applying each other's lipstick, glitter eyeshadow, and highlighter. Then sprayed their makeup to set it.

"You look lovely, ladies. Your hard work paid off."

"Thanks, Liew. It was crazy hard throwing it all together last minute. But the Aussies brought it home."

"Oi, Oi, Oi," answered Josie, hooting with her eyes closed.

The shuttle was flying toward the water planet, which was a relief for the girls.

"I'm assuming we are heading toward Triton, Liew," said Josie, sneaking a quick look out of the window. She was applying the finishing touches to her sisters' bright red lipstick, while her sister stretched.

"Yes, Ms. McQuenzy. That is correct."

"Ya never know around here! I was fully prepared to swim in space again, FYI," stated Jodie, expertly lining up sticky jewels on her sister's forehead. "Wow, we are close."

"The ship moved during lunch. After Jen's event."

"Never felt a thing," said Josie, putting on her sequin-trimmed sheer gloves and unrolling them up to her elbow.

As they entered the atmosphere of Triton, there was a slight bump of the shuttle.

"Felt that," laughed Jodie, "Luckily for us, weren't putting on any makeup!" She was stretching along with her sister.

The girls finally finished their prep and joined Liew at the viewscreen. "Wow! There is nothing but water as far as the eye can see."

"It's a little daunting, isn't it, Jos."

"Yeah, poor Amy, down here all alone," finished Josie.

"She was never alone," stated Liew boldly.

"Oh yea, sorry Liew." She touched his arm. "I meant I'm happy we have each other." She winked at her sister.

They saw the blue waves splashing and swirling as they approached the sea's surface.

"I don't see the pool," first stated Jodie, glancing around.

"Or any stands," reaffirmed Josie.

"Or for that matter, a stadium," finished Jodie.

The shuttle continued at full speed toward the surface of the water.

"Ah!" the girls shrieked in unison.

They grabbed each other's hands as the shuttle dived underneath the surface at full speed, and continued down into the water. Further and further it went, going from light blue water to dark blue, until it stopped dead in the middle of the ocean.

"We're underwater, Liew," stated Josie in disbelief.

"Yes, we are. I hope we made it in time." Liew touched a button on the viewscreen. "Yes, we did," he was giddy with excitement.

"I hate to state the obvious here, Liew, but we can't breathe underwater."

He looked at them both confused. "Of course, you can't. Why would you say that?"

"'Cause we're in the middle of the bloody ocean," answered Jodie.

A beeping sound emanated from the control panel. "Perfect timing." Liew pressed a button and the viewscreen folded back into the wall. One side of the shuttle became transparent. It felt like standing in the middle of an aquarium.

The twins gasped in shock. It felt as if they were underwater. The sun's rays filtered down just far enough to send light through the water. It was beautiful.

"Forgive the rush down girls; I just thought you both would like to watch the other contestants in your heat."

All of a sudden, two creatures appeared in the water, frozen in place. They looked like a combination of an angelfish body with lionfish spines, a long tentacle, and long flowing fins. Music began playing and the fish, in perfect unison, started moving. It was mesmerizing.

The fish turned around in circles, mirror images of each other. Zooming around from left to right, lifting a fin, flaring it out, and turning around, and completing the same move backwards. With each turn, and each flare, the fish would reveal a new scale or tail, or fin that glimmered in the light. The fin would catch the sunlight and a rainbow of light would shimmer back. Loopity-loo, they turned to a deep base sound in the music, and then they swam together so they appeared like one large angelfish. At the crest of the higher-toned sonorous music, they separated and flared a new silver fin from the tentacle at the top of their head.

The girls gasped.

The new fin wrapped around the pair, engulfing them in a rainbow of sparkles. Then it all stopped.

They retracted everything, just as they began, and raced away back into the dark sea.

The girls were left speechless. It was one of the most exquisite displays of synchronicity they had ever seen.

Liew clapped then said, "All right, girls. You're up next."

They remained motionless.

"Jodie, Josie! Let's go!" Liew hurried. He raised his voice, but not in a stern manner.

The twins snapped out of their stupor and unzipped their warmup suits to reveal absolutely stunning sequined costumes.

"Oh, how lovely," said Liew. "You both warmed up?"

The girls nodded yes, still not able to speak. They stretched just a little more as Liew stepped over to the door of the shuttle. It opened.

The girls yelled, then braced for the wall of water to pour in. But instead, there was a tunnel of air through the water, and a small platform leading out from underneath the shuttle.

Liew walked out into the tunnel, which was illuminated and gave the sea the most beautiful royal blue hue. The girls hesitantly followed but stopped at the shuttle door.

He turned around, "It's perfectly safe. Please hurry, we only have a small amount of time allotted before the beginning of your program. If you are not on time, you'll both be disqualified."

Jodie stepped out first. It was a surreal experience. She touched the water, which remained in a perfect tunnel around them. There was no glass, no visible shield, no anything, that held the water back.

Josie stepped onto the platform with her toe and tapped it a few times. It seemed solid enough.

"Girls, you both had no problem stepping out into space for the qualifications." He smiled reassuringly at them both. "Please. You don't have much time."

The girls grabbed each other's hand, took a deep breath, and walked behind Liew.

"Do your best. I know you will make Team Earth proud."

When they reached the end of the tunnel, some twenty feet away, Liew threw a small green ball into the water. It started swirling and spinning, creating a small air bubble. With each turn the bubble grew and grew, until they could see it was made of air. And at each end of the bubble, light emanated clearly giving a better view underwater.

The twins stepped up beside Liew as the water was pushed away by the swirling vortex. It had created a large air bubble in the middle of the ocean.

"Wow," was all Jodie could muster.

"This will be a mid-water start, ladies," stated Liew, since most synchro-swim programs begin out of the water, poolside with a platform part of the routine.

"Understatement of the year…" interjected Jodie.

"Jump in, and when you hear your music please begin your freestyle program."

"Will the bubble hold?" asked Josie looking nervously around her.

"Yes, it will, but the air tunnel will disappear when I return back to the shuttle. Please don't worry, I will come and get you both when your routine is finished." Liew smiled at the twins, who were a little shaky on their feet.

"Take a deep breath."

They did.

"Again."

Jodie and Josie inhaled deeply.

"There is more than enough air for both of you—for an entire year—in there. Imagine this bubble is the surface of the pool."

The twins shared a dubious glance.

"I know you can perform your program beautifully." A beep sounded from the patch screen on his sleeve. "Plugs on." The girls set their nose plugs in place to close their nostrils. "Patches on?" Both girls lifted up their hands with the patch. "Good. Jump in, you have two minutes."

The twins grabbed each other's hand. "On three," said Jodie. "One, two..."

They jumped in unison and swam to the middle of the bubble that had about a thirty-meter circumference.

"I'll be right here when you're done," yelled Liew from the air tunnel. "Good luck," He waved from the tunnel. "Go Team Earth!" Then he turned around and walked back to the shuttle. The air tunnel disappeared behind him, leaving only the sea.

The twins were left alone in a giant air bubble, under the sea, on a strange planet, in the middle of an unknown solar system. They both looked up at a sound above them. The bubble extended about eight meters above them. They could see the faint glimmer of the sea's surface far above. A whole world of creatures and large objects moved back and forth in the water over them.

"Don't look up," declared Jodie.

Josie looked down into the deep fathoms, which was even worse. A long dark snake-like figure slithered by only meters below their feet. She gasped.

"JOD!"

"Keep your eyes on me!" exclaimed Jodie, the older of the two sisters and generally the one in charge. You wouldn't think that two minutes would be enough time to delineate older versus younger, but in the McQuenzy case, it did. Jodie's words echoed in the bubble and a few drops of water came down. "It doesn't matter what is going on around us. It's always us."

Josie looked her square in the face.

"Focus here, McQuenzy." Jodie pointed to her eyes. It was a saying their dad had always said during family meetings.

Josie looked at her sister. She was about to be in tears.

"Hi," said Jodie in a calming happy voice.

"Hey."

Jodie smiled. "I love our eye shadow."

"Thanks." It was Josie who designed the artistic side of the twin's routine.

"It does our theme justice." The swirling dark blue glitter exploded from the eye.

"Yeah…"

They tread water silently, head-to-head, like they had done a million times before, surveying the bubble. It extended fifteen meters to the right and fifteen to the left, about the dimension of an official Artistic Swimming Olympic pool. There didn't seem to be any current that would affect their routine. The temperature of the ocean felt like their pool in Sydney: warm and comfortable. The occasional drop came down from the top of the bubble. The sound of their breathing echoed loudly.

The beginning beeps of their music could be heard. It came from everywhere.

"You ready?" asked Jodie

"Yup."

"Love you, kid."

"Yup."

"Set." stated Jodie.

They turned their backs to each other.

"Love you, Jod."

They put their heads down waiting for their music to begin.

"Aussie, Aussie Aussie!"

"Oi, Oi, Oi!"

With the elephant horn blaring, their music began! A whistle blew loudly.

Jodie dove down far below, and like a bullet turned and torpedoed up to her sister, who was waiting, underwater for their first opening lift.

The Flyer, Josie, was raised up almost fully out of the water, spinning to perform a perfect upside-down twirl that turned into a cradle. Josie caught a quick breath.

Josie dove back into the water. In perfect unison and in time to the la, la, la's of the music, they popped only their legs up into the air bubble. Their torsos lifted out of the water past the collar bone. As they sculled their arms, turning and spinning their legs in alternating positions, they were doing a toe point dance that any ballerina would be jealous of—except it was upside down, underwater, and while holding their breath.

They rotated, circled, and swayed about to the only kind of music that seemed appropriate for the occasion, the Spice Girls. Classic Pop. Both girls were a bit shocked when they heard the full vocals of the pop song itself rather than their usual instrumental version of the music. The singing gave them that extra jolt of confidence and excitement to their routine.

With each rotation, and split, and craning of the legs, they perfectly mirrored each other's moves making perfect complicated figures. After almost half a minute, the girls finally popped their heads back into the air bubble for the first deep breath. Their routine continued with the girls tightly woven together as two ballet dancers in close proximity, legs crisscrossing, and then looking like pinwheels. But with every twist, turn, and twirl, they never moved apart. Their legs effortlessly executed knight, crane, and split positions all to the beat of the lively music.

They both had perfect extensions, height, and stability. They knew what the other was doing, instinctually. Five spin downs in a row with a 360° rotation and they were never more than a foot apart. They both descended and traveled fast across the bubble's surface together.

The view under the water was just as captivating as the view above. The girls had hands that were as agile as seals fins; Josie and Jodie's stationary, propeller, torpedo, barrel, spinning, and support sculls pushed water around like any marine evolved mammal. The swimmers took a side fishtail position, which turned into a crane, and made a flamingo into a final split element. At the pinnacle of the song, the girls, and the Spice Girls, all at the same time, joined together in a big… AHHHHHH! The twins dove down deep, and returned together, in an epic final lift, which is what won them the gold in Nairobi.

It was very rare after a long free program, for swimmers to have enough strength and energy left to perform another lift that would be just as perfect and "fresh" as the first lift. But the McQuenzy twins had legs and energy to spare. As Josie swam down for the final time, she caught sight of the dark slithering snake creature in the fathoms again. It took her attention away for a moment, and she winced underwater, which broke her synchronized position for a split second. Jodie, who was squatting, grabbed Josie's body and began to push her up to the final throw, legs up and over.

Above water, in the bubble, it was a spectacle to be seen. Jodie threw her sister, tossing her even higher than her first lift. They popped up together for the final bridge of the song. In perfect unison, their hands, smiles, and all their moves hit the notes of the song after the lift. When the spice girls hit their "Hold tight" last lyric, both girls were clutching each other, hands in synch in an arch above their heads. The eggbeater kick stabilized them to their collarbones. The end position was a work of art; hands wound together like an ancient Hindu statue. Both as unmovable.

It was probably one of the most perfect routines they had ever performed, both above and below water. The music finished, and within ten seconds, the air tunnel opened on the other side of the bubble.

"Hello! Girls!" yelled Liew waving. "Over here."

The girls gently swam over to the tunnel and Liew helped them out of the water.

"How'd we do?" asked Josie.

Liew wrapped each girl in a towel that seemed larger than he was. It sucked up the water and warmed the girls' aching muscles instantaneously.

"We'll know when we get back into the shuttle." Liew pointed the way back down the air tunnel to an open shuttle door.

When the girls stepped inside the shuttle, they were shocked to hear not only shouting and cheering, but also to realize that they were now inside the large shuttle, not the small one they initially came down in. The whole team, sans, Oni and Dmitri, were clapping and cheering.

"You rock, girls," shouted Ari.

"That was unbelievable," said Amy who came up to them. "I thought I had it crazy pants down here. But this was beyond!"

Both twins were delighted and exhausted at the same time. Luckily, the larger shuttle had chairs and benches to sit.

A beeping sound emanated from the control panel.

Liew stepped over and looked down. He touched a button.

"Well?" wondered Jodie.

"I'm sorry girls. You came in second this heat."

Josie stomped her foot and stood up! "Why?"

Liew pressed the control panel. "It seems there was a slight out of synch move at the end, 'underwater deduction.'"

"It was ME!" howled Josie. "I saw that snake thing, and it made me jump out of synch."

"Wait? We were judged for our moves both above and under the water?" asked Jodie.

"Yes, you were," answered Liew.

The shuttle door tried to close the air tunnel, but almost caught both Jaysen and Pappie's hands, which were touching the water side of the air tunnel.

"Mind the gap," shouted Liew to the gentlemen. "Going up."

The twins were devastated and slumped on the bench.

"What did we lose by?" asked Josie.

"Two-thousandth of a point."

"Hey," smiled Jodie rubbing her sister's back. "We almost beat fish."

*   *   *

Josie and Jodie followed behind Liew to the Recovery Room. It was hard to miss their slow sullen steps; where there was usually glib non-stop humor filling the halls, now there was absolute silence as they walked hand in hand. They had not let go of each other's hands since leaving the air bubble under the sea.

As they slunk into the two Recovery Chairs, they remained hand in hand, refusing to let go, only switching hands once they laid down side-by-side. A tear ran down Josie's face; she quickly wiped it away.

Amy quietly walked into the Recovery Room, feeling that she didn't need to talk or add anything to this solemn moment. Hopefully, just her presence and support would be of help to the twins. She was there if they needed her.

Liew walked over to the wall with the 3-D diagnostic hologram, and instead of each person's hologram being head to toe, the twins were almost directly one on top of the other. Liew zoomed in on Josie's brain. There was a dark blue patch, centered in the amygdala and hypothalamus.

"Don't be so hard on yourself, Josie. I can literally see the dejection and sadness in your brain."

Josie didn't even glance up to wipe away the slew of tears as she took a deep breath.

Liew zoomed into Jodie's diagnostic hologram, which was also blue. The color flowed from Josie's right hand into Jodie's body, creeping closer toward her heart.

"Girls, please." Liew turned around and faced the twins. There was a soothing calm to his simultaneous higher and lower register voices, but he purposely let the lower register take the lead when he spoke. "Try and elevate your spirits. There is no reason for both of you to be so sad."

"We just got the pants beaten off us, Liew," answered Jodie. She turned to her sister waiting to see if the wide-open joke opportunity would be taken by her. Josie remained silent, which stung Jodie's heart—the blue color had now fully entrenched the holographic 3-D diagnostic around her actual heart.

"We lost and it's my fault." Josie sounded both disgusted and disheartened at the same time.

Liew glanced back at the diagnostic and could now see the deep blue color spreading throughout their bodies. "Now Josie, Jodie, I can literally see how hard you are taking this loss, and I'd like to share something very important with both of you."

Both twins looked over at Liew in unison.

"Without you, we wouldn't be here."

The girls looked at each other confused.

"What do you mean, *we*?" Jodie motioned to the ship. "Like the ship or the McQuenzies wouldn't be here?"

"No, Team Earth."

Amy pulled her chair closer to the twins' Recovery Chairs, wanting to be a part of this conversation. The twins were left speechless, which was a rare thing.

"You *both* are the reason Humanity made it past the qualification round and into the Universe Olympics."

Josie wiped away a lingering tear. "But I thought the goal was to swim to the other side of the platform."

"And not drown in space," finished Jodie.

"Yes, that was a small portion of the event. But that wouldn't have been enough."

"What did we do?" pondered Jodie with a genuine curiosity in her voice.

"The octopus thingy," guessed Amy with a smile on her face.

"The Ciapor, yes," answered Liew.

"That thing whose mommy grabbed it up with a tentacle," stated Jodie.

"Yes, and you both saved him."

"It wasn't the best swimmer, poor lamb," said Josie.

"You'd think an octopus could swim?" finished Jodie.

"But *HE* was part of the qualification."

"Ya lost me, Liew," said Jodie quizzically.

"You both stopped what was your designated event and goal, and you took the time to save the Ciapor from drowning by stopping a further descent into space. By saving this unknown 'alien' creature—

unknown to you that is—in an unfamiliar place and space, you both showed great compassion."

"Just doing the right thing, Liew," stated Jodie.

"Exactly." Liew smiled and pointed at her. "That act of compassion was the primary task for Humanity to gain official entry into the Universe Olympics. By showing that you care for others just as much as yourselves, you helped Earth qualify as an advanced cognizant planet. The 'benevolence task' was specifically picked for Planet Earth. Now many—not me of course—were convinced that humans couldn't pass the first qualifier. But I chose you two, plus Amy…" Liew walked over and put his hand on Amy's shoulder, smiling at his team members. All three girls had dumbfounded looks on their faces, "For the tremendous hearts you all have. You three are the greatest examples of human compassion alive."

"And sassiness…" interjected Josie, who had finally found her inner jokester again.

"And that too. Yes, tremendous intellectual capacity and quips are also among your strong suits, Ms. McQuenzy, as well."

The twins finally turned in perfect unison and smiled at each other.

"Wicked sassy," answered Jodie. They high-fived. It turned into a pinkie swear.

"So, you both getting terribly upset and feeling down right now is simply misplaced emotion. When in fact, your single act of compassion, kindness, and caring, are what qualified your planet, your people, and your team, to be entered in these games. Congratulations."

"Thanks for sharing, Liew. It kind of takes the sting out of the loss," said Josie.

"To... FISH!" finished Jodie. "Never living that fishiness down."

"That was a momentary blip in a lifetime of achievement, Ms. McQuenzy. Both of you sisters, working together, will accomplish extraordinary feats, both in and out of the water."

Josie smiled at Liew. "And don't forget, Amy did turn back Liew. She just wasn't as close to the Ciapor as we were."

"Yes, she did," said Liew, silently noting to himself that only a truly compassionate person would refuse to take the full credit for their achievements but would share the credit with others. The girls had proved his point, yet again.

"Now, you two. Please rest and recover, physically, but most importantly, mentally, emotionally, and spiritually. *WE* have big plans ahead. I need all of these higher aspects in tip-top form soon."

Josie grabbed Jodie's hand as she had done a million times before—while sharing a crib in infancy, in their twin beds as youngsters, and sharing almost everything until they were teens. Their tight grasp reminded them of home, comfort, and support, and love of family. They closed their eyes and basked in the healing light of the Recovery Chairs. When they closed their eyes, the Australian desert-like terrain of Kings

Canyon appeared on the walls, with accompanying atmospheric sounds and arid smell of dirt and ghost gum trees.

Amy suddenly jumped up and hurried over to Liew, whispering. "I thought you said never to touch anyone while inside the light, Liew."

"Yes, Amy, I did," he whispered back.

"But they ARE! They're holding hands, you know, touching."

"Amy, that rule was to make sure the DNA of another person doesn't fuse in with another person's during repair. This recovery takes place on a cellular, actually, down to mitochondrial DNA level."

"Yeah," she said, worried and shifting anxious eyes back towards the girls.

"The girls are twins."

"Yeah," said Amy confused.

"Their DNA is the same. They are identical, so it's allowed."

"Oh yeah!" said Amy, laughing quietly. "Guess that's a real thing then, isn't it?" She smiled at the Ambassador, who nodded for her to return to her friends, who were still holding hands even in their sleep.

*   *   *

Later that afternoon, all of the athletes gathered around Liew, who was waiting at the front of the observation lounge. Liew was staring out at each of the four planets of the event arena. The ship was currently closest to the blue ocean planet. The ever-blazing Olympic

Flame sun was off in the right corner. One by one, the members of Team Earth gathered together in the lounge.

"What's up, Liew?" asked Jaysen.

"Going to watch another sun explode?" joked Eric.

"No," answered Liew, as he glimpsed the last person (Ari as usual). She was again in her wetsuit pulled halfway down, dripping with water, and apologetic for her tardiness rushing in.

Liew turned around to face the team. "Ms. Foxx, have no worries about the water; please sit down."

Ari sat in the last row, in the last chair (which just happened to be plastic, that way she could wipe it off afterwards with her towel).

"Anything wrong, Liew?" asked Margit.

"We meeting another turtle?" teased Pappie, winking and elbowing Ramon.

"No, not this time. It has come to my attention that the team has been…" Liew struggled for the correct words, "Blue. No, disheartened, discouraged, and downcast, as of late."

"Yeah, in case you didn't notice, Liew. We've been losing," replied Jen, with a straightforward strength to her voice.

"Like, big-time," finished Stoke, nodding to Jen.

"Team Earth hasn't made a dent in the Universe Olympics, Liew," stated Margit.

"Yes, in the last few events you all have participated in so far, but there is still so much more to go. You as a Team have only just begun…"

"…losin'," quipped Amy.

"Now, stop! Ms. Ride, take that back. Please. You don't know what the future holds. Why taint it with a negative forecast," Liew said pleadingly.

"I apologize, Ambassador," she said, surprised with his impassioned retort.

"We are losing hard here. All our competitors are literally adapted for the terrain we are competing in. How can we compete with that?" asked Ramon.

"That's true. We aren't snow penguin-seals," started Stoke.

"…or whales," finished Amy. "I had *NO* chance against the submarine."

"Ladies and gentlemen, boys and girls." Liew raised his voice louder than he had ever done before. "Please, let all of your frustrations out now, but it's important to keep your heads high, your spirits elevated, and your thoughts intellectually positive and not be emotionally mired by fear, anger, and sadness. Humans have done their worst with such intentions. If you all continue on this negative spiral, we are going to do just that."

"Liew, we are Olympic gold medalists, we expect to win. All of us." Jen looked around and caught eyes with Ramon, then noticed her mistake. "And Ramon has a heart of gold, and that counts as exactly the same, in my book. We are the best of the best here. We're used to being number one."

"Indeed, Mrs. Washington Lee, you are. But let's take that moniker, that expectation, that pride point, and rid ourselves of it. Let them go, now. We need to take these temporary, momentary, losses and mourn them properly, and learn from these event trials, please. Adapt to your mistakes or circumstances and motivate yourselves onward as a team."

Liew surveyed the room. There wasn't much of a budge from the sullen crowd. It seemed as if almost no one was swayed by his motivational speech.

"Dude is this why you called us?" asked Stoke, confused.

"Yes. It also leads me into my next motivator. Since things haven't been what you planned or expected, I thought perhaps a surprise might be in order to put a smile on all your faces."

"What is it?" wondered Ari.

"You have a visitor coming."

"Is it the turtle?" asked Pappie, curious to get a better and closer look at the being.

"No."

"Is it *another* alien?" asked Margit, curious since the rules stated otherwise.

"No, it is not, Margit."

"Well, who is it?" asked a still-dripping Ari from the very back of the room.

"You'll see. Come with me, please." Liew glanced down at his patch. "The shuttle is about to dock."

Every athlete who was present, sans the healing twins, calmly got up and followed Liew out of the room.

Finding their way down to the main shuttle bay had become routine. Each athlete had been there, as either a contestant or a spectator of the competition, at this point. The bay had three shuttles. The small one Liew took down with whomever was the athlete of choice for an event. Another somewhat larger one that was used to transport the whole team. Tucked in the corner was the largest shuttle of all, one that had yet to be used by the team. But there was room enough in the bay for a fleet of other shuttles.

When the gang meandered into the bay, no running was necessary this time.

"Hey! Look! There's a fourth one Liew!" noticed Stoke.

To their surprise, a fourth shuttle was already docked in the middle of the bay. It was about the same size as the medium size shuttle—white with a black tipped nose, ruddy brown underbelly, and white on the sides and wings—and looked like the other American space shuttles, only a mini version.

The athletes froze when the new shuttle opened its main door. There was quiet expectation in the bay.

A small figure stepped out.

Liew spoke loudly across the floor ahead of the group. "Good afternoon, Director Xi."

The light from above hit the small Asian woman as she stepped down the stairs. "Greetings, Ambassador. And hello to all the athletes from Earth."

"Thank you for coming. It was a perfect time for the team," announced Liew.

As she stepped into the shuttle bay, it was hard to miss the shadowy figure behind her waiting in the doorway.

"I hope you don't mind Ambassador, but I brought your two 'stowaways' with me."

The first person descended the stairs, while another filled the doorway behind them, standing motionless.

"And did you bring everything we mentioned?"

"Of course, Ambassador, and more. It's all here for the team."

"What is it, Liew?" asked Yosi, very quietly in Chinese.

"Some goodies from home," he answered in Chinese.

"From China?"

"Yes, items from all over Earth. Even a little something for you from your grandma, Ms. Zhang."

Director Xi turned and spoke to the entire group, "I've brought the members of Team Earth some special food, clothing, and drink requests. Also, some care packages from coaches and loved ones for each team member."

Liew looked over at Jen who got a slight tear in her eye, beaming. She needed to hear from her husband and her baby.

"Wonderful, Director Xi. It is exactly what your team needs right now. A little bit of home."

The two people in the shuttle followed behind Director Xi, and the light finally hit the top of their heads.

"Welcome, Mr. Al-Nair Shabbat." Moses stepped forward into the light, descending the rest of the stairs.

"Mo!" yelled Jaysen. "Oh my God! You decided to come!"

Jaysen walked up and grabbed Moses in a combo of a handshake, hug, and thump.

"And welcome aboard Ms. Von Strither. Team Earth is proud to have you here," said Liew to the person in the shadows.

Blond hair caught the light from above as she stepped down. "Thank you, Ambassador. I'm kind of surprised to be here, myself."

Margit could barely contain her excitement. "Gretta! You decided to come too!" she yelled.

"As far away and foreign as this all seems, I realized pretty quickly I made the wrong decision, Mar," answered Gretta. "I hope it's not too late to join the team, Ambassador Liew?"

"As did I, Ambassador," responded Moses, "I would like to assist Team Earth in any way I can."

"You already have. Just by showing up here, Mr. Al-Nair Shabbat. You already have." Liew smiled. "Wonderful! Let's go eat dinner. You can catch up with the team there."

"Off to the JUNGLE!" bellowed Amy, leading and pointing the way. "Are the twins coming?"

"Yes. I'll go get them," answered Liew with a smile on his face.

"The Jungle?" whispered Gretta to Margit, with a grim look on her face.

"You'll see. You're going to love it," replied Margit, laughing, as she hugged her friend, "Howlers and all!"

"Ambassador, thank you for allowing us to intervene at this late hour. My visit here will be short. I also wanted to check on the team members to report back to their world leaders at home, now that each was briefed on the competition," said Director Xi officially and formally. "Are the McQuenzy twins well?"

"They are fine and well," Liew spoke loudly enough so that each and every member of the team heard what he was saying. "We are just ending the first heat of the games, Director Xi, with many more events and heats to be played, where Earth's athletes will have their chance to show what Humanity is capable of being and doing. They will adapt, gloriously."

"And you just added two more," said Director Xi.

"The more the merrier, Director. Or have you not heard that old Earth saying?"

"I have and know it well, Ambassador. You have your team of twenty."

"Yes, I finally have my full Team Earth, as it was meant to be. They are complete and are the finest human beings from your planet. And *now* the Universe Olympic Games can truly begin."

TO BE CONTINUED IN HEAT 2

Nasula will soon be publishing Universe Olympics: Heat 2

www.Nasula.com

Publishing Tomorrow's Stories Today

Also, soon to be in print is Amanda Dubin's first novel

Assassins Wall.

http://www.assassinswall.com

Follow Universe Olympics online

www.UniverseOlympics.com

Follow Universe Olympics on social media

YouTube: Universe Olympics

Instagram: UniverseOlympics

Twitter: @UniverseOlympic

Facebook: UniverseOlympics

<u>ACKNOWLEDGMENTS</u>

First, I'd like to thank my wonderful editors: Sharon,

Susan, Lucinda, and Amy. Without you all, none of this would

have been possible.

Second, I'd like to thank my family and close friends.

Your love and support lifted me up and helped me ride this

creative wave.

Finally, I'd like to thank Tillie Timmes, may she rest in

peace. She always believed in me and told me never to give

up. She was my greatest cheerleader.

Universe Olympics Heat 1

ABOUT THE AUTHOR

Amanda Dubin is an author and independent filmmaker. Her first novel, *Assassins Wall*, is based on her original script. Her second, *Last Stop, Earth*, is a children's science fiction novella.

Universe Olympics Heat 1 is her latest release.
She currently resides in Alexandria, Virginia. She attended film school at Boston University, winning a grant for a short film from Miami Light Project.

Follow her on social media

Instagram: DubinAmanda

Twitter: @DubinAmanda

Facebook: AmandaSue.Dubin

Youtube: Amanda Dubin